ADVANCE PRAISE FOR
AMISH GUYS DON'T CALL

"*Amish Guys Don't Call* is a rumspringa of a novel: a delirious, fast-paced spree with a deeper emotional purpose. You won't be able to put it down."
- Marc Acito, award-winning playwright, novelist, and humorist

"A great story of acceptance and the pain of love."
- Harry Hannigan, writer/producer (*School of Rock, According to Jim*)

"Debby Dodds nails it. What begins as a smart coming-of-age romantic comedy unexpectedly veers into horror and heartbreak, and the storytelling is as sharp as the humour. This is a story about loneliness and turbulence that rewards the reader with its insight and wit."
- John Fugelsang, actor, television personality, and comedian

"Novels like Debby Dodds' *Amish Guys Don't Call* are scarce gifts: this is a story with most excellent stuff that happens while also being a book **about** something."
- Brian Bouldrey, author of *The Sorrow of the Elves*

"At once charming, hilarious, and deeply intelligent, the characters in *Amish Guys Don't Call* will grab you by the heart. Debby Dodds is a shining light and an exciting new voice."
- Ariel Gore, author of *How to Become a Famous Writer Before You're Dead*

"Dodds' book is filled with humor, warmth, and real emotion while exploring a culture clash that surprises and provokes. Samantha is witty, engaging, and flawed. I was laughing from the beginning to the end."
- Shanee Edwards, writer (*Sheknows.com*), actress

"*Amish Guys Don't Call* is entertaining, insightful, and moving, as it adds new levels to the world of teen romance and bullying. Author Debby Dodds blends warmth, humor, and dramatic punch into the tale, along with an intriguing glimpse at a rarely-viewed part of society."
- Michael Reisman, author of the "Simon Bloom" series.

COPYRIGHT INFORMATION

AMISH GUYS DON'T CALL

By Debby Dodds

BlueMoon
PUBLISHERS

This book is a tribute to all the strong women in my family.
To my Nana Ade Crosby and my Nana Mary Dodds, two smart
and inspirational women who loved to read.
Both attended college at a time when it was rare for a
woman to do so. I wish you were both here to celebrate
my first novel with me.
To my mom: a teacher, a librarian, and a wonderful mom
(who has nothing in common with Sam's mom at all, except for
the thin layer of plastic I found on her stove!).
To my daughter, Dory, a voracious young reader,
talented writer, and my heart.

CONTENTS

ACKNOWLEDGMENTS

Writing this acknowledgements section is scarier than taking any final exam or stepping onto any stage to perform. I'm wracked with anxiety that I might forget someone. Heck, I'm sure I will. If it's you, please forgive me. And let me know, because I plan to write more books with *many* more acknowledgements, and I will include you next time.

Some fantastic teachers made my becoming an author possible. At Lancaster Country Day School: Mrs. Luttrell, Mrs. Lewis, and Mrs. Musselman, all three I owe a debt of gratitude because they told me I was a writer before I believed it to be true. When I won the English Award at graduation, I was floored. I identified myself as an actress, not a writer. In college: Dr. Charles Turney (creative writing) and Alan Langdon (acting), and in grad school: Susan Taylor Chehak, Brian Bouldrey, and Jim Krusoe all challenged me and elucidated the esoteric, and my classmates at Antioch (Mustards and Mangos both) were/are wonderful. I'd be remiss if I didn't also mention the fantastic Mrs. Long and Mrs. Shultz at Kissel Hill Elementary. My writing group in Portland: Warren Easley, Alison Jakel, LeeAnn McLennan, Janice A. Maxson, Lisa Alber, and Kate Scott, for bolstering me when I needed it and giving me blunt feedback even when I thought I didn't want it. At various times in my life: Ariel Gore, Marc Acito, Vaughn Patterson, Judy Henry, Gary Izzo, Gary Smith, Neil Dreibelbis and Stan Wells all taught me things and fed my creative life. And I'm devoted to Joss Whedon beyond the telling of it, because his work has given me so much.

Thanks to all my students from my creative writing classes (most recently Ink and Magic and the Goodtime/Sunshine crew), my various prep classes, and especially my one-on-one students; I appreciate how much teaching you has actually taught me. Naming you all would be a book in itself. I've been privileged to have your trust, and working with you has been perfect for me, because in many ways it's allowed my inner teen to stay vibrant and unforgotten.

My parents (David and Dale Dodds) and brother (Rob) gave me their love and tolerated my reading so much—at meals, up until late most nights, at World Series games, and on car trips (even though it made me puke). And for loving me. Also, my appreciation to my extended family of Bill, Peggy, Abby, Adam, Claire, and all my relatives (blood and otherwise) in the families of Crosby, Dodds, Black, Andersons (x2), and Cool.

My friends from LCDS, Lititz, Catawba, NYU, Disneyland, and Disney World, The Empty Stage, Spilt Milk and Time Out, indie films and theatre plays, LPAC, Tigard Mom's Club, ComiCons, Buffy Fandom, Portland Public Schools, Prophecy Con, Kaniacs, Catlin Gabel, Riverdale, The Attic, Willamette Writers, etc. (Does that etc. get me out of jail for forgetting something?) Seriously, my pals are the best. xo

A sky-full of gratitude to Blue Moon Publishers: Heidi, D.W., and Talia, and my editor Allister Thompson for their guidance, valuable feedback, and belief in me.

Finally, I need to thank Deke and Dory for all the laughter. You put up with my gourmet crockpot meals, crazy work hours, and "papers and books everywhere!" messiness. I couldn't write without your adoration. You ARE the wind beneath my wings, you two cheeseballs. You're my everything.

Debby Dodds

CHAPTER ONE

It wasn't like we'd seen them pull up in a horse and buggy or anything, but their Amish-ness was unmistakable.

Madison and I couldn't help but stare at the group of teens in odd-fitting clothes shuffling into the movie theatre lobby. Huddled so close together, they moved almost like a single organism. A dead giveaway of their status as Plain Folks: the guys sported bowl haircuts, and the girls had hair hanging down past their armpits. One girl's was pulled severely into two braids that hung almost to her elbows, without any sense of irony. Standing in line at concessions, we watched them scurry by. Madison wiggled her eyebrows at me.

"Look, even the Amish girls have boyfriends, Sam!" Madison nudged me a little, teasing. I smiled at her, stealing another glance at the backs of the Amish kids, because surreptitious subgroups of society have always intrigued me. Madison caught my eye again and held it. "And you're way hotter than they are. A helluva lot hotter than you give yourself credit for."

I couldn't help but feel a thrill when she said this, like I had Mexican soda running through my veins. The kind of cola made with pure cane sugar. She had my back like nobody else ever had before.

Madison Caulfield was the kind of friend I'd always craved: beautiful, stylish, and funny. She had it all figured out. This time, I wasn't letting opportunities pass me by like I was a hunk of inert matter. I wanted to change to be a reactive and bonding chemical, like carbon. I was ready to make connections.

But I also knew that Madison's friends had to be convinced I was worthy to hang with them, so I needed to lay off the dorky analogies like the carbon thing I just did there.

"I know, Mad, but I keep telling you, the guys in our school... I just don't know what to talk to them about. I don't like deer hunting or the Penn State Nittany Lions or goofing off all afternoon at the quarry." We moved forward two inches in the popcorn line, though nobody had left. The kids at the counter seemed to be having serious issues deciding between Whoppers and Milk Duds.

"Puh-lease. At least you just moved here last winter. I've known all these idiots since elementary school, when they used to pick their noses and try to wipe them on me." Madison rolled her eyes. Lancaster County was the kind of place where people lived for generations, so everyone knew each other, and one person's aunt was another's godmother.

"The guys weren't any better at my old school in Philly..." I didn't want to talk too much about my experiences at any of the three different high schools I went to in King of Prussia, because I knew an air of mystique always trumped the scent of loser. Also, Madison's clique seemed to like that I'd lived in a big city, not *the suburb* of a big city.

"Look, finding guys is like scoring weed or booze. You just need to know where to look." Madison's eyes glittered, playing with me again. She knew that all the partying she and her friends did freaked me out even more than the pressure they put on me to date. She coolly appraised my rapid blinking. Then a smile broke over her face, like pink dye spreading through silk. "Oh, Saint Sam, Plan P is supposed to be fun! If you wanted to stay home watching old *Firefly* reruns on Hulu while eating sharp cheddar cheese all the time, you wouldn't have started hanging out with us, right?"

I laughed. She stuck out her tongue, but it didn't make her look like a petulant kid as much as it did a 1940s pin-up girl.

By "Plan P" she meant our plan to find a boyfriend for me. I knew it was silly. But like many things Madison proposed, it was also exciting.

"Fun is good. I like fun. Fun can be..." Mercifully, my babbling was cut short by our turn to order our sodas and popcorn.

We headed into Theater 4, where the newest horror film, *Blood Space*, was showing.

Turns out the group of Amish kids was already seated in our otherwise empty theatre.

"I bet they have bad B.O." Madison snickered a little. "Let's not sit too close to them." I hoped that nobody had overheard. No other groups seemed as mercilessly and blatantly stereotyped as the Amish were; the kids at my school got downright brutal. I heard a story of some boys shooting paintball guns at the Amish while calling them "Yonies" and others setting off fireworks near their buggies.

At least Madison wasn't as rude as her friend Hillary could be. Arguably, Hillary took shots at people pretty unilaterally, though, so there was that. For me to hang with Madison, Hillary had to think I was cool enough. I still wasn't exactly sure how Madison got the other girls to give me a chance, but I'd learned sometimes it's better not to know everything about everyone around you. Then it can be hard not to be judge-y. My mom's over-sharing during my parents' divorce had taught me that.

"Mad, be nice," I begged in a hushed voice. But I snuck another peek as we passed by the Amish kids. I had to admit, what she was saying about the pungent aroma might be true. Amish people often didn't seem to wear deodorant when they were out in public. I'd noticed it myself at the downtown Farmer's Market.

"Their clothes don't seem homemade, though," I said, looking them over.

"Hillary's mom says that stealing's a big problem," Madison told me. "Amish teens come into stores all the time and grab stuff and run because they don't have the money." Hillary's mom owned a clothing store, so she'd know.

"But why didn't they get better clothes?" I was genuinely curious, but Madison giggled snarkily.

"That's funny, Sam!" Madison gave me an approving nod. "If they're taking things anyway, why not pick the expensive brands?"

I hadn't meant it that way. The Amish teens just seemed to be wearing spring fashions, pastels and light fabrics, and it was fall. But I was happy I'd made Madison laugh.

I ate a big handful of popcorn. I liked the artificial butter better than the real stuff.

She continued, "If they're caught shoplifting, they just play dumb. There's no way to call their parents, because the Amish don't have phones." She sipped her Diet Coke.

I wished I'd known this back in ninth grade when I lived in the suburbs of Philly and went through my "five-fingered discount" phase. I guess I could've claimed I was Amish and gotten away with it.

Although I also knew I should just be grateful that I didn't get worse when I'd been caught. I'd lucked out; I was only given probation. Yet from the way my mom acted when she found out, you'd have thought my "life of crime," along with an accompanying photo of BOTH of us, had been reported on every freakin' major media outlet.

Not that I was still thinking about shoplifting, of course. I knew that stealing was wrong, whether it was out of desperation like the Amish kids or the result of compulsion like me. Just wrong.

I wondered for a second if Madison even remembered me telling her about my shoplifting. She'd been pretty drunk this past summer when I did. At the time she'd laughed and called it "racking." But she didn't show any signs of remembering it now. Probably for the best.

The Amish kids were still looking around the theatre, wide-eyed. It was kind of endearing.

The Amish didn't go to our schools or talk to us; they stayed in their communities, and we stayed in ours. It was some weird modern-day, mutually-agreed-upon segregation. Except that sometimes Amish teens would sneak out and pretend not to be Amish for a little while. They just weren't very good at it.

The commercials for TV shows that come before the previews finally started. We soon forgot about the Amish when the cute guys appeared on the screen.

"Gosh, Chaz Lore is hot, but Hillary says he's gay." Madison flipped a piece of popcorn into her mouth.

"Uh, he's married," I said.

"Like that matters." Madison rolled her eyes. "That image, the marriage thing, it's all his manager's deal. The managers set up 'beards' for their gay actor clients."

"Huh? Beards?"

"Oh, Sam, how can you be so naïve?" Madison chuckled. She liked it when I was clueless, which happened too much when it came to the slang words she used so easily. But I was more than happy to fulfill her need to have a "project."

She continued, "Beards are what they call the women who pretend to be the wives and girlfriends of the gay dudes. They're a disguise… like a beard. Get it?" She licked her fingers.

"Hillary's sister, Teagan, the one who's working in a Cheesecake Factory restaurant in Los Angeles until her acting career heats up, has all the real dirt."

"Oh." I felt a pang of jealousy talking about Hillary. Madison thought Hillary knew everything there was to know about everything. Especially celebrities.

Hillary recently announced that she would also move to Los Angeles after graduation to be an actress like her sister. We all told her we knew she'd be a giant celebrity.

"I think it's stupid anyone needs to have a disguise," I said, gnawing on my Red Vine. "Why do people try to be something they're not?"

"Agreed… well, sometimes." Mad grinned like a Davric demon. "I mean, who cares if someone's gay? But what if a person naturally kinda sucks because they're clueless? Shouldn't they try to change this heinously dense loser-tude like you did?" We both laughed. Her harder than me.

"Wow, now that guy… *he's* so on fleek." Madison had lowered her decibels, so I knew she was referring to someone nearby, not just a face on the movie screen. "A definite candidate for Plan P!"

I turned and looked down the aisle to the entrance. Three guys had shuffled in. All of them were pretty cute, but I knew immediately which one Madison was talking about. One of the guys looked like he could be on *The Librarians*, our favourite TV show. He had dark hair, longish and swept to the side, but not drastically like he'd been in a windstorm or anything, with high cheekbones and kinda squinty chestnut eyes with lashes that I'd kill for. He was perfect. So I did what I always did when I was attracted to something: I lied.

CHAPTER TWO

"He's ok, I guess." I sighed as Madison ogled the dark-haired guy who'd just strolled into the theatre with his crew. "You know, if you go for the Christian Kane type." I shrugged, pretending to be spellbound by the premovie commercial featuring waterskiing energy-boost drinkers rapping about their love for overly sweet caffeine shots.

Madison snorted. "And YOU do! He's one of your favourites! I totally saw you joined his 'Kaniacs' fan page the other day!"

Ugh. That was right. I'd forgotten I did that. And that she could see it. Oh, well. It was true. I thought he was super-foxy. I both hated and loved that Madison had grown to know me so well in the few months we'd been friends. "Whatever. Facebook is so over." I rolled my eyes.

I, like a lot of kids in my school, tried to pretend I never went on social media. But of course I did.

Luckily, the guys who'd just come in sat a few rows behind us. I was distracted enough by the idea of them. If I'd been able to steal glances at them, I'd have missed the whole movie.

I really did want to have a boyfriend. Plan P wasn't just to impress Madison.

After my dad left my mom and me, I had a therapist who diagnosed I might have "trust issues" and "a hard time bonding with others." I hated it when she told me this, because it felt as if she was casting a witch's curse on me, like in a Disney movie. What if the idea of me "not trusting guys" became true, just because she had spoken it out loud?

More audience trickled in. A group of tweens in matching "Team Tay-Tay!" shirts came in and sat in front of us. They ranted about some Instagram diss their idol had received from a baseball player. Yawn.

A guy and a girl about our age, but not from our school, sat across from us; they were so stiff they resembled mannequins. He had on an Ephrata Bible Church baseball cap. But about five minutes into the movie, they started making out pretty aggressively. I didn't blame them. The movie didn't make much sense.

The plot of the flick centred on a group of beautiful twenty-somethings doing stupid things and getting bit by the undead, toothy villains. So the Pretty People decided to hide. In space. Unfortunately, the vampires stole a spaceship, too, to chase them.

The Amish kids seemed totally transfixed by the big screen. I wondered if this was their first time at a movie theatre. Newbies.

I stole another look at the kissing couple, trying not to seem like a creeper. I wondered if I'd ever get kissed like that. Getting contacts and growing my bushy brown hair longer had made me feel a little better about myself. Madison taught me to use lemon to bring out some highlights. And I wasn't quite as skinny or nearly as flat-chested as I'd been in tenth grade. But still, I was no Madison. I thought she looked like an even sexier version of Ariel, the Little Mermaid. Who was already the sexiest Disney Princess, no contest.

Me? I didn't look like anyone but *me*. Certainly not like a princess.

After the movie, I assumed we'd head home. I'd had my driver's license for eight months now but still didn't love driving after dark. But Madison said she didn't want to get in the car, that she needed to stretch her legs a bit. I should've known that was just an excuse to scope out guys.

So we stood in front of the theatre in the middle of downtown. Lancaster wasn't a big city like Philly or NYC, but it had some dangerous areas. The streets around here were almost all one-way, and the row houses and businesses were packed tightly together. There seemed to be a lot of people cruising "The Loop," a track that kids liked to drive around as if they were in some M.C. Escher picture. A few guys in a low-rider car with lots of primer patches decorating its doors beeped at us. The whistling and yelping dudes inside looked like they were in their twenties. We weren't interested in them, but we liked that they were interested in us. Then I saw the cute guys that we'd seen in the audience at the movie hanging out in the parking lot. I abruptly turned to walk to my car down the street.

"Hey... What's the big hurry?" Madison smiled. "Let's walk over to House of Pizza for a slice before we head home. We have time, right? Oh, what am I saying? Your mom isn't home tonight!"

"I guess, but I'm not that hungry..."

Madison watched the guys from the theatre watching us.

"But I *am* hungry. And thirsty. And the thirst is real!" She laughed and linked arms with me. "Come on, Saint Sam, it's time for you to stop acting so squirrely around boys! It's fun to flirt. Besides, remember Plan P!"

I knew she was right. If I ever wanted to be totally accepted by Madison's A-list friends, I needed to step things up.

We left the movie theatre and crossed the street. Then something happened that was more terrifying for me than anything I'd just seen in the idiotic vampire movie we'd just been to: the group of guys talked for a second and made a decision.

And they followed.

CHAPTER THREE

On the walk to the pizza place, Madison was telling me a story about how last week Britt and Hillary had been trying to open a wine bottle with a shoe, just like they'd seen on YouTube. But instead of sliding the cork out smoothly, they goofed it and ended up getting Britt's white shirt all stained and...

I must admit, I tuned my friend out.

I needed to quell my building panic, so I started a little list in my head.

8 Things I Like to Do That Calm Me

1. Lie on my bed and look up at the glowing stars I put on my ceiling outlining the shape of the constellation Cassiopeia.
2. Go to the mall and watch the people in the food court and make up their backstories based on their clothes, food choices, friends, quirks, etc.
3. Take a long bath with an unjustifiably expensive LUSH bath bomb that I steal from my mother's ridiculously large stash of them.
4. Watch amateur short horror films about nasty things that hide in the dark.
5. Go to a salon and read all the cheap movie magazines in the waiting room, even though I don't have an appointment.
6. Watch videos of kittens trying to fit into too-small spaces.
7. Estimate and then count the steps between things, just in case I go blind some day.

8. Cut out pictures and make collages without intended themes but then try to find patterns after.

After making the list, I wouldn't say I felt "ready" to go in the door of the restaurant. But I did anyway.

CHAPTER FOUR

"I want just cheese on my half," I told Madison. We stood in line behind someone picking up a takeout order of five pizzas.

The guys from the theatre had claimed the booth near the door. They must've decided to wait until there wasn't a line before they got up to order. There was no waitress at House of Pizza. And no slices. Whole pies only.

"Seriously. That is so freakin' boring." Madison rolled her eyes at me. "What's up with you always wanting the plain? Get some mushrooms or something. It's weird enough you don't like pepperoni, but *plain*?"

"It's got mozzarella cheese and tomato sauce; I like those two things together without the complication of other flavours. And I don't get pepperoni because I don't eat things that used to have a face." I felt a little defensive around Madison's friends, but when it was just her and me, I didn't mind sharing my quirks.

"Yeah, yeah, the vegetarian thing. So late '90s." Madison shook her head.

"No, I'm not a vegetarian. That sounds like I'm super high maintenance/ militant about what I eat. I'm not. I just..."

Madison mimed a big yawn. We both laughed. Madison was good for me. Before her I used to sit at home, just going online to read fan pages and fashion blogs, wishing I had a life. I doubted Madison ever had a day in her life when she felt lonely. She ordered our pizza: half with mushrooms, pepperonis, and olives for her and half plain for me.

There's no such thing as a bad pizza, but there are definite levels of "good." I once ate almost a whole small pie by myself. My mom always tells me I have a ridiculously high metabolism and that when I'm an adult, like her, I'll have a rude awakening when I have to learn to diet. That relentless nagging compounded by an obsession with looks sums up my mom right there.

I watched the blonde guy from the theatre pretend to consider songs on the retro jukebox. The machine itself had a vintage exterior, but the interior was digital. A T-Pain song had been shaking the machine when we'd come in, but the current tune playing was acoustic, one I loved but didn't hear much by the band Anime Eyes, "Buried".

Alone in my room, nobody sees my soul
The secrets I keep, I long to let go
Grim and concealed, they weigh me down.

It was like the singer was perched on a windowpane in my heart, able to see into my soul.

After ordering, Madison and I scooted into a booth kitty-corner from the guys' table. The tiny restaurant should've probably only had six tables, but there were eight jammed in tightly. Madison kept boldly eyeing the one she thought was "my type." When she wasn't trying to catch his eye, she was making up nicknames for the boys and sneakily pointing to them so I'd know who she was talking about. The light-blonde, stocky but muscular guy was "Blondie Bear." The tall, thin one with the darker, stringy hair was "Scowly Dude." The one who was supposedly perfect for me was "Cheekbones."

Madison and I watched Cheekbones order their pizza. He seemed nervous, the way he kept looking down at the counter. Madison got up to go to the bathroom and again tried to make eye contact with him but didn't succeed. I hoped Madison didn't have her flask with her; she usually didn't spike her Cokes when it was just the two of us. When Cheekbones sat back down, Blondie Bear picked up a conversation they must have been having about the movie.

"Screw that! I'd have punched that vamp in the face and gone out on the surface," Blondie Bear enthused, showing his not-very-impressive punching technique. Cheekbones smiled and shook his head. Scowly just scowled. Hard to tell if the comment had registered with him, because he only seemed to have that one expression.

"Great plan, then, what would you do when your oxygen was all…" Scowly took a bite of his pizza. "You'd have to go back to the ship, and they'd be waiting for you, doncha know?" He paused and then solemnly stated, "Violence is never the answer."

Cheekbones laughed. "Mox nix. Vampires in space, not very schecklich." *What language is he speaking?* I thought it sounded Swiss or something. Or maybe it was some skateboarder slang. It wasn't like I'd know. Fact was, there were so many phrases I was clueless about. So I was used to just nodding knowingly.

"You two are still stuck in the past. We live in the real world now!" Blondie Bear said. I didn't know quite what to make of that statement, as the movie was so *not* the real world.

"I think it's you two that are deceiving yourselves about reality and English temptations," Scowly said, glaring at Cheekbones and Blondie Bear between slurps of his root beer float. I gathered this dude was the opposite of an Anglophile. An Anglophobe? Not sure why he hated the British.

"And I still don't think going out onto an alien planet would've been the best bet!" he sighed as if trying to school his friends exhausted him.

"Hey, couldn't help but to overhear that thing you were saying about the vamps," Madison said, returning to the table. She was brilliant at flirting-but-seeming-not-to-care-about-anyone's-reaction and employed her talent often. "Since the vamps are technically dead, they don't breathe, right? So they could track you anywhere on the planet's surface without having a rover. I think the only chance you'd have would be to stay in the ship and fight." She slid into our booth. "They were just too passive about it."

"See?!!" Blondie Bear laughed appreciatively at Madison's analysis, even though she'd kind of contradicted his original plan.

"Or you could lock yourself in the control room and fly the space ship toward the sun and just hope the Undead Space Hitchhikers got burned up before you did," I interjected. This was so unlike me, but my idea just popped out. "I mean, vampires are more light-sensitive than we are, right?" I wish I could claim this outburst was part of the "new me," more confident and ready for a boyfriend, but honestly I surprised myself.

Cheekbones laughed. "I love that idea!"

My insides felt as gooey as the cheese on the pizza that the counter guy had just plopped in front of us.

Madison nodded slightly and slyly winked at me. "This is Sam, and I'm Madison," she told them. I was happy to note it didn't smell like Madison had done shots in the bathroom.

"Oh, I'm Zach and this is Josh." He pointed to the blonde guy. Before he could introduce the permanently cranky looking one, Madison cut him off. That girl was focused when she was on a mission.

"What school do you guys go to?'" The boys exchanged looks. "I figured you're from around here because of the way you talk."

"Actually, I go to a private college... um, not around here. It's in Ohio. But I did spend my childhood here." Blondie Bear seemed to be blushing a bit.

"I'm from Manheim," Scowly dude said without specifying Manheim Central or Manheim Township as either his current school or alma mater.

"And I'm out of school," Zach tossed off casually.

"Oh, *we* finally get out of prison... um, I mean high school, this spring!" Madison lied. I didn't know whether to be happy or upset that she'd included me in her deception. We'd just started our junior year.

"Oh, it's not so bad," I mumbled and then stuffed half a slice of pizza into my mouth.

"Do you guys Facebook or Instagram?" Madison asked in an of-course-you-do way, sipping seductively at her Coke straw.

The boys smiled at each other. "Josh does. Facebook. Snapchat." Scowly nodded at Blondie Bear.

Madison took out her phone and typed in his name. "Josh what?"

"My page is under Josh Farmer, but that last name isn't my..."

"How about you?" Madison winked at Zach.

"I used to… but who needs the drama?" He shrugged and then looked over his shoulder like drama might be sneaking up on him. I figured he must have a crazy stalker ex-girlfriend or something. Not that I'd blame her for not being able to let go. Or maybe he was a player. There was no way he hadn't had tons of girlfriends. I knew I should stay away from him. But then he made eye contact and smiled at me. Madison did a double-take but then smiled at me, too. We talked for about another few minutes while we all ate our pizza. Josh seemed pretty amped about some big party he was going to next weekend.

"If you girls want to go, I can PM you the address on Facebook."

Scowly said, "Count me out."

Zach rubbed his neck a lot and looked at the exit. But he did smile at me when Madison said we'd maybe go.

I couldn't get rid of my nagging feeling: *Zach's a guy with secrets.*

CHAPTER FIVE

While dining, monarchs of old used to like to be seated in the centre of the room to be able to see and be seen. Even though we were located on the far side of the lunchroom, near the food line, the same concept applied. Everyone who bought their lunch had to walk by us, giving Hillary and her crew the opportunity to judge them. And they had the privilege of admiring Hillary in all her fabulousness. She often wore green to set off her natural corn silk hair, turquoise eyes, and smooth porcelain skin. She resembled a trendier version of Botticelli's Venus painting.

Hillary had been named not for Hillary Clinton, but for Edmund Hillary, the first man to ascend Mount Everest. She made sure everyone was clear on that. Her parents expected great things from her, and she was confident that she'd deliver.

Hillary referred to her group of friends as her "Sherpas."

Sherpa Roll Call!

1. Madison: Hillary's right-hand bestie since kindergarten. Also my only real friend. Eats a salad most days.
2. Me: The newest Sherpa. Or maybe I was still a wannabe. Not sure. Seated by Madison at the end of the table, across from Delia. Perched on the edge of my chair, carefully trying to balance. Used to routinely eat pizza or pasta until Hillary asked me if I was "carb-loading for a marathon" and everyone laughed. Now I eat fruit and granola or a protein bar.

3. Britt: Cheerleader who sits on Hillary's other side. Doesn't ever smile at my jokes. Would stab Madison in the back if she thought it'd please Hillary. Loves to eat chicken and turkey, no sauces.

4. Delia: A big reader, maybe more than me even. Dark hair in a pixie cut. Often quiet but very observant. She's the only one of the Sherpas in some of my classes (English and History). Unabashed carnivore who loves her red meat. But I don't judge.

5. Kensie: The athlete among us. Misses a lot of school because she's a synchronized swimmer on the Junior National team. Eats two lunches a day but weighs less than most fifth graders.

With Monday's Special Guest Stars...

6. Grace: Wrote Hillary's paper analyzing John Donne's "Batter my heart, three-person'd God" and got an acceptable but not suspicious B-plus. Hair, skin, and eyes so light she'd disappear on the famous white sand beach of Siesta Key my mom raves about. She'd packed an egg salad.

7. Lauren: Chinese-American girl with extra short bangs who'd just started dating a senior linebacker on the football team. On her plate: an apple, a pack of goldfish crackers, and an oatmeal raisin cookie.

I'd started out as a Special Guest Star myself at the beginning of the year. I suspected Madison convinced everyone that because I came from Philadelphia, I possessed some special cool cachet. The Sherpas quickly ferreted out that me having a cosmopolitan attitude was far from the truth, but they also found out I was practically always alone on weekends. The benefit of being able to tell their 'rents they were sleeping over at my place so they could stay out all night if they wanted was not lost on them. I assumed that was why I was allowed to keep sitting at the table in my seat.

CHAPTER SIX

"Wow, Petra is trying to rock the purple velvet pants, huh? Interesting fashion risk... if you don't mind looking like The Hulk." Hillary was unparalleled in the way she threw shade as the self-appointed style doyenne of the cafeteria.

I secretly thought Petra's pants were awesome, but I knew better than to try to challenge Hillary. She'd turn on me in a heartbeat. I couldn't risk it. To stay in this group, to be popular, to be Madison's friend, I had to make some sacrifices.

I knew I needed to be ok with that.

Most of the time Hillary was funny, kind of like one of those comics who judged the fashions celebrities wore on the red carpet. Once she had us in hysterics in a mall food court by pointing out, "See that guy? You can tell he's a douchecanoe by the way he eats that tomato." It was so absurd. But she often went too far, and it didn't matter where on the "humorous to cruel" spectrum she fell; we were expected to find the funny in whatever she said.

Hillary must have sensed my unease, in spite of my mighty effort to seem blasé. She turned her attention to something that would involve me. "Hey look, Sam, 'New Couple' alert! That halitosis-challenged dweebasaurus, Simon, that you used to hang out with in your little Loser Patrol seems to have a new girlfriend!" She speared a pineapple slice smeared with cottage cheese with her fork and popped it into her mouth.

I knew my response mattered, and this was some kind of test. Madison seemed obsessed with her kale and strawberry salad all of a sudden. I guess I appreciated the fact that Madison didn't laugh at this particular joke of

Hillary's, but it did sting that she didn't at least send a consolatory glance my way. Then again, it's not like any of us were brave enough to challenge Hillary.

I especially wanted to point out the fallacy of Simon having bad breath... but I didn't.

"Good for him." I shrugged, hoping this would be perceived as complacent rather than combative, preventing me from having to directly diss Simon.

When I first came to Lancaster at the end of April of sophomore year, all the groups felt pretty tight and impermeable, so I had trouble finding anyone to hang out with. Except the kids who were the outcasts anyway. But when I'd left my old school, I'd grown apart from all my middle school friends after my dad left, so having anyone to hang out with at all was a big change for me. But now that I was friends with Madison, I knew I couldn't also be friends with anyone Hillary dubbed to be in the "Loser Patrol," and that definitely included everyone in Simon's group. I also couldn't expect to keep being Madison's friend without being a Sherpa. And that meant working harder to get Hillary to like me.

I assuaged my sense of guilt about not hanging out with my old acquaintances anymore because I felt like we weren't *that* close. My love of fashion and horror movies irritated them. They preferred to talk about global warming and quantum mechanics.

But Simon had been a true pal.

"Jea-lous of your old boyfriend, Simon, and his new Basic Bae?" Hillary's eyes sparkled. She had me squirming under her paw and wasn't about to let go.

Simon and I had never dated or even had a thing for each other. Frankly, I was psyched for him because I hoped he'd finally found someone who appreciated that he knew how to enumerate pi out to its hundredth digit and could recite all of the words to every Duran Duran song. I'd never heard of that '80s band until Simon once slipped me the lyrics to "She's Come Undone" after I'd hinted that we'd left Philadelphia because my mom wanted to get me away from "bad influences." I think he'd assumed I'd been doing drugs. Only Madison knew the story about my shoplifting.

"No, it's no big deal. We don't hang anymore." I heard my voice, but it didn't sound like me. I had a strong sense I was failing Hillary's test, but I wasn't sure. I could do challenging math proofs, but as far as reading people goes, I'd be put in a remedial class.

"I'm still shipping Simon and Sam! We can call them Sam-mon," Britt said and waited to hear Hillary's derisive laugh before she joined in. Madison smiled but shook her head too, so I wasn't sure where she stood on Britt's comment—did she think it was funny or caustic?

"This chocolate chip cookie is good!" Lauren offered in her high-pitched voice that could probably get her a lot of work in animation voiceovers if she wanted. Hillary rolled her eyes. It didn't look like Lauren would be asked back to the table tomorrow.

Hillary redirected her laser-like focus to me. "Don't you think it's about time you hooked up with someone yourself?" Hillary smiled, showing lots of pearlies. "Even the derpiest of your nerd friends seems to have found someone."

I finally saw her endgame. Hillary had laid a trap for me, and I'd fallen right into it. If I didn't want to be worse than a loser, I needed to name who I was crushing on. Whoever I stated would be fodder for mockery, but not saying anyone would be worse. This wasn't the first time she'd gone after me, but I still didn't know how to prevent the hot flush creeping up my neck like a snake slithering up a tree.

I chose my words carefully. "I haven't found anyone I'm into yet, is all..." I hoped she'd make some comment about my expectations being too high for what I had to offer and leave it at that. But part of me knew better.

To calm myself, I took a breath and mentally started listing the things I needed to do:

1. Stay cool. Don't get up and walk away or you'll lose Madison.
2. Try to have a sense of humour and not be so literal about everything.
3. Stop blushing. You probably look like a tomato.
4. How would Cordelia Chase or Lucinda McCabe or Supergirl handle this? Try to be more like the kickass girls on TV.

"What about Cheekbones? I mean Zach," Madison blurted.

Everyone at the table fixed their gazes on Madison, then on me. I couldn't come up with a reply, so Madison continued, addressing the group. "You should have seen this guy! He was so into Sam. Now all she needs are the cojones to pursue him. And we've all gotta help her light this fire."

Of course, I hadn't told Madison *not* to tell anyone about the other night at the movies. Honestly, I hadn't thought I needed to. But what the heck was she doing? I couldn't tell if her allegiance was to Hillary and she had a great piece of gossip to share with the table or if she was actually trying to help me out. I had to remind myself about what my old psychologist told me. I was overly sensitive to things like this. Friends teased each other. That was part of being a teen. Madison probably just wanted what was best for me. And hadn't my life been pretty miserable before she befriended me?

"So did you get his digits?" Britt wiggled her eyebrows. She thought she was funny. Mainly because her older sister, a senior and the captain of the cheerleading squad, told her she was. Britt was pretty, but just 10% less pretty than her sister, and that drove her crazy. Her nose was just a wee bit pointier, her lips a bit smaller, and her thighs a tiny bit wider. I thought she was a better cheerleader than her sister, though. She jumped higher and screamed louder.

"Nah, that's so boring. Sexting is stupid," Madison answered. "This is even better! We know about a party he and his friends are going to this weekend." Part of me couldn't fathom why Madison would think we should go to the party that Josh had talked about. We didn't know anything about these guys. And we certainly didn't know their friends who were having the party.

"Ooooh, I love me a party!" Britt squealed.

"Oh, yeah? Who invited you to come?" Hillary laughed. Britt looked like a kid who'd just had his caramel apple fall off its stick and into a mud puddle.

Hillary winked at Britt. "No, just joking! We'll all go!"

"Can't. Have a meet," Kensie volunteered. Bad move. Hillary glared at her. Something like that would normally get you booted from Hillary's inner circle. But Kensie was safe for now because everyone said she had a shot at the next Olympics. Hillary loved having people around her with prestige.

"That's why I do Drama instead of sports. Play rehearsals are only Monday through Thursday, so I can be social on the weekends." Hillary kept her eyes on Kensie. "But I guess it's fine to have extra-curriculars on the weekends if you care more about that than a social life." I felt bad for Kensie, but wasn't about to put my neck on the line. We all knew better than to do that.

"Bye, Felicia!" Britt added mirthfully, following Hillary's lead. When Kensie didn't react, Britt started over-explaining. "That's, like, a joke, it means, like, who cares…"

Hillary interrupted, "So… are you going, Sam?"

"I guess if we all went, I'd go," I hedged, not wanting to be the uncool Debbie Downer.

Everyone knew that I could do almost whatever I wanted to do on the weekends. My mom had just rented a studio apartment in Philadelphia to stay Fridays and Saturdays because she was exhausted commuting back and forth from Philly to Lancaster for her job as a real estate agent. She showed high-end properties only on weekends. She said that now that I was almost seventeen, she thought she could trust me. Her business was making so much money, she didn't want to cut back on her hours. She called and texted pretty regularly, and the neighbour, Mrs. Bullock, was supposed to check on me. But she only ever did that once. Her glaucoma "medicine" and Frank Sinatra records seemed to keep her pretty distracted.

Madison jumped in just as the silence was getting unbearable. "Zach was totally hot, not gonna lie. And he had some cute friends, too! Though this one dude, Josh, has the most boring Facebook page ever. He only had one check-in the whole summer, a monster truck show. And maybe four pictures in his album, and, like, fifty friends. Weird." Madison poked at her salad while she was talking but never took a bite. I chewed the inside of my lip a little, because I didn't have many more friends than that myself on Facebook.

"Will there be college guys there?" Delia asked predictably. Delia had big dark-chocolate eyes that opened even wider when she asked a question.

She'd just broken up with her boyfriend, a college freshman, and made it clear that the thought of dating any high school boys disgusted her. "Dating down," she called it. We were seeing more of Delia now that she and Roger had broken up. That wasn't a bad thing, because I liked Delia.

"Pretty sure." Madison ran a napkin across her pout. "Zach is definitely older than us, I know." I felt a weird anger bubbling in my stomach, because Mad was acting like she knew Zach better than I did

"He said he'd already graduated, so I'd guess eighteen," I offered. It sounded defensive, like I had to show off I knew more about him than Madison did.

"You might have some competition for Zach, then..." Delia pointed her spoon at me, insinuating that any guy over seventeen was her potential quarry.

"No way," Madison exclaimed, looking at Hillary for backup. "Zach is Sam's."

"Yes, end of discussion." Hillary smiled at me with her mouth, but the corners of her eyes stayed uncrinkled. "We need to respect that."

"I'm not..." I started, but Hillary ignored me. Her eyes were now locked on Madison.

"I'm glad you found someone to go to the movie with this weekend after I turned you down," Hillary said to her. "You know how I hate horror movies. They're so stupid. But I guess everyone's allowed their opinion."

I knew this was a lie. I hadn't been the backup. Madison and I had always planned to go together. I wondered if Hillary was jealous of our friendship. She had so many other friends. Why couldn't she let Madison have me? Why begrudge me having a real-life fidus Achates?

"Well then, it's a plan!" I smiled at Madison, hoping to help change the subject. It worked. We talked about our plans for Friday's party. But a tiny voice inside me asked, *What the hell are you getting yourself into?*

I knew they'd all be watching me. And Madison would be expecting me to put Plan P into action.

CHAPTER SEVEN

"This can't be the place! There's nothing here but corn!" Madison scrunched her nose up like she smelled fresh fertilizer, but fall wasn't the season for that. We were only a few miles outside of the city of Lancaster, headed toward Manheim, and it was a totally different landscape. There seemed to be more barns than houses out here, more tractors than cars.

"Pipe down back there." Delia laughed, but there was an edge in her voice that signalled she was serious. "These roads are hella curvy, and there aren't any street lights."

Madison and I sat in the back seat of Delia's Prius. Delia was the richest girl in our group, but she always played it down, like, "Oh, it's not my car… it's a family car." Right. But her family was only three people, her and her parents, and they owned six cars. Her dad had designed some software program and sold it for a ton of money.

My mom did well with her real estate commissions, a born saleswoman, but we had nowhere near the kind of money Delia's family did. I appreciated that Delia seemed reluctant to flaunt her money. To be totally honest, I often craved some impossibly fluffy blue cashmere sweater or a delicately beaded Buddha silk wrap bracelet that she wore. Although I was relieved I wasn't so enamoured that I was tempted to find a similar one to steal.

Unfortunately, items still faintly called out to me to take them when I was shopping, but they weren't always the things I coveted in my everyday life. The lure of shoplifting a certain object wasn't necessarily congruent with its price tag or the results of a crowdsourced beauty poll. Once I even stole a five-inch ceramic cat knick-knack. It was right after I'd heard from my mom that my dad got a shelter cat when he moved out, and that pissed me off.

"Hillary, you put the cross streets Josh gave me into the GPS, right? I'm sure we're going the right way." Madison leaned forward to ask Hillary, who was sitting shotgun. Of course she was. "He did say it was a Harvest Party, so maybe it's in a cornfield?"

Britt and her older sister Sasha, a senior, were in the red Geo Prism right behind us. They'd texted Madison a few times in the last couple of minutes to ask us where the heck we were going and if we were sure this whole party thing hadn't been a prank. We'd met up with them before heading out to the party for dinner at Freeze and Frizz, which had the best fries and chocolate shakes in the world. I'd been surprised to see Britt and Sasha had both been wearing short pencil skirts and boots with spiked heels. I'd just worn jeans and a new faux leather shirt with embroidered flowers on it that I'd bought at Park City Mall. It was my first time wearing it. Nobody mentioned they thought it was cool, like I'd hoped they would.

"There's a few cars and a big bonfire up ahead on the right," Madison announced after we rounded a curve. Sure enough, there was a clearing with some vehicles, mostly pickup trucks, parked haphazardly nearby.

Hillary sulked. "Oh, great, a redneck hoedown."

"Aw, come on, it'll be fun!" Delia enthused.

"Bet it smells like badussy." Everyone laughed at Hillary's pronouncement except me.

When I asked what "badussy" was, Madison flashed me a look that told me I should've kept my mouth shut.

"God, Sam, you can be so ridiculously twilight!" Hillary had called me "twilight" before, and Madison explained it meant "pathetically stupid." I made a note that I needed to spend more time on Urban Dictionary.

"Bet they'll for sure have moonshine," Madison coaxed a diversion, and Hillary twisted around to make eye contact. They laughed. They both liked to flaunt what big partiers they were. But unlike them, Delia would usually take a beer and, if you watched her closely, nurse the same one all night. I knew this because I watched *everyone* carefully. I, myself, always declined the booze or other party favours, using some excuse like, "Oh I went overboard last night" or the vague, "Already good, thanks." After that, most people would drop it. If a jerk persisted pressuring me, Madison usually came to my defense with either, "More for us, right?' or "That just means Saint Sam can do a snack run for us!" But if it was someone who irritated Mad, she'd cut them off at the kneecaps with, "What the heck? You can't let people make their own decisions? Leave her alone, she's cool." When Madison spoke up, almost nobody dared to challenge her. Even strangers. I guess that's why it always confused me why she let always Hillary go unchecked.

We found a spot to park where it didn't seem like we blocked anyone in, close enough to the dirt road that we wouldn't get trapped ourselves, and out of the way enough that we wouldn't be hit by anyone driving crazy in the dark. Britt and Sasha pulled up right beside us. Britt jumped out. Instead of getting pissy about her stilettos sinking into the mud, her eyes were all wild-excited.

"Sasha went to a party around here once a couple of years ago when she was a sophomore and said it was off-the-hook-CRAZY!" Britt loved danger.

"I didn't recognize this area until I saw the big purple-and-black Hex sign on that barn over there." Sasha threw her keys in her purse while getting out of her car. "It's because I didn't drive here the last time. I came with some of the Cheer Squad. If it's the same dude throwing the party, or maybe his little brother, watch out!" Then she lowered her voice for dramatic effect. "I saw more drugs floating around than I've ever seen at a party before. Coke, pot, 'shrooms, spice, bath salts, even meth."

"Seriously? That sounds like trouble," I whispered to Madison.

"WE like new adventures, remember?" In the low light, I could barely make out Madison's distinct features, but she either winked at me or rolled her eyes. "You need to put yourself out there if you want Plan P to work."

Sometimes I wondered if Madison expected me to just bone the first guy who paid me some attention. Was that what *she* meant by Plan P?

"Remember that babe magnet, Zach is going to be here." Madison softly squeezed my scrawny bicep. It made me self-conscious; I really should work out more.

I started to object again but then caught Hillary's eye. I was sure she hadn't heard what we'd said, but she was scrutinizing me. She didn't like people keeping secrets from her.

CHAPTER EIGHT

We walked over to the twenty or so people gathered around the bonfire. The air had a cool snap to it, like biting into a Honeycrisp apple fresh out of the fridge. Hillary spotted a gap in the group and manoeuvred us in so that we had a spot with the best potential to make an impression. I still hadn't spoken to anyone. Scanning the twenty or so people gathered at the fire, I saw only two other girls, and the rest were guys. I knew my friends would be liking these odds. There seemed to be more people in little clusters in the shadows, but my eyes hadn't fully adjusted to the dark yet.

"Wait here. I'm going to check everything out. Go see if any guys here are snack-worthy," our fearless leader, Hillary, instructed us. She sauntered off, sporting a pair of skinny J Brand jeans. I knew they retailed for about two hundred dollars because I'd seen some last week at her mom's store, Now and Forever. Most of the dudes did double-takes as she passed.

After the guys checked Hillary out, they turned their attention to Madison, who glowed in the firelight. She looked positively ethereal. I knew that when Madison was standing directly next to Hillary, most people didn't notice Madison's more subtle beauty. I wondered sometimes if that was why Mad started hanging out with me so much lately instead of Hillary. Next to me, Madison could really shine.

That wasn't fair. I knew that. Madison had never been anything but a good friend to me. But sometimes I just couldn't figure out why she'd want to hang out with me.

I stared into the fire.

Madison and I had gotten to know each other at the end of sophomore year. Our school required us to do sixty social service hours to graduate, and Madison and I had both signed up to volunteer at a Head Start preschool on the list of approved organizations. I recognized her immediately during orientation. She was a Sherpa. A popular girl. It took her a little while longer to realize we were even from the same school, because students from a few different schools were there volunteering.

A lot of the student aids just sat on the sidelines, "putting in their time." Not Madison and me. We were pretty into it, gung-ho about playing hide-and-seek and tag on the playground and helping the kids learn their letters and numbers in the classroom. We also both loved art time at Creation Station. We cared about the kids; I think that's what made us appreciate each other.

After that, Madison and I started talking a bit at school, too. But over the summer, that was when we got close. Hillary was down in Los Angeles with her family, getting her sister settled into her new life. When Hillary came back, Madison got her to accept me, or at least tolerate me. A new life began for me then. And I wasn't about to let Madison down. I could do this popular girl thing to keep her as a friend. I knew I could.

I was knocked out of my fire trance by Madison elbowing me in the ribs.

"Hi, Josh!" Madison excitedly waved Josh over.

"So this is Josh." Britt batted her eyelashes like some film noir femme fatale. "Josh, did you help start this fire?"

"No, ma'am, but I've been putting some logs on it to keep it going." Josh smiled. He had a nice wide smile. I heard some mutterings from my friends about how he could start their fires but tried to ignore them and focus on the dark beyond the flame.

I couldn't help it. Part of me was scanning the faces for Zach's. I wanted Zach to see me, to come over and talk to me. But then another part of me hoped he'd ditched going to the party so I wouldn't have to see him again, because he made me feel all weird and nervous. I knew the best way to deal with rejection was not to let it happen to you in the first place.

Yeah, and THIS kind of thinking is why you've never had a boyfriend!

I resolved not to be such a damn coward.

"Hi, you must be Josh!" Hillary said, returning to the group from her scouting expedition. She remembered our descriptions of the guys very well.

"Hi, I..." Josh started, but Hillary was already done with him.

She put her hand on her hip and took a step toward me, asking a little too loudly to be called discreet. "So Sam, where's this Zach of yours?" I didn't reply quickly enough for her, so she flipped her head to Josh. "I want to meet Zach, too!"

"He's around here somewhere..." Josh answered, looking around.

Flustered, taking a step back and looking away from Hillary, I saw Zach. He'd just walked up, across the fire from us. He was talking to one of the two girls who were here before us. Of course he was. It was so silly of me to think he wouldn't have a girlfriend. Before I could look away, he looked straight at me and caught me staring at him. I felt a surge of energy pass through me unlike anything I'd ever felt before. I managed to cut the flow of it between us by tearing my eyes away from his.

"Anyone bring marshmallows?" I asked Josh with a fake cheerfulness that made my voice sound an octave higher than it was.

"OMG, really, Sam? Marshmallows? That's what you're going with?" Hillary laughed. I was relieved that nobody else had seen Zach.

"I think I'd like something stronger than sugar." Madison looked pointedly at Josh. *Oh, so it was going to be one of those nights with Madison... one that she was going to get wasted.*

"We have beer, peach schnapps, some other stuff... What are you looking for?" Josh drawled. I was beginning to think this farmboy thing was just an act as Josh sauntered around, taking everyone's drink orders.

While the other Sherpas were distracted ordering their "adult beverages," I backed slowly away from the fire and found a hay bale to sit on behind a wooden cart. Until recently, I'd spent a lot more time alone, and old habits were hard to break. I needed to regroup. The pressure of small talk weighed on me like an elephant butt. But I knew if I wanted to be a full-fledged Sherpa like Madison, I'd have to up my social game.

The hay pricked me, even with my jeans on.

A guy with a very large chin who was wearing suspenders approached me. "Hallo! You are Elizabeth Yoder's cousin, yah?"

"Huh, what, me?" I stammered. *Yes, Sam, who else? Do you think he's talking to the hay bale?*

"Oh sorry, you are not her." He smiled, revealing a missing incisor. "At least a mistake is evidence you tried!" He grinned wider, and I saw he had a missing back tooth, too. I was trying not to get too creeped out when a divine intervention occurred.

"Hey, I didn't think you would actually come." It was Zach. He stood right beside me. He nodded to the chinny-chin-chin guy, who nodded back before he took off.

I was glad I was already seated, or I think my knees might have buckled.

"Do you mind if I sit down here with you?" he asked. I was hoping the earth would swallow me whole at this point.

"I don't mind, but your girlfriend might." *Did I actually just say that?* Oh jeez. I was such an asshat.

"Girlfriend? I don't have a… oh, wait, you mean my cousin Rachel? That's who I was talking to a couple of minutes ago when I saw you. Sorry I didn't come right over. It's her first party, and she's a little ferhoodled."

Ferhoodled? After that whole Hillary calling me "twilight" thing, I didn't want to ask what yet another word meant. But I think Zach sensed my not understanding.

"Uh, that's overwhelmed and you know, uh, shy."

"Oh, well then, you probably shouldn't leave Rachel alone, right?" I shrugged. What the heck was wrong with me? I totally wanted him to stay, but I kept acting like the biggest ice queen in the world.

"She and her friend Beth were feeling pretty awkward until you and your friends showed up, being as they were the only girls for a while. But I think she's fine now." Zach hadn't sat down and was now pulling back a bit from where I was perched. "But hey, if you want to be left alone, that's cool, too."

Say something! Don't let him go!

"No, no, sorry, just teasing you a bit." Great, now I sounded like Hillary. She always covered with a *Just joking!*

I tried again. "Also, that guy kind of freaked me out. Was he Amish or something?"

"Old Order Mennonite, I think." Zach looked away. He seemed eager to change the subject from that guy who'd been chatting me up. *Could he be jealous, too?*

"Look, parties just aren't easy for me. Anyways, I'm used to feeling out of place. Awkward is my jam!" He didn't laugh at my goofy joke. Great.

"Yeah, I'm not a big party guy myself."

"Sorry, I assumed you and your cousin were dating..." I scooted over and left more than half the bale beside me open, hoping he still wanted to sit down but also worried that he would.

"No problem. Some around here do date their cousins." He didn't laugh, so I wasn't sure how serious he was. I couldn't suppress a discomfited snigger. I worried he'd think I was being contemptuous, but he didn't seem insulted. As he lowered himself down next to me, his right thigh gently brushed my left thigh, leaving a trail of tingly-ness on my leg. "I am never sure what to say or do." I was pretty sure he was totally just telling me what I wanted to hear. I mean, he was gorgeous. But I didn't care. I was kind of flattered he'd lie to get in good with me.

"So what college do you go to? Millersville? F&M? Or one farther away?"

"Oh, no, I'm not in college." He looked up at the stars. "Not that I won't go someday, but right now I'm just working and saving up my money."

"Doing the gap year thing, huh? I might be going that route myself." The fib just popped out. Frankly, I couldn't wait to go away to school. Also, I was doing everything I could to make sure I got a full-ride scholarship so I wouldn't need to feel indebted to my mom for tuition. I wanted to be completely free of her. Good grades, good SATs, lots of academic awards;

that was my plan. My dream school was Columbia. I loved the idea of diving into the sea of people that made up New York City but still having the safety net of attending college at the same time.

"I'd like to make movies some day. The kind of films that make people want to change the world," he said.

Was he for real? I couldn't tell if he was the most snarky, drily sarcastic person I'd ever met or the most earnest. I didn't know how to respond, so I didn't. I was the master of creating uncomfortable silences.

"Do you want a beer or something?" he asked. Great, now he'd find out what a super-dork, nondrinker I was. "I don't drink, but if you want something..."

"No, uh, no, but thanks. Not for me." I couldn't believe it. He didn't drink either! I was giddy. Or maybe that feeling was just the result of second-hand pot smoke that had been wafting around. Someone was smoking some serious skunk.

"Faschnaut?" he said.

Huh? Did he think I'd just sneezed?

"Excuse me?" I asked.

"Oh, a faschnaut is like a donut, it's uh, just slang, I guess." He dipped his head a bit. "My aunt makes them with apple cider. They're pretty good. My cousin brought some and put them on a table over by the beer."

"Sure, thanks, that sounds yummy," I replied. I wished I could take the "yummy" back. What was I, a five-year-old? I'd never wanted to impress a guy so much and had never been failing so miserably. He smiled and left to get me a donut.

After about five minutes, I heard someone come up behind me. I turned with anticipation. I'd been thinking of some things to say and felt more prepared to dazzle Zach this time. But it wasn't just Zach looking down at me like I'd expected. Instead it was a very smashed Madison with her arm locked around Zach's, grinning at me like a deranged jack o'lantern.

CHAPTER NINE

"Hey, look who I found!" Madison said, pointing at Zach like she'd reached the end of a glorious quest. She also sounded like she had peanut butter in her mouth or something.

"This was a surprise to me, too." Zach raised one eyebrow.

"Oh geez, sorry." I directed my comment to Zach, who, despite the low light, clearly looked embarrassed. "Huh. She hasn't had enough time to get drunk on beers... was she doing shots?" Then, before giving him the chance to answer the first question, I fired off another. "Do you know where our other friends are?"

"No, I have no idea. She came up to me while I was looking for the table with the faschnauts and told me we needed to find you. I thought that was a good idea, because she seems a little... uh..." Zach couldn't seem to find the words, so he started again. "There is much more at this party to take than just alcohol... if someone's wanting to get addled."

"Oh great, could someone have put something in her drink?" I asked, but knew that the idea she'd been the innocent target of some jerk who'd spiked her drink was probably just wishful thinking. *What a whack thing to be wishing for.*

Madison seemed to be slumping a bit, head hanging into her chest, but then suddenly snapped to attention. "Hey you guys, I'm right here!" she said, slurring much less than before. "I can TOTALLY HEAR YOU! Hello? Right? Can I get a whoot, whoot?" She laughed. "Anyway... nobody tricked me or roofied me. I wouldn't let that happen." She put her hands on her waist like Wonder Woman and made a tough-girl face. Then she dissolved into giggles. "Dudes! I just took some bath salts some guy gave me. It's cool. I've always wanted to try it."

"Oh, crap, seriously, Madison? Why did you do that?" Madison high and Madison sober were so different.

And this was Madison beyond plastered.

"And by the way, you're WELCOME! I just totally found your boyfriend for you. What the hell? I should get some I should get some gratitude! I mean, I'm helping with Plan P!" Madison tried to stand in a sassy pose, her left hand on her hip and her right finger up in the air like she was hailing a cab, but stumbled while trying to pop her hip out to the side. Zach had quick reflexes; he moved in and caught her, preventing her from taking a massive header. It was good he did. Her "boyfriend" comment had paralyzed me.

"I'm not sure what she's talking about…" I muttered, blushing. But Zach didn't seem to have heard.

"Wow!" Madison fondled Zach's triceps. "You work out a lot, doncha? That's nice. Sam, feel these!" She was acting all Amazonian princess-y again. Madison's attempt to channel a warrior goddess inspired me to wish I had the superpower to erase Zach's mind regarding the last few minutes.

A loud boom pierced the air, followed by some crackling. I felt the impact of the sound in my chest and instinctively ducked my head between my shoulders.

"Just fireworks." Zach smiled at me sheepishly. "These guys love them for some reason." I found it odd that he didn't refer to the people at the party as his "friends."

"Hey, let's go dance! All of us! I'm feeling ROWDY!" Madison laughed and started doing a mambo like a rhythmically challenged competitor on *So You Think You Can Dance*.

"What should we do?" Zach asked me, wisely ignoring her. "I'm afraid she's going to kutz."

"Kutz?" I asked.

Zach took a breath. "Uh, yeah, sorry. It means vomit. But maybe getting all that junk out of her system would be helpful at this point…"

"Oh, right. Makes sense. We just want to make sure it's not all over herself." Zach nodded solemnly. "Well..." I paused, thinking of options. "We can't take her home, obviously, but I also don't think it's a great idea to stay here, because it'd be hard to keep her out of trouble in this stupid dark cornfield. Besides falling into some sharp farm equipment, she could keep taking other drugs or hook up with a stranger... or you know, something." My tongue stumbled, because I didn't want to seem like I was judging Madison or that I thought Zach's friends were gross or anything. "So... maybe take her somewhere where she can sober up. I wish I knew where our other friends went."

"Hill was showing everyone how she could ghost a hit of weed," Madison offered.

"Really? Really?" I massaged my eyebrows to help me think. What the heck was I going to do with two messed-up friends? I hoped I found Delia to help me with the rest of them.

"Do you want to look, and I'll stay here with her?" Zach asked. "I'd offer to go look for the other girls, but I'm afraid I'd have a hard time recognizing them because...." He cocked his head. "I was kind of distracted by looking at you."

Did he just say he was into me? I didn't know how to react with my face. *Smile? Wink? Roll my eyes?*

"No, I agree, it's better if I go, I think," I said, acting like I hadn't even heard.

Madison was still rubbing Zach's arm and purring a bit. I didn't like that Madison was flirting with Zach. I knew she was bombed and wasn't really trying to make a play for Zach, but it still pricked at me. "Are you sure you can handle her, though?" I asked Zach.

"My head hurts," Madison mumbled.

"Yeah, maybe I can just take her somewhere where she can relax?" He was scanning the area. More guys had been showing up, and it was getting noisy.

"How about your car? She can lie down if she wants," I suggested. "And also, she can't get away in case she tries."

"Who'd want to get away from this dreamy goodness?" Madison's garbled comment was again ignored by us. But inside I seethed.

"Uh, I don't have a car... here... uh, my car..." Zach stammered.

A nasty, completely unjustified part of me wondered if he was lying and he just didn't want to get puke all over the inside of his precious car. I knew how guys could be about their rides. But I realized I wasn't being fair. Zach was going out of his way to help me when he didn't need to. He barely knew me.

"Ok, how about we take her to Delia's car? She has a combo lock on the door, so we can get in without a key." Luckily I had a great memory for numbers, and I'd seen her punch her code in a few times. Zach took one of Madison's arms and put it over his shoulders, and I did the same with the other.

Madison Is Wasted: My Options

1. Call a cab and just go home without her. Except I don't know if cabs come to cornfields. Also, that'd make me a coward and a bad friend.

2. Stay and hang with Zach and let Madison deal with her own decisions. But how horrible would I feel if she got hurt?

3. Call Madison's parents to come get her. Yeah, THAT would actually make me the worst friend ever.

4. Ask Zach to help me babysit her until she stopped acting so weird. But I didn't know him that well, so expecting him to deal with her craziness seemed unfair.

5. Try to handle sobering her up all by myself. Nope. I was so out of my depth. That'd be like asking Hillary to give a lecture about compassion to a bunch of Buddhist monks.

6. Find my flaky friends and beg them to help me. Unfortunately, that was the only option that made sense.

After we got Madison settled into the shotgun seat of Delia's car, Zach got in the driver's seat to watch her. We agreed that letting her totally fall asleep probably wasn't a good thing. She seemed to be swinging from hyper to almost comatose and then back again, pretty quickly.

"Hey, thanks," I said to Zach. "I mean it. I don't know what I'd do without you here helping me."

"It's not any trouble," he replied. "Besides, maybe it'll be a great story to tell our grandchildren one day, how on our first date, I couldn't try to sweet talk you like I'd wanted so I had to wait to try to win you over another time."

I'd never heard a guy at school talk like that. Was he playing me? Damn this dark. I couldn't read his face to see if he was being facetious, flirty, or serious. He was one inscrutable guy. *Maybe too mysterious?* But I didn't have time to think about him. I had to find the Sherpas.

CHAPTER TEN

B ritt was easy to find. She was, predictably, hitting on Josh. I told her what was going on with Madison and that she needed to help me find the others. She reluctantly walked away with me but kept looking back at Josh.

"I can't believe he goes back to Ohio in two days," she said, her little feet stomping on the ground. "That sucks! He's yummy."

"Well, he needs to get back for classes, I guess." I grabbed her hand and pulled her through the crush gathered on the outskirts of the bonfire, all the time scanning the faces for the other lost members of our tribe. "Keep your eyes open for the others," I instructed Britt.

"He didn't mention his classes. Which college did he tell you guys he goes to, again?" Britt asked.

"Come on. PLEASE. Focus!" I begged. I wanted to be more forceful, but I didn't dare offend any of the Sherpas. "Sorry, but we need to find everyone and get back to Madison and Zach."

"I don't think it's Madison you want to get back to. I think it's Zach! True story. Boom!" She said it all sing-songy, like we were in third grade.

Before I could tell her how crazy-pants she was, I spotted Delia and Hillary in line at the keg. It was a long line, and they were in the middle of it. Lots of guys stood around waiting, too, but a few more girls had shown up. Most of the new girls were clearly with a guy, holding hands or standing very close. I also noticed many of the guys wore tight shirts, and a lot of the girls sported trendy maxi skirts and stylish high boots. I felt like I was at Opa, my mom's favourite upmarket Philadelphia restaurant.

"Hey!" Hillary waved to us. When we got closer, she used a fake stage whisper that was loud enough for everyone around us to catch. "My god, I don't know if another beer is worth this. The dude in front of us has the worst freaking stank ever!"

"And check out the Justin Bieber look-a-like a few people in front of him!" Delia laughed.

I glanced down the line. I was certainly no expert, but it seemed like there might be more than one Mennonite kid here. Mennonites came from the same background as the Amish, but most weren't as extreme. I did a little reading up on this when I moved here. I found out that though the Old Order Mennonites avoided cars and electricity, many other Mennonite groups assimilated, and some even went to local high schools and colleges. Obviously, from what I was seeing tonight, some partied quite hard, too. That fact hadn't been in any of the books I'd read.

"Farm boys." Hillary stuck out her tongue and rolled her eyes.

"Where's Sasha?" I bluntly interrupted their catty chatter. "Britt, have you seen your sister? Look, Madison is in bad shape, and I think we need to get her outta here."

"What's wrong?" Delia asked, brows furrowed.

"Madison took some random drug she got from a shady dude she just met!" The admiration in Britt's voice pissed me off. I'd had to tell her about how trashed Madison was to tear her away from Josh, but leave it to Britt to make the drama rival some *Real Housewives* episode.

"Bath salts, I think," I added, trying to sound more casual than disapproving, but I'm not sure if I pulled that off.

"No way!" Hillary snickered. "So she's having a total freak out? Hilarious AF!"

"Not literally a meltdown or anything, but she is seriously messed up, and let's face it, we don't know exactly what or how much she took," I told them. "So we need to find Sasha and all get back to the cars."

"Where exactly are they?" Hillary asked but had already turned her attention from me, her eyes locked on the keg that she was now only about two people from reaching.

"She's in Delia's car with Sam's new boyfriend!" Britt squealed. "I think Sam's so uptight right now because she's afraid Madison's putting the moves on him, and he might be into it!"

Britt was tap dancing on my last nerve at this point. I felt myself grinding my teeth, something I hadn't done in ages. Not since my shoplifting days.

"Maybe we should head out." Delia shrugged. "I'm totes snoozing here at this hootenanny."

"Well, Delia, why don't you just go with Sam, then?" Britt said. "Hill can come back with Sasha and me. It's all good." Britt grabbed a cup by the keg and let Hillary pump some beer into it. Then they switched positions.

"You guys are seriously staying?" I knew they were selfish, but their apathy about Madison taking unknown drugs from some stranger floored me.

"Look, if it's bath salts, she'll come down soon, couple of hours max. Probably," Britt said. "It's pretty short-lived if she only took a regular amount. I've seen people on it before. You guys might just want to wait it out, too. Then we can all stay!"

"Yeah, don't take her home, or she'll get in a shitload of trouble," Hillary agreed. "Besides, it sounds like you're over-reacting. I know Madison, and she can handle anything."

I was getting pissed. I'd only been to one other party with the Sherpas, and I'd never seen them behaving like such douchecanoes. Getting drunk was one thing; I knew how to deal with people who were drinking wine or beer, and I'd watched my mom tip back her wine enough times to know what to expect. But bath salts were outside my wheelhouse.

Remember, this is what you wanted. Friends come with problems. I told the nagging voice in my head to STFU. But I also swallowed my irritation. It tasted like arugula.

"Lead the way, Sam." Delia nodded at me, ignoring their comments.

As we walked away, Britt called after us, "Hey Sam, looks like you'll have to wait to be alone to make out with your boyfriend some other time!" Then lots of laughter. *What were they implying? Did they know I'd never made out with anyone before?*

Hillary sighed and added, "I really wish some people would learn the art of ghosting away. You don't always need to say goodbye." More laughing.

I didn't turn around to give them the satisfaction of a reaction. Delia and I had to go deal with the chaos that was Madison.

CHAPTER ELEVEN

When we arrived at Delia's car, we were surprised to find it empty. "I swear… they were right here inside the car when I left a few minutes ago." I scanned the area, straining my eyes to see in the dark between the cornstalks.

"Maybe Madison got away from him and went back to the party. She can be sneaky and quick… especially when she's hammered," Delia said.

"Oh, great. She's probably got Zach chasing her through the cornfield."

"Or he didn't want to deal with her anymore, so he just took off."

"No, that doesn't seem like him." I didn't know why I was standing up for him. I barely knew him. Zach didn't strike me as a wuss.

"Yeah, you're right, I'd have definitely chased her if she tried to escape. Although if she'd done a serpentine move she might have gotten away," came a familiar voice from behind me. I turned, and there Zach stood with Madison. I loved that he made a joke in such an awkward situation.

"I had to pee!" Madison blurted and then giggled. "Geez, whaddaya want me to do, pee on Delia's front seat?"

"Absolutely not," Delia said. "How are you feeling?"

"Fine. God. Stop making such a federal case of everything. You're not my mom!" She continued, muttering unintelligible things about her mother under her breath.

"Where did you take her?" Delia asked Zach.

"Over by the trees. It was a challenge, giving her enough privacy but also making sure I was able to see the top of her head well enough to know she was still there," Zach said.

Even though I was contributing nothing to the conversation, standing there like a stupid garden gnome, Zach hadn't taken his eyes off me. His words were a reply to Delia's question, but it was me he grinned at.

"So who says that I wanted any freakin' privacy?" Madison said, wiggling her eyebrows and then pouting. Was she making a joke or actually trying to be sexy right now? Gross. *What about her telling everyone Zach was "mine"?* Then I reminded myself that she couldn't help herself; she was high.

"I guess the discretion was more for my benefit than hers, then," Zach said, and I couldn't help but to grin back at him.

"What-EVER!" Madison said. "Hey, Delia, did you bring me a beer?" She ran her fingers through her somewhat matted hair, obviously still caring how she looked. *I guess that's a good sign?.*

"That's the last thing you need. Let's get some soda or coffee or something. And you need some food in you." Delia opened her car door.

"House of Pizza!" Madison shouted.

"Sure, if that's what sounds good to you. I'm fine with that. Ok with you, Sam?"

"Yeah, cool," I replied. Zach helped me get Madison into the front seat, and I buckled her up. I noticed he had bigger, stronger hands than any boys I went to school with.

"Here's a plastic bag if you feel like puking," I heard Delia say to Madison before we closed the passenger door.

"Hey… thanks a lot," I said to Zach, embarrassed to be almost alone with him for the first time since he'd told me he wanted to chat me up.

"Not a problem. I enjoyed being able to help," he replied. I wondered what it'd feel like if he just wrapped his arms around me and pulled me close.

I snapped back from my petite paracosm. "No, seriously, I don't know what I would've done without you." I didn't want to get in the backseat, but I knew I'd have to soon if I couldn't figure out something else to say. Then we'd drive away, and that would be that.

"Well, it was kind of my fault. My friends and I did invite you here, right?" *Is it my imagination or is he stalling saying goodbye, too?*

"No, it wasn't your..." I started to say, but then the passenger window next to us rolled down.

"Geez, Either kiss him and give us something interesting to watch, or get your ass in the car!" Madison demanded. I got flustered. I'd just been trying to figure out a way to ask him to meet us at House of Pizza, but I knew he didn't have a car here.

"Oh. Ok, ok." I fumbled with the backdoor handle.

"Sorry we couldn't talk more." Zach's voice sounded wistful, but neither of us had a clue how to stop this train from leaving the station.

"Yeah, uh, me too. Well, bye, I guess. And thanks again." I lowered myself into the seat, closed the door and sat, looking straight ahead. I wondered if he was still looking at me. I was hoping he'd yank the door open and tell me he wanted to hang out with me tomorrow. I've always been a fan of the Hail Mary plays. I heard something, and my heart leapt. I lowered the window.

"Huh? Did you say something?" I asked. Delia had started the car.

"Nope!" He smiled blithely.

Not exactly what I'd been hoping for. "Oh."

"Hopefully I'll see you again," he offered, probably feeling sorry for me. I clearly misinterpreted everything as usual.

I smiled weakly and said, "Sure," and then pushed the button to roll the window back up.

We left the cornfield slowly, and nobody talked for a good five minutes. Madison had slumped over, leaning against her window—I figured she'd probably passed out—and Delia was concentrating on not hitting any drunk partygoers who might stumble in front of her car. Then suddenly Madison piped up.

"Oh geez, don't be so bummed out, Sam." She relished loudly breaking the silence. "When we were alone, I told Zach you liked him, and I gave him your cell number. I'm sure he'll be calling you soon."

CHAPTER TWELVE

The weekend had been uneventful after Friday night's memorable gathering. Because the pizza had only partially straightened up Madison's faded self, she stayed over at my mother-less house. She slept fine and wanted to go get breakfast together the next morning. But even though she was sober, I felt itchy to get her home the next morning. I liked my alone time on the weekends. Saturday I did homework and rearranged my room. That afternoon I watched Hulu, some '80s flick called *Fast Times at Ridgemont High*. And I kept checking my cell every hour.

Zach never called.

Part of me resented Madison's presumption, giving Zach my phone number. Especially since he probably wasn't interested.

But another part of me wished Madison had gotten *his* number for *me* instead of the other way around. When I told her that, she just laughed.

"Yeah, right! Like you would've been brave enough to call him!" she said. That girl was smarter than a lot of people gave her credit for.

By Sunday, I couldn't help myself. I checked my damn cell every ten minutes. Nothing. I was losing it. I wanted to go to the mall to steal something so bad, it made my head buzz. Instead I did some yoga and made a list.

Reasons Why Zach Hasn't Called

1. The most obvious—he's just not that into me
2. The second most likely—he lost the number (because... see reason #1)

3. He lied. And already has a girlfriend and decided not to be a Man-Tramp.

4. Madison told him of my "racking" past, and he doesn't want to date a thief.

5. He hates that my friends liked to get hammered, because he doesn't, so he's steering clear of me.

6. An Elf on a Shelf doll came to life because of an evil curse, and its first act was to eviscerate Zach to make cookies from his entrails...

My dark humor served as a drop of antidote in a sea of poison, but it helped. I was still bummed about Zach not calling, but I also felt free from the stress of this drama.

I was feeling more serene until right before bed Sunday night. I remembered my mom telling me, "Men always want their freedom more than anything." Maybe Zach thought about it and decided to dodge a bullet by not calling me. He could be unencumbered. I imagined that sense of relief was what my dad felt when he left my mom and me.

CHAPTER THIRTEEN

I sat in my first-period math class Monday morning, barely paying attention to Mr. Carter, who was droning on in his pedantic way about concepts I'd learned years ago. My dad was a math genius who'd taught me theorems beyond what any of my school math teachers had. Other kids and their dads played Yahtzee or threw a ball around while my dad and I challenged each other to math games. Of course, that was before he left. Now that he wasn't around, I was on my own with high-school math. And everything else. But I was doing just fine without him.

"...An asymptote runs tangent to a parabola's curve for an infinity, the function's line, getting closer and closer but never actually touching or intersecting the asymptote..." Mr. Carter's monotone continued to describe computation techniques involving "knowing and using limits" and the importance of "ascertaining the orientation."

The metaphor was not lost on me.

I was a human asymptote.

When people tried to get close to me, I didn't let them. I'd come a long way from the introvert I'd been in middle school but still never had a boyfriend. It was like I emitted a faint whiff of, "Beware, hot mess here!" I'd never even had a guy try to kiss me. Why would I think Zach was any different? I had no idea what his "orientation" or "limits" were, but it didn't matter. I knew I was the one with the invisible force repelling everyone.

I was depressed. Plan P was hopeless. I was hopeless.

Maybe if I'd thought more about *Zach's* possible limits, things would have started making sense sooner for me.

But I pushed the doubts aside. "I'd be ok coming to pick you up."

"No, it's fine. I can come straight to the restaurant from work downtown. I'm so close anyway," he said. "Why don't we just meet at Lombardo's?"

Now the Madison voice in my head and my own snarky inner voice both laughed at me. *Great. He probably lives with his girlfriend, too.* I told the Faux Madison in my mind to stop being so paranoid.

"Oh, ok, so Friday then?" I looked down at the paper on my desk and the pen in my hand. I'd been doodling vortexes. I had no clue what that meant, but a shrink would probably have a field day with it.

"Is that best for you?" His voice coming out of my phone snapped me back.

"Well, you said you'd be coming from work, so I guess I just assumed…"

"Oh, yes! Right. Certainly." Then he paused. "Well, actually I work both Fridays and Saturdays, so either night would work for me."

"Do you work on Sundays too?" I was hoping he'd tell me more about what he did, without me coming right out and asking like one of those horrible girls on the stupid reality dating shows my mom liked to watch.

"Sundays? No!" He laughed then broke off abruptly. "Oh, wait that's not funny. Some do work Sundays. Do you?."

"Uh, no. I don't have a job yet." Awkward to the power of ten. I didn't get why working Sundays would be funny to him. But I laughed too, anyway. It felt good to have a joke between us. This time my laugh sounded a little closer to my true laugh, and a little less like a crazed hyena-girl's.

"So, Friday it is then. I will reserve a table for seven o'clock if that's good for you?"

"Sounds great!" I replied. Just then a clicking noise, different from cell interference, almost like someone had picked up separate land line but a little different from that sound too. I wanted to ask what it was, but before I could, he answered.

"Ok, I must go now! I am looking forward to our date Friday. I'll see you then. Goodbye!"

"Bye," I said to a dial tone. Weird. He definitely seemed to be hiding something whenever he flipped into that peculiar speech pattern. It kind of reminded me of the uptight Rupert Giles on the first season of *Buffy*. But I couldn't worry about his hasty signoff for too long because I'd just said yes to my first date! I guess I wasn't so geeky after all. I was filled with hope. Maybe my days of being an asymptote were behind me.

CHAPTER FOURTEEN

I woke up Friday morning with a stomach cramp. I thought my dinner last night might have been the culprit. My mom had eaten a Jenny Craig frozen dinner, like she did every Thursday night, so I'd made myself a grilled cheese and tomato sandwich with some super-sharp cheddar we'd gotten at the farmer's market last month. Maybe it had gone bad? But I'd scraped the mold off it and had only eaten the part that seemed ok. Neither my mom nor I was big on grocery shopping, so we never had much in the fridge. It was always a random collection of weird stuff like garlic-stuffed olives, rye bread, and Dr. Brown's diet cream soda. Even a contestant on *Chopped* would have a problem in our house. Though arguably any real cook would have loved all the ultra-modern appliances, granite countertops, and subzero fridge that my mom had bought for the place but never touched. I think our oven door still had a layer of thin plastic on it from when it had been delivered six months ago.

I'd gone to bed early last night. My mom knocked back a few glasses of red wine after dinner, and she got weepy like she does sometimes, saying things like, "You know I'm doing the best I can, right? I didn't ask to be a single mom! It's not what I chose." And the perennial favourite, "Is it my fault your father sucks at everything, including parenting? He's always been such a disappointment… in so many ways." I particularly hated when she hinted how unsatisfying her marriage had been in the bedroom. It made my cheeks burn like they were leaves under a giant magnifying glass in the sizzling sun. Sometimes I'd pat my mom's arm and tell her I was fine, though most times I did that, I wasn't sure I was selling that cliché very effectively. Others, like last night, I just left. I slipped away to my room, where I read Stephen King or Chelsea Cain and slept like a baby... fitfully and erratically.

The next morning, I couldn't stand up straight without a pain like a knife twisting in my core. I walked to the bathroom all hunched over to brush my teeth. My mom had gotten up and left for work already. I tried, but I couldn't stand to take a shower. I was in such agony.

I considered that my stomach pain might be psychosomatic. Maybe I was nervous or wary about the date I'd made for tonight, and that was manifesting in a "pain." I tried to take deep breaths. I attempted to will it away but wasn't making any headway with that mind over matter absurdity.

I went online to check out some medical websites. It looked like I either had a gas bubble, Crohn's disease, or a black widow spider bite.

I knew I could stay home from school. My mother wouldn't care. She knew I liked school, so if I stayed home, she'd figure I must seriously be incapable of going. I was more likely to lie to avoid staying home than the other way around.

Ultimately, what made me decide to stay home was that I realized I wouldn't have to lie to my girlfriends about my plans for the night. Hillary, Madison, and Britt had been talking about going to the football game at Manheim Central and assumed I'd be going out with them. I'd be off the hook. I didn't know why, but I didn't want to tell Madison about my date yet. I knew she'd get so excited about me making strides toward manifesting Plan P. But I just didn't want the pressure, I guess.

At noon, I panicked and considered cancelling, so I called Zach's cell that I'd added to my contacts from our only conversation. Only the phone just rang and rang without going to voicemail. *Suspicious.* But I won't lie, I also felt kinda excited knowing I couldn't back out. Because deep down, I didn't really want to.

I drank a bottle of Coke. I felt much better after burping while resting on the couch, watching an *Angel* marathon. I especially enjoyed the one that featured a doctor/stalker-creep detaching his body parts and using his eyeball the peep on the poor girl that was his obsession. Of course, Angel made sure that twat-muffin got what he deserved.

I was glad that I was meeting Zach at the restaurant instead of going there with him, because I remembered reading in an article in *Marie Claire* magazine titled "First Date Tips" that you should always drive yourself to a first date. You should also never leave your drink unattended at the table or bar. And you should have a friend scheduled to call you an hour into it in case you want to leave. I thought the first two tips were good, but the third was kinda cynical. What kind of person plans to ditch a date if bored? Seemed like a move from the Hillary playbook.

I decided to wear the Desigual purple tunic I'd just snagged at Goodwill with some black leggings. Sometimes I managed to get into Goodwill or the Salvation Army before the upscale vintage shops sent their buyers in to cherry-pick. It was more fun to do that than to buy online. The thrill of the chase. I loved Spanish designers like Custo Barcelona, Desigual, Mango, and Agatha Ruiz de la Prada. Stuff that was too cutting edge for Hillary's mom's shop, though I'd never dare say that to Hillary. You'd see some of these labels every now and then in Lancaster's resale stores, because the city was only three hours to NYC by train, and lots of people went in to shop.

I know, nerdy girls like me aren't supposed to care about fashion. But I spent many evenings on Hautelook.com, RueLala.com, Giltgroup, etc. Madison and I would pore over the items that would be our top picks if we won the lottery. She went for Michael Kors, Kirna Zabete, and William Rast. Me? I liked colours. The world was bleak enough. But I never wore my most unusual clothes to school; I wasn't ready yet to face Hillary's probable derision. I just wore safe stuff to blend in. But I was feeling more daring tonight.

I found parking a block and a half from the restaurant, which seemed like a good sign. The area of Lancaster the restaurant was in was an "up-and-coming hot spot" with lots of new art galleries and bistros, near the train station. Our three-storey condo, replete with all the latest technology like heated bathroom floors, was only about two miles away. I'd have preferred the charm of an older row house with built-in bookcases and cupboards in the old School Lane Hills area of town, but my mom liked having the newest and sleekest.

I saw Zach standing in front of the restaurant, waiting, before he saw me. I didn't know whether to wave or to act distracted, like I didn't see him. I didn't want to seem too eager. Desperate. A second after making the decision to play it cool, I waved anyway. With both hands. I must have looked like a nutcase being dive-bombed by bees. He smiled and waved back.

When I reached Zach, I felt like the wind had been knocked out of me. He looked great, like a guy out of a PacSun ad: khakis, a dark blue shirt that matched his eyes, and a big smile pushing those cheekbones even higher. *A gorgeous older guy and I am going on a date.* I felt like I'd just slipped through a wormhole into an alternate reality. But there was an Agent Scully part of me waiting for the real explanation for this phenomenon. Like maybe his friends would all pop out from behind a bush and laugh at me for thinking Zach would want to date me.

"I love the eggplant parmesan at this place," he said, opening the door for me. "The spaghetti carbonara is pretty good, too."

"I don't eat bacon," I replied, but then I worried he'd think I was judging him. "But eggplant parm sounds awesome. And hey, you order what you want, don't think twice. Wait…. except veal. If you could not get the veal, I'd appreciate it. That would bum me out to be seated at the table with a dead baby cow. I hope that's ok. You weren't going to get veal, were you?"

"No, the way they're kept before they're killed upsets me, too." He stopped at the wait station. "Stoltzfus. Table for two."

I thought it was a funny last name, but I knew it was not an uncommon one in this area. So many kids at my school had Pennsylvania Dutch backgrounds. My first hint that they did was in their references. Every now and then I'd hear about someone's grandmother serving "pig's stomach" or "scrapple." Britt once told me her parents had Belsnickle visit a couple of weeks before Christmas. Belsnickle, a PA Dutch tradition, was kind of like

Santa's evil twin, a dirty, mean dude who carried a switch that was supposed to scare kids into being good. Having the last name of Lapp, Yoder, Beiler, Stoltzfus or any of the other common names didn't mean a person knew or respected their PA Dutch history, though. For instance, this sophomore, John Beiler, seemed to purposely target Amish and Mennonite farms when cow-tipping and tagging barns.

On the way over to our table, I saw a familiar face. Luckily it didn't belong to Hillary or any of her Sherpas. It was my old friend from The Loser Patrol, Simon, having dinner with his mom and dad in the front corner of the restaurant near the window. That surprised me, because at school he always tried to pretend he didn't know his dad.

His dad, Mr. Evans, was a counsellor at school, but I didn't know him very well. It was always weird to see teachers or adults from school outside of school. I don't particularly like knowing they have another "outside" life and I think my friends feel the same way. I'd met Simon's mom once or twice at school functions, and she'd always seemed nice—a bit of an aging hippie lady, but not too goofy. Although I hesitated for a second going by their table, Simon didn't see me, which was a relief. I had a twinge of guilt that I hadn't spent much time with him since becoming friends with Madison over the summer. I resolved to try to talk to him in school, though it'd have to be sometime Hillary wasn't around, because she'd go after me mercilessly. But now was not the time, either. This was my first real date, and I wanted to focus on that right now.

"So what are you doing this weekend?" Zach asked after we sat down.

"No big plans." I dove into the bread basket for the parmesan-crusted focaccia.

"You work on the weekends, right? Where?" So much for trying to be subtle.

He paused, seeming a little flustered, he but recovered quickly. That seemed odd. It wasn't like that was a mega-private question. *Oh no, maybe he thinks I'm trying to find out how much money he makes. Like I think his job is an important factor in deciding if I want to go out with him again.*

"Not that it matters to me where you work." *God, could I be more tacky?* I was sure it was obvious I didn't have any experience with dating small talk. I loaded up my thick slab of yeasty goodness with butter.

"I have two jobs, actually. My Friday/Saturday gig is only part-time, helping out with my cousin's business. Monday through Fridays, during the day, I work over at the Armstrong factory trying to save up enough for college."

"Your parents didn't put some aside for that?" I regretted it almost as soon as the words left my mouth. My mom was always talking about money, budgeting, investing, etc. She was the one obsessed with money, not me.

"Well, they didn't go to college themselves, so they don't see the point. Also, I have eight brothers and sisters, so they don't have a lot of money." He looked like someone told him he'd have to settle for only one bowl of oatmeal, mouth thin, chin lowered.

I felt even worse now. Wow, nine kids in the family. That was just begging for a reality show. But I figured it'd be rude to suggest they pitch themselves as a TV show to Lifetime as a way to make some cash. "Hey, I've got some books on how to score college scholarships, if you ever want to look at them."

"Definitely." He smiled at me, giving me hope I didn't totally ruin this date. "So many of my friends are only concerned with 'boozing and cruising.' It's nice to talk with someone else with goals."

"Your friend, Josh, has goals though, right? I mean he's in college now, didn't he say?" I asked. But before he could answer, the waitress brought our eggplant entrees. Zach wasn't kidding; these were heavenly. We mmm-ed and ahhhh-ed through our first bites and giggled at the way the stringy cheese hung from our mouths.

I laughed. "I feel like a zombie eating someone's unmanageable intestines."

"Don't zombies only eat brains?" He cocked his head.

"Depends. In some movies, yeah. But I've been watching *The Walking Dead*, and on that show, the zombies like to chow down on any kind of human flesh. Doesn't have to be brains."

"I like how you can talk about zombies chewing people but still get upset about people eating cows." Zach put down his fork and gazed at me.

Could I have finally found someone who got me? Or did I just have a giant flake of oregano in my teeth?

I had no time to try to figure it out, because my blurt mechanism kicked in again. "Madison and I lied to you!"

Then I did feel like dying and letting myself become a zombie, right then and there, so I wouldn't have to face him.

CHAPTER FIFTEEN

"**M**adison made it sound like we were seniors when we first met you at the pizza place, but we're not. I'm a junior—I'm only sixteen." I braced myself for his inevitable disdain.

"Oh." Zach laughed. "Is that all? I'm only seventeen. So we're not that far apart."

A wave of relief swept over me. "I'm actually going to be seventeen in a couple of weeks! I thought you might be a lot older, because you're out of school and everything."

"Graduated young." But before he could say any more, the waitress came over again.

For dessert we split a flourless chocolate cake. I wasn't a big tiramisu fan, and Zach didn't like cannolis, but we agreed that we both loved chocolate. Truthfully, I knew I was too full from the eggplant and bread to do much more than pick at the dessert, but I didn't want the dinner to be over. So when Zach had suggested splitting dessert, I'd enthusiastically jumped on the idea. He must have thought I had a tapeworm.

"I don't normally lie to people," I told him when the waitress left. I expected a laugh, but instead Zach looked away for a brief moment. *Is he lying to me about something?* Then he looked back at me and gave me that smile again, the one that made my toes tingle.

Then this led to a conversation about whether we'd lie or tell the truth to our friends and family if we found out we were werewolves. The choice was: lie and hope we didn't eat anyone on the full moon or tell the truth and ask for help but risk having the proper authority take us away or chain us up for the rest of our lives. It was a conundrum. I said I'd tell someone, but that was actually a lie. I knew deep down I'd never tell anyone. I had nobody to tell that I'd trust 100%. I knew I'd be surreptitious and take my chances. Zach admitted he wasn't sure what he'd do.

"So have you ever played Two Truths and a Lie?" I used my fork to scrape a little icing off the top of the giant cake slice the waitress had just brought. I'd remembered seeing this game played in a movie once, and it looked fun.

"Two Truths and a Lie? No, how do you play that?" He seemed hesitant. *Crapola.* Things had been going so well. I hoped I wasn't screwing anything up.

"Well, you tell me three things about yourself. Only two of those things will be weird true things, things that might be hard for me to believe, and then one thing will be a lie. You don't do them in any fixed order. Then I have to guess: which one is the lie?"

"That sounds fun." Zach still seemed wary, but willing. He scraped a little icing off the top of the cake with his fork. It struck me as impressive how his big hands could so delicately grip the utensil. Then he drank some milk. It was adorable he'd ordered a large glass of milk with dessert. He said he couldn't imagine eating cake without it.

"Can you go first?"

"Oooh-k." I took a deep breath. "Number one, I had a black and white rat with an extra toe named Elvis for a pet when I was a kid. Number two, I went to Costa Rica when I was eleven and saw an active lava flow on a volcano. Number three, I once threw up on Cinderella at Disney World."

I heard Zach's belly laugh for the first time. It was glorious. It made me feel warm and protected. I was sad when it was over.

"Oh, this is the best game ever! I almost don't want to know the lie! They are all so wonderful." He leaned back and narrowed his eyes as if trying to psychically read me. I arched my eyebrows and tried to look like a blank slate so he wouldn't be able to read any of my "tells."

"Um, I'm going to say that Number Three is the lie," he said, "but I don't want it to be."

"Good, because I *did* throw up on Cinderella! I was eight and had just eaten churros, an ice cream bar, and a frozen lemonade. Right after that, I went on the teacups. Then, as soon as I got off, my parents shuttled me over to the autograph station, where Cinderella and the Fairy Godmother were. The whole thing is a bit of a blur, but I remember Cinderella just kept smiling, even after I spewed chunks down the front of her blue satin dress. Didn't get mad at me or anything. Just smiled and excused herself." I didn't mention that this was the last big vacation that we'd taken as a family. My childhood always seemed to involve incidents of ridiculous splurges followed by poverty and bills.

"Wow. That's hilarious." Zach smiled. "So which one was the lie?"

"Ah, the rat named Elvis. I've never had a pet. Always wanted one. My friend Graham who lived in the same apartment building that I did when I was ten had a rat named Elvis, and I was very jealous."

"Never had a pet? Really?" Zach shook his head and smiled in a bemused way as if I'd said our family didn't have a TV or something. *It isn't that rare not to have a pet, is it?* Then he asked, "So… you got to see an active volcano?"

"Yep, Arenal. I still remember how beautiful the lava looked at night from our cabin porch." What I'd intentionally left out of that story was why I was stuck out on the porch at night for a few hours. My mom and her boyfriend, Roger, wanted the three-room cabin we were staying at in Costa Rica all for themselves. Roger was her third "serious boyfriend" after Dad left. (I've stopped keeping count now, but back then I still did.) Roger was not the worst of all her man-candy; I remember he bought me a coral necklace in San Jose on that trip.

But sitting on the porch was gross and uncomfortable. It was a balmy night, and I had mosquito repellant on, so being outside wasn't that bad. But I was old enough to know what was going on inside between my mom and Roger. To avoid a confrontation with her, I pretended I was too naive to understand. The whole thing was a million times more disgusting than the Cinderella/vomit incident.

"Your turn!" I took the smallest bite of the cake I could.

"Um, all right. I just think my life is probably not as interesting as yours, so this might be hard." Zach looked up and to the right and then to the left. "So, for number one, I have milked a cow. For number two, I can play the guitar. For number three, my oldest sister once made a shoo fly pie with no egg in it!"

He looked at me expectantly. I had no idea what the third one even meant. I knew that shoo fly pie was a treacly pie beloved by locals in Central PA, but it smelled like a moldy basement to me. I wasn't sure why leaving an egg out would be a bad thing. And the other two weren't very shocking things. I'd probably not explained this game well enough. I must have forgotten to say that you were supposed to be trying to trick the other person into guessing the wrong thing. Either that or Zach had had an oddly plain life. Or maybe he was just guarded about how much he wanted me to know?

"I guess, I'd say number one, the cow milking thing, is a lie?" I ventured, laughing a little.

"Nope, I did that every morning of my childhood! I grew up on a farm." He leaned forward. "But you know how you always wanted a pet? I've always wanted to play music. The guitar especially. So number two was, sadly, the lie."

I was about to ask him why he didn't take lessons at school but then thought better of it. I remembered how he said he had a big family. Maybe because his family was super-poor, they couldn't have any extras. I didn't want to embarrass him.

"So, your family had a farm?" Now it made sense. That's how he knew the people who'd had that party in the cornfield.

"Yes, tobacco mainly, but we have cows and chickens and barn cats, too." He seemed a little uncomfortable again. Interesting how he used the present tense to describe his family, even though he wasn't living there any more. Then the waitress came over.

"Hey guys, I need to clock out before closing tonight to relieve my babysitter. Would you mind settling up your bill? You can stay as long as you want, but it'd help if I didn't have to transfer your check over to one of the other wait staff to collect…"

"Of course." Zach snatched the bill before I could see it.

"Oh, I brought money! Let's go dutch," I offered.

"Dutch?" Zach's eyes flew wide.

"Yeah, split it?" I hoped I hadn't offended him. He didn't seem like the kind of guy who would be so old-fashioned.

"Oh, no, please let me." Then he proceeded to pull out a wad of cash. Twenties. No wallet. Just all folded up neatly in his pocket. He grabbed a bunch and handed them to the waitress. "The extra is for you," he told her. Wow. He had a lot of cash. Odd. I had the random thought that maybe he was a drug dealer, but then I remembered he didn't drink, so that was probably unlikely.

"Thanks." She gave him a big smile that let me know he'd been very generous with the tip, and then she hurried off.

"What is your curfew?" Zach asked.

"I don't have one." I smiled, a little smug that I could say that when I knew not many of my friends could.

"Oh. Good, then. I'd like to show you something, if you don't mind. It won't take long."

"Ok, sounds like a plan. Where is it?" I stood up next to the table. In truth, I furtively hoped it *would* take a long time. I never wanted this night to end.

"Oh, the garage my apartment is over. I want to show you something underneath where I live. It's only a few blocks from here." Zach stood, too. "We could walk there if that's good for you."

I hesitated. Then I agreed. My heart was racing.

CHAPTER SIXTEEN

We'd walked six blocks. Zach had offered me his jacket three times. And my teeth had noisily chattered at least 550 times. I kept turning his kind suggestion down, but not because I didn't like the idea of wearing his jacket. I loved the thought of having a piece of his clothing touching me. It was stupid, but some misplaced sense of ostentatious stubbornness kicked in. It wasn't unlike what my dad used to do when I was a kid and he'd refuse to let a friend pay his way. We were broke back then, and my mom was always nagging him about us being poor, but he wanted to show the world he wasn't a helpless moocher.

Because I was only eight, I remember thinking he was foolish. *I'd never argue with someone if they want to buy me a toy!* But now here I was acting all weird about taking someone's generosity myself.

"I wish I would have thought to let you drive us in your car." Zach shook his head. "I hardly ever get cold, but it was doplick of me not to consider you might feel cold on the walk."

Doplick? I didn't remember seeing that word on any of my SAT vocab study lists. I wondered what the root was. It sounded German in origin. I made a mental note to look it up when I got home. Or maybe it was another for the Urban Dictionary.

"It's only one more block. Please wear my coat?" Zach asked.

That's four times, I thought. To Zach, I tried to smile sweetly and gratefully while shaking my head. But I worried my smile looked more like a grimace. I was pretty sure my chilling grin, coupled with the fact my eyes had been watering copiously from the cold wind, washing all my mascara down into dark circles under my eyes, probably made me look like some sort of deranged clown. Or the Joker from *Batman*.

I was going to Zach's apartment. OMG. I was following a guy I barely knew to his apartment, and I'd told nobody that I was out with him. I couldn't help but wonder if I ended up "missing," how long it would take for the criminal profilers from the FBI's BAU to figure out what had happened to me.

More worrisome, because it seemed more likely, what would happen if he lit some candles, put some Adele on his iPod, and expected some naked couch wrestling to ensue?

He did say he wanted to show me something… *Yeah, I bet he does! And it's a trouser snake!* the hyper-wary voice in my head hissed. I tried to ignore it. It used lame genital metaphors.

The Ways I Could Escape a Serial Killer or Other Big Bad

1. If something seems suspicious, ask to go to the bathroom and climb out the window.
2. Start laughing maniacally and chanting in Latin so he'll think I'm a witch like in *The Coven*.
3. Shove my finger down my throat and puke on him. He's not Cinderella so probably won't "just smile."
4. Use some of the moves I'd learned off of my mom's Aerobic Kickboxing Wii Fit game.
5. Offer to join him on a murder spree, wait until he's distracted, and run to the cops.
6. Hope that the added adrenaline finally brings out my latent superpower. And have faith that my surprise is something cool like being able to fly or turn invisible at will.

Zach beamed at me. "I just hope you think it's worth the walk!"

I stifled an inappropriate nervous giggle and realized I hadn't stopped smiling. My facial muscles were probably partially frozen now.

This frozen face thing wasn't all bad, though. It kept me from reacting to something I hated seeing. Something that made my face squeeze into a sharp scowl.

As we passed by Hillary's mom's shop, Now and Forever, I saw my mom's engagement ring was still on display in the front window. Every time I passed by it was a nice little reminder of my parents' broken relationship. After that little torture nugget, we walked another few blocks, took another couple of turns, and I was totally lost.

"There it is! Finally, huh?" Zach pointed at a garage attached to the side of a townhouse, which appeared to have a room over it. "I live up on top, but I wanted to show you something in the garage." He took out a key and inserted it into the side door on the garage. "It's been hard keeping this a secret, but I wanted it to be a surprise. I can't wait to see the look on your face."

Great, what if it's his severed head collection?

But I reasoned, what kind of head collector would be so concerned with making sure I'd gotten my share of cake for dessert at the restaurant?

After we entered, I felt immediately warmer. The garage wasn't heated, but inside at least I was sheltered from the wind thrashing me raw.

To my right, stairs led to what I assumed was Zach's apartment. The faint scent of oil and paint lingered in the space. To my left, Zach clicked on a light that illuminated the rest of the garage.

My eyes adjusted quickly. Under a tool bench in the far corner, I saw some fur. I realized it was one full-sized cat and a bunch of squirmy little ones!

Kittens. Tiny little newborns. That's what Zach wanted to show me.

"Oh my gosh! They are so adorable!" I wanted to rush over and cuddle them so badly, but I held myself back, not wanting to startle them.

"The pregnant mama must have scooted in a few nights ago when my landlord drove in. He's been gone the last three days, and I discovered them here on Wednesday. There are four babies. Their eyes aren't yet open, so they're pretty helpless."

"Are they going to be ok?" I asked.

"Thankfully, it's a small litter, so I think so. I put a soft blanket and my sweatshirt down here for them to cuddle up in and have been bringing the mama water and food."

"She doesn't have a collar or anything?" I asked, slowly inching a little closer for a better view. The cats didn't seem to mind.

"Nope, but she's very tame, so I think she was once a house cat, not a barn cat."

"But what happens when your landlord returns?"

"I'm not sure." He hesitated. "I don't know if he would allow me to keep any as pets. But even if he does, I doubt he'd allow me to keep all five cats. I'm sure when they're a bit older I can find them work as mousers…"

"Gosh, they should stay with their mom for at least six weeks though, right?"

"Would you want to take them?" Zach studied me intently. "I hadn't thought of that before, but you said you'd always wanted a pet."

"For reals? Oh, Zach. I'd love a cat, or two, but my mom…" I bit my lip, "…she's not a big animal lover." I knew my mom had great disdain for people who had pets. Whenever she had to show a house that had been occupied by people with animals, she'd have a fit about the pet hair or the smell.

"Well, they are fine here for now," Zach said. "I certainly would not want to cause conflict between you and your parents."

I still didn't want to explain to Zach yet about my dad not being in the picture. That didn't seem like a good first-date conversation. So I blurted out the first completely random thing that popped into my head. "Why don't you have a voicemail on your cell? Or is it full?"

"Oh," Zach paused, "I'm not used to… um. I'm not sure."

I nodded. It didn't seem that important now. So I just nodded. I wondered why I always had to ruin moments by saying stupid things. "The fur babies are really adorable."

"So I guess if you can't take a kitten, you can come visit them any time," Zach said.

"Yeah, I shouldn't..." I started, but then I lifted my chin, and Zach and I made eye contact. He was so darn cute! My heart fluttered. "But then again, I'm getting tired of always doing things because I should or *shouldn't.*"

I was thinking of my friends always calling me "Saint Sam" and how irritating that was. If I was going to change my life, I should start now. Not to impress Madison. Not for Plan P. But because I wanted to.

"I think I know what you mean about always trying to fit someone else's expectations." Zach winked conspiratorially at me.

"Oh, you do, huh?" I said. And before I could think about it and stop myself, I lunged forward and kissed him.

CHAPTER SEVENTEEN

My first kiss. I'd always thought it would be like the ones I'd seen in the movies. You know, the short peck with the mega-awkwardness after. Lots of stammering and blushing. But nope, wasn't like that at all! My first kiss lasted over thirty minutes. It was better than anything I could have imagined. In my opinion, what Zach and I experienced shouldn't share the same moniker as that quick lip press I've always thought of as a "kiss"—the kind you do with parents, if you have a mom and/or a dad. Or friends, if you have a squad. And don't even get me going on the stupid slang I've heard for the passionate kind of kiss to try to delineate it: Frenching, making out, macking, first base—all seemed so inadequate. *Ineffable*. Our kiss felt like we were speaking a new language, one that no one else would ever be able to speak except us, one that we created with our lips.

I never thought I'd find something better than the high I used to get from surreptitiously sticking a jewelled necklace in my pocket or sneaking a tiny bottle of an exquisite perfume in a jewel-toned bottle down my top and walking out of a store with it without being stopped. Well, this thrill surpassed it by a mile. I was sure it was better than getting drunk or stoned or anything I could imagine. What I couldn't figure out was why anyone wanted to do anything but make out all day long? Time both sped up and slowed down. I flew, floated, and flipped as if in another dimension.

When I got home that night, I made some mental lists to calm down to go to sleep. Because that's what I do.

10 Things I Like About Zach

1) He's the first guy to ask me out.
2) He knows a lot about horror flicks and doesn't get grossed out or think I'm weird for liking them.
3) He respects I'm a vegetarian, even if he isn't. And he likes kittens.
4) He splits desserts fairly.
5) He was polite to the waitress (didn't I read that this was a sign of how to judge a guy?).
6) He's seriously gorgeous. Those warm eyes and strong arms...
7) He's not into drinking or drugs.
8) He doesn't go to my high school, so he doesn't know anything about my nerdy past.
9) He's smart but not ostentatious about it.
10) He's an amazing kisser. Amazing.

10 Things I Don't Like About Zach

1) His enigma front is getting old.
2) He doesn't return my emails quickly. Also, I hate not texting with him, which brings me to...
3) He gets so many messages his voicemail is full... all from other girls?
4) Sometimes he doesn't get my jokes. Awkward.
5) He's older (intimidating).
6) He's maybe TOO gorgeous. Other girls probably throw themselves at him.
7) Seems to have issues with his parents. (Yes, I see the hypocrisy in this, but it's my list, darn it!)
8) No car! Why?
9) I don't get his friends at all.
10) What if he just wants to move too fast? After that kiss in his garage, he probably thinks I'm DTF. (Ugh, I hate that acronym, but Mad uses it a lot and it gets stuck in my head like a bad song lyric.)

On Saturday, I managed to get all my homework done and do some grocery shopping for my mom, even though I couldn't stop thinking about Zach. Madison called, and we talked for an hour about what I'd missed at school and the football game. But I didn't tell her anything about my date. She asked if I was feeling better, and I told her I was and we left it at that.

Lying in bed Saturday night, I found myself thinking more about my kiss with Zach and our conversation afterward. How after we shared this amazing magic together, we were so much more comfortable with each other. Like this palpable bond had formed between us. I liked playing the little movie from last night over and over in my head.

"Oh, wow," one of us had said after the crazy-long kiss. *Me?*

"Yeah. Wow." *Him?*

The coldness of the wall, the hardness of it against my back, his hand on my arm, the other moving to my waist... then he pulled back.

"It's so late," Zach said. "I'm sorry..."

"No, it's ok." I smiled at him and realized my lips stung a little, like when I'd used some of Madison's lip gloss that was supposed to plump up your lips because it had cinnamon and ginger in it.

"Good. Because I'm not really. I'm the farthest thing from sorry right now!" He laughed. I laughed, too.

"Can I see you Sunday night?" he asked.

"Sure," I replied.

"Six? How about a movie at my place?"

"Great." The kittens caught my eye. They were in a snuggly pile, all intertwined with each other and their mom.

"How about I order a pizza? You like just cheese, right?" He remembered my order from House of Pizza the first time we'd talked!

"Sure! I'll bring the soda. What do you like?" My mind wasn't as clear as his; all this kissing had made me delightfully fuzzy.

"Regular Coke, not diet."

"That's what I like, too. My favourite is in the green glass bottles. I'll try to get those."

We both knew why we wanted to meet at his place. It was the most obvious thing in the world at that moment.

As I drifted off Saturday night, still wearing the big, soft wool sweater he insisted I take home after he walked me back to my car, I thought of Zach.

I dreamed about him that night.

All day Sunday I tingled with anticipation of our second date. That was, until four on Sunday afternoon. That's when I started feeling zero chill.

What the hell am I doing? This isn't me! I'm not a "go to a guy's apartment to make out" kind of girl.

What would we possibly talk about while eating the pizza? Was he even going to bother to get a movie? What if he wanted to do more than kiss? Good gosh, he had no idea that that my first kiss happened on our last date! I certainly hadn't acted like it was my first kiss. Gone was all the self-confidence I'd had. All the ease I'd felt with him after the kissing. I was a fool. I'd gotten in way over my head.

But who could I talk to? Not my mom. While yesterday I'd felt so much more understanding of her and her need for weekends away, I still had no idea how to broach this topic with her.

Maybe I should call Madison. Would she be able to understand my fear? Did I have a choice? The answers to these two questions, respectively, were "Probably not" and "No." but then I rationalized that a double negative in both math and grammar makes a positive. Besides, Mad deserved my trust that she wouldn't tell the other Sherpas. She'd kept secrets in the past when I'd specifically asked her to. So I called her.

CHAPTER EIGHTEEN

"Hey Mad, it's Sam." I held my cell with one hand and raked the sand in my mom's mini Zen garden with the other.

"Sam! What's up? Two phone calls in one weekend from my favourite resident saint. To what do I owe this honour?" Madison didn't pause for me to answer. "I think I've told you all the dirt from the football game. I told you we found out Tracy was dating this guy from Penn State, right? Delia is still so jealous! And that Britt twisted her ankle..." This gossipy conversation we'd been having so far was doing nothing to bolster my faith that I was safe confiding in Madison. Most of our talks were very one-sided. Madison told me stories, and I asked follow-up questions. So I couldn't blame her for assuming this was why I called.

"Look, sorry to interrupt but... listen... I'm... I..." There was no way for my words to express the chaos swirling in my mind.

"Just take a breath and chill. Are you in some kind of trouble?" She sounded genuinely concerned. Of course she was. *She's my friend*, I reminded myself.

"I'm ok." I made perfectly parallel straight lines through the sand of the Zen garden with the little wooden rake. "Madison, can I tell you something, something private, and not have you tell anyone?" I heard my voice shake. I put down the tiny garden tool.

She was silent for a beat. "I can keep secrets, Sam."

"I know! Of course you can. I just don't know what to do..." I started, and then to my complete mortification, I started crying.

"Do you need me to come over? I can borrow my mom's car and be there in fifteen minutes," she said.

"No, no." I sucked in some air and steadied myself. "I'm just being stupid."

"No, it's not stupid," Madison reassured me. "Sam, are you stealing stuff again?"

It was the first time she'd ever mentioned my confession. I guess she did remember our first sleepover, when we'd stolen some beers from her dad's garage refrigerator and I'd purged my soul about my problems back in Philadelphia. That was the first and last time I got drunk. It made me totally vulnerable, and I hated that feeling. But maybe that's when I knew Madison was a true friend. She'd never told any of the other girls about it, never joked about it, never even hinted at it. Until now.

"No, no, nothing like that," I whispered into the phone, "but something did happen. Something that feels much better than shoplifting. But maybe that's why it terrifies me."

"Look, whatever it is, I won't judge. Hell, I've probably already tried it myself."

"Yeah, you for sure have." I laughed a little, and that helped the pressure that had built up in my chest. "I'm a drama queen. Ok. You know that guy, Zach? Well, we went out."

"Sam, that's great!" Madison squealed. "Swaggy! I… wait a minute. Be straight with me. Did he hurt you? Did he do something to you that you didn't want to do?" Madison sounded like she'd kill him for me if he had.

"No! God, no! Not at all. He's nice, super-nice. But we kissed for, like, an hour and, well…"

"Oh my god! You're serious? What a relief! Oh, that's awesome! That's how you put Plan P in action, baby! But wait, why are you so messed up? Oh, let me guess: he didn't call after."

"No, he didn't call, but it's ok because he didn't say he would. We already made plans. We're supposed to go out again tonight. Well, actually, not 'go out.' I said I'd go over to his place." When I heard myself say this, I wondered why the heck I was making such a mountain out of a molehill.

"Oh, I'm getting it. He doesn't know you've never been with a guy?" Madison was so straightforward. I was glad she couldn't see me blushing.

"No, that never came up."

"Hmmm… so did he try to grope or hump at all?" Madison asked very matter-of-factly. It occurred to me that she'd make a great family doctor if she'd only focus more on her studies. She had a nice "objective yet kind" tone coupled with a frankness that would serve her well in that profession.

"No. He wasn't like that at all."

"Hmmm. Ok. Good kisser?"

"Amazing. Not that I have any basis for comparison." We both giggled. "But I can't imagine any better."

"So you think he's sexy?" Madison goaded.

"Well, let's just saw he's like a walking endothermic catalyst, yes!" I giggled at my own wit.

"Uh… yeah. Ok. Don't tell him that."

"But it's a compliment…" I said, but before I could explain it was like saying, "He's making me warm and tingly," with a science analogy, Madison cut me off.

"So it's really true you didn't ever date that brainy guy, Simon?"

"No! I told you I didn't! We were just friends." I was surprised that Madison thought I lied to her. "Why would you think that?"

"Oh, ok. It's just you never hang with him anymore, so I thought maybe you'd had a bad break-up, and it was weird."

"No." I was ashamed that I hadn't talked to Simon at all this fall and embarrassed to admit why. "You know how Hillary makes fun of those guys. I guess I just… I mean, I don't want her to…"

"Say no more. I get it. She scares me, too, sometimes. You have no idea." Madison paused. "Anyways, back to more pressing business. You say you kissed Zach and you loved it, huh? So is it that you trust him to stop when you want, but you just don't trust yourself?"

"I guess…" I replied. That wasn't exactly it, but I didn't even know myself why I was acting squirrelly. I just felt completely overwhelmed, miles from my comfort zone.

"Ok, here's what we'll do. You go, but keep your cell's ring tone on loud. I will call you every hour." This strategy was sounding familiar. I wondered if Madison had read that same *Marie Claire* article on dating that I had. "If you want me to get you outta there, just say 'Caramel Macchiato,' and I'll figure out an excuse why you have to leave. If you want me to come over there, just say FROZEN Caramel Macchiato. You can text those code words to me too, if you need, ok?" Madison paused. "Boy, now that I think of it, I could really go for a Caramel Macchiato right now."

I told her that clandestine language idea was a good plan. I gave her his address. She commented that it was not too far from the train station.

"Close to the Hi Ho Comics shop," I clarified then remembered that Madison didn't share my love of comic books. "And the train station, yes."

"One last little tip," Madison said just as I thought we were about to hang up. "Put a tampon in."

"What? Why?"

"Well, it'll give you time to think about whether you are sure you want to do something. If things are getting hot and heavy, you'll know it's there, so you'll need to excuse yourself to go to the bathroom to take it out, right? That'll give your inner fire a chance to settle down so you can consider what you're doing."

"Oh," I said. "Kind of like a self-inflicted chastity belt?"

"Hey, it's kept me from getting naked and then later regretting it many times!" she said. "But then again, I've also taken it out when I felt like it, too!"

"Good tip." I had no idea what else to say.

"But before it gets to that point, I'd tell him you want to be sure everything is right this time. If you don't want to blow his mind with the whole 'virgin' thing, you could tell him you had your heart broken recently and need to take it slowly."

"Sure." I was lucky. Madison knew so many tricks.

"Great. I'll talk to you at seven. And make sure you answer your phone! Otherwise, I'm coming over there. Oh, and if at any time you want me to stop the hourly check-in, just say, um, 'pickle.'"

"Pickle?" I laughed. "Really?"

"Yeah, it's not very subtle, but it'll work." We both collapsed into silly giggling again.

CHAPTER NINETEEN

After looking at the kittens for a while, we went up to Zach's apartment for the first time. It had only a few pieces of furniture, most notably a huge bookshelf, completely full. Draped over the faded couch was one of the most colourful and intricate quilts I'd ever seen.

He had a bunch of DVDs for me to pick from. He said he collected them from garage sales and bargain bins.

I'd picked one with cover art that featured a buxom vampire lady in a bloody bathtub. It was one of the most horrible yet hilarious B-movies I'd ever seen, with the very literal title of *Bloodbath*. Zach and I both howled with laughter when during a suspenseful moment one of the female victims walked into a room looking for the killer vampire, and because of bad editing, you could see the camera and sound guys behind her in a mirror, but she shrugged and exclaimed, "Nope, no one is here!"

"Wow, I haven't seen a movie that cheesy since *Sex, Chocolate and Zombie Republicans!*" I said.

"That sounds like one I have to see." Zach shook his head. We'd eaten all the pizza except one lonely slice, and I noticed him eyeing it.

"Oh, please, go ahead and eat that one," I said. "I'm so full, I think I'm going to pop."

"Don't do that until I can get a camera to film it," Zach said. "Then we can make our own horror film!" We laughed.

"If I was going to make a horror film, I think I'd like to make a sorta funny one along the lines of *Shaun of the Dead* or *Zombieland* rather than some nasty one like *Hostel*," I said. Zach didn't reply, so I went on. "Oh, so are you more of a docu-horror fan of ones like *Paranormal Activity* or *Blair Witch*? Or maybe you're more of an old-school aficionado—do you prefer the original *Halloween, Nightmare on Elm Street,* and *Friday the 13th*?"

"Uh, actually, I just started watching horror films in the last year or so." Zach looked down at his pizza. "I haven't seen many old ones yet."

"No kidding? Wow! Why?"

"My parents, were… strict."

"Oh, so they didn't let you see rated R stuff? And you guys didn't have cable? I mean, I think they show edited versions of some of the old classics on regular stations at Halloween…" I said, not trying to make him feel bad but just rambling, as I do sometimes.

"We didn't have a TV." He said this so quietly, I almost didn't hear him.

"Yikes. I had a friend like that in elementary school. Her parents were old hippies. She had to go to a Waldorf School through third grade. They espoused this anti-commercialism stuff. Was that the deal with your parents?"

"Sort of. It is maybe more complicated than that…" he said and then quickly shifted the conversation. "You are lucky. Your parents seem to let you be very independent and free."

"Well, it's just my mom and me." Now it was my turn to get uncomfortable.

"Oh, I am so sorry. Your father, he passed away?" Zach reached out and put his hand on my knee. I liked it there. So much so, I was tempted to say yes and let him comfort me more, but I couldn't tell him another lie. I'd dodged a bullet with the age bluff, and I wanted things honest between us. Or I wanted at least no barefaced deceit. What he didn't know about my past wouldn't hurt anyone.

"No, he left us. Divorced my mom. Now he lives near Baltimore, Maryland, and we don't see each other. Or even talk."

Zach was quiet. "I think that's very sad. I'm so sorry. I can't understand how a parent could ever turn his back on a child. Whatever the situation is. And yet they do sometimes…" He stopped talking, and I didn't know what to say. So we just sat in silence for a second that seemed like a decade.

"It's no big deal." Wow, this conversation had gotten serious. I didn't like "serious" but had no idea how to redirect it. What I wanted to be doing, and what I thought we'd be doing by now, was kissing. Maybe he didn't like last time as much as I'd had? Or maybe I'd needed a mint or something.

"I am probably speaking more from my own experience, I suppose," Zach said. "I can't presume to know how it feels for you, I guess. Just how my parents make me feel."

This floored me. After our dinner, I'd gotten the impression Zach's was the quintessential close-knit farm family. Maybe his dad was British or something, and that's why he sometimes said "can not" instead of "can't," and him living in England caused a rift. "You're not close with your parents now?"

"No," he said simply, and for once I let the topic drop without pushing. He seemed to be hurting. And anyway, if I asked why he wasn't getting along with his parents, we might not end up kissing. It was selfish of me, but my desire was making me into more of a Freyja than a Gaia.

Then he asked, "It doesn't bother you about your dad?"

"Well, I hardly ever think of him anymore. Honestly, I'm glad he doesn't send me things on my birthday, so I can totally forget about him." I curled my left leg up under me, which had the unfortunate consequence of making Zach remember his hand on my knee. He removed it self-consciously. *Drat.* Then my cell rang.

"Hello?" I knew it'd be Madison.

"So how's it going?"

"Oh, hey, no, I don't know the math pages we had to do for homework, sorry!" I said, looking at Zach, who was looking out his window that had a lovely view of an alley.

"Cool! Well, have fun and don't do anything I wouldn't do! Which leaves you pretty open!" Madison snickered. I quickly hit the button to hang up, hoping Zach hadn't heard anything. I smiled at him.

"My crazy friends. So what were we talking about?"

"So... you were talking about your birthday... when is it?" Zach asked.

"The day before Halloween. Maybe that's why I like horror films so much," I said. "I'm a Scorpio. What are you?"

"That is in a couple of weeks!"

"True, but you didn't answer. What are you?"

Zach looked confused. "I'm a March birthday."

"Pisces or Aries?" I was hoping for Pisces. When he cocked his head, I realized he had no clue what I was talking about. When's your birthday?"

"March 9th."

"Pisces!" I said triumphantly.

"Ok, now what does that mean?" He moved closer.

"Ah, well, it's supposed to mean you have a great imagination and are sensitive and creative. Spiritual, not into materialistic things."

"Interesting... and what does your birthday date predict about you?"

"Supposedly enigmatic, attracted to luxurious things, and passionate." I ticked off these qualities without thinking about what I was revealing.

"Passionate, huh?" Zach leaned forward more. Then it happened. I got my wish. We were kissing again.

When my cell rang a few minutes later, I answered, "No! This is not the PICKLE store!" and hung up.

CHAPTER TWENTY

There she was. My mother. Sitting at the breakfast table waiting for me. On a Monday morning. I was totally blindsided. She hadn't come home the past few Sunday nights, and, more remarkably, she'd never been a morning person.

If I'd guessed she'd be there, would I have given myself a quick once-over in the bathroom mirror before coming downstairs? Possibly. But I guess I'll never know. I like to think I would have at least changed out of the clothes I'd worn out the night before on my date with Zach. And I possibly would've pulled a comb through my hair. Why does making out on a couch turn your hair into a rat's nest anyway? Washing under my mascara-smeared eyes would have been a good idea, too.

"Wow, what the heck happened to you? You look like a truck ran over you." My mom was wearing a bright new orange top under her favourite Michael Kors blazer. She was multitasking as usual by texting with one hand and eating her cardboardy bran cereal with the other.

"Oh, I was studying late," I mumbled. "I guess I just forgot to wash up before bed because I was so wiped out."

"You study way too much, Sam." I could tell my mom was about to launch into one of her famous "When I was your age..." speeches highlighting her great social life as head cheerleader of her high school in upstate New York or explaining how she couldn't miss a dance because everyone counted on her showing up to make it an event to remember. Or regaling me with the story about the time when she once made three dates for one night and managed to juggle them all by having an early dinner with one guy, seeing a movie with another one, and going to a late party with the third.

In retrospect, I wish she'd given me the same old boring speech that implied I was a giant loser compared to her. But instead my normally oblivious mother glanced up and then looked at me. Really looked at me. For the first time in a very long time.

"Oh my gosh, Sam," she gasped. "What happened to your neck? Oh, hon, is that red blotch the start of another of your stress rashes?"

"Huh?" My hand involuntarily moved to the spot on my neck that my mom's eyes were glued to. It was a little sore and tender. "I... I don't know..."

Then my mom's tone changed from amused frustration to something that almost seemed like concern. "Did you try to pop a zit or something?" She narrowed her eyes and had an almost-furrow between her brows. Must be time for a new shot of Botox; her forehead wasn't as perma-smooth as usual.

"No, don't be silly. Why would you think that?" I turned away from her and walked to the bathroom to get a better look. My mom followed.

When I got to the mirror, I pulled back my hair and saw a faint purplish bruise about the size of a small, flat walnut under my left ear. "I have no idea what that is!" But even as the words were leaving my mouth, it was starting to dawn on me what the mark might be.

"It's a hickey!" my mom squealed from behind me. Now I've read about whackjob moms embarrassing their daughters by displaying unmitigated glee while on the first trip shopping for a training bra or the kooks who get all psyched about their daughters getting their first periods. But MY mom was getting all freaky-happy about me finally getting my first hickey? *Kill me now.*

"No, I don't think... No!" I said as emphatically as I could but failed to convince her.

"Oh, honey, who was it? Do you know his name? How did you meet? Come tell me all about it! We have so much to talk about." She all but clapped her hands in delight.

Did I know his name? Good Lord, I'd rather eat an extra large tub of maggots than tell her all about it. I was unnerved, though. I couldn't remember when I'd last seen her so excited.

"A curling iron burn. It's only a curling iron burn," I sputtered. I haven't used a curling iron on my hair in years, but there was no way in hell was I going to let my mom know about Zach. It was none of her business.

"Oh, hon, now that I got a good look at it… well, I know what a love bite is! But ok, if you need some space on this, I'm cool with that." My mom shrugged and backed out of the bathroom, and I couldn't help but get the feeling she was trying to guilt me with her faux meek retreat.

"I'm not lying." I heard the whine in my voice, and it repulsed me. "Seriously, it must be a curling iron burn." I realized I was talking to empty space.

"Sure, whatever you say," she called back to me in a pathetic, hurt way. There was a pause, but I knew better than to fall for her games again.

Then, when she didn't get her way, I heard the bedroom door slam.

I started the shower, peeled off my stale clothes, and sat down in the tub. I let the water pelt me from above while I cried as softly as I could. I hated her. I didn't want her dead or anything, but…

Things I Wish Would Happen to My Mother

1. A tragic yet painless illness would strike her that would make her tongue fall out.
2. She'd marry a benevolent billionaire who would give me my own private wing of his mansion. He would also provide a distraction for her so she never saw me.
3. An old gypsy lady would see her heartlessness and would put a spell/curse on her to restore her soul.
4. She'd get herself to a nunnery.
5. Her *real* memory would come back of how hard it is to be a teenager.

I don't know why, but the idea that this hickey was what my mom finally found interesting about me, that this was what she felt we could "bond" about, that this was what made her proud, made me profoundly depressed. My grades, my friends, my college plans, none of this meant anything to her. But the fact a boy saw me as worthy of kissing my neck... well, now that was really something. Kudos to me! Finally, I wasn't so repulsive to the opposite sex! I could actually entice a boy to a certain amount of passion.

I began to regret my stupid Plan P. What if I became just like my mother, obsessed with sex, physical attractiveness, and money? As I often did when she pissed me off, I started thinking about how coldly she'd put her engagement ring up for resale without even asking me if I might want it. Her lack of sentimentality disgusted me.

As the water inched up around me, I wondered where my dad was at that moment and if he ever thought of me. I wondered why he'd never cared enough to try to save me from being raised by her.

CHAPTER TWENTY-ONE

I know you're hiding something, I'm just not sure what it is." Hillary appraised me as if she was a CIA-trained expert in the Facial Action Coding system and could read my expressions to tell what was *really* going on, despite my claims of innocence.

"I was sick all weekend," I repeated for the third time. I willed myself not to touch the fuchsia scarf I'd tied tightly around my neck to hide the fading hickey, my very own scarlet letter. I also tried to make steady eye contact with Hillary and not look away. Like a wolf, she could smell fear.

We were standing in our usual spot under the big oak tree near the deserted baseball field. It was 7:55 a.m., so first bell would be in ten minutes. Ten more minutes of shrugging and hoping someone would help me change the subject would be torture.

"Where's Britt?" Madison asked. She knew Britt had early cheerleading practice, as she did every Monday morning. We all knew it. It was the stuff of legends: Britt never missed it, even going last spring after she'd sprained her ankle, claiming, "There'll be time to rest it when the season's over!" So this was Madison's way of bailing me out, not brilliant but nevertheless effective in its own way.

Before Hillary could snarl what was sure to be a rude comment about Madison "lunching" this morning or being "drain-bramaged," two of her favourite insults, she was interrupted by a group of the most popular senior girls. Sasha, their leader, made a beeline to Hillary and hugged her. Unlike her sister, Sasha skipped cheerleading practice when she felt unenthused, caring more about what cheering could do for her than what she could sacrifice for cheering. It didn't matter that Sasha's little sister, Britt, was also going to be a senior next year and that popularity at our school was usually affected by the older sibling's status at our school. It was a done deal. Everyone knew it would be Hillary who ruled the school next year. She practically did already.

While they gossiped, my mind wandered. Hillary possessed that indefinable Queen Bee quality that made the other students strive to be with her, even as she crushed them under her feet. She had her choice of boyfriends; no senior could match her. She had the lead in the school play this fall. Next year, Hillary would be both Homecoming and Prom Queen. She would call every shot. It would be "Hillary-now" on steroids. I shuddered at the thought.

After the seniors exchanged catty remarks with Hillary, they sauntered coolly away. Then Hillary wheeled back on me. Only two more minutes until the bell…

"So you didn't do anything this weekend? That's so sad." Hillary's voice dripped with mock pity.

Madison interrupted, "Hey, Hill, did you tell Delia about those college guys we met who couldn't hold their tequila? It's such a hilarious story!" *Madison just risked a bullet for me. Wow.*

Delia perked up at the mention of her name and stopped peeling the bark off the poor oak tree. She'd been away over the weekend looking at colleges, so she hadn't been able to go to the game with Hillary and the other Sherpas. Her parents wanted to motivate her to get an early start thinking about her higher education. She'd done so well on the PSATs when she'd taken sophomore year. She often let it drop into conversation that she'd broken 1400. I'm glad nobody asked me what I'd gotten. I had scored a 1500, which was almost a perfect score, branding me a giant geek. You wanted to get a good score, not a perfect one. It was the difference between a candy bar and a fried candy bar with ice cream on top. The first was a treat, the second was too much—gross. The old me would've been proud of my scores. And truth be told, a little part of me was still psyched. But it was more important not to give the Sherpas any reason to resent or reject me. I hoped they wouldn't ask what I got on my upcoming PSATs when I took them.

"Oh, Delia, it was soooo DISGUSTING!" Hillary laughed with genuine enthusiasm. "We were thinking these guys were hotties, right? They graduated from Township last year and are at Penn State now. One of them looked kinda like Sasha's ex, Cody. We were totally considering hooking up with them. That was until they started slamming tequila shots in the back seat of one guy's Prius and then soon after started barfing under the bleachers! I swear Madison and I got laughing so hard. Especially at this one dude who peed himself while heaving!" She and Madison both dissolved in giggles.

"It was fun. It felt like old times," Madison said, winking at Hillary.

I felt a pang of jealousy. I'd never had a bestie in middle school, preferring to hang out with my dad rather than kids my age. And then I thought of my first real friend in Lancaster, Simon, who'd tried to talk to me in the hall last week. But I'd been too busy, running to claim my seat with the Sherpas at the pep rally in the gym, so I just told him to text me. He did, and I forgot to PTB.

"I loved that it was just us hanging out together again." Hillary smiled back. "It makes everything so much simpler."

"Wait, I thought Kensie was there, too?" Delia cocked her head.

"Oh yeah, she was I guess… yeah, she was! Ooops. It must be she's just easy to forget." Hillary laughed again. Disturbingly, Madison joined in on this one, too.

I knew I should just be grateful that Madison was keeping my secret about Zach, but I couldn't help but to be bugged that my absence this weekend seemed to be Hillary's opportunity to move in and reforge her bond with Madison. But how petty was I? I'd just spent two amazing evenings with this gorgeous, sweet, funny guy who was a wonderful kisser and who seemed to genuinely like me. Someone with whom I felt totally comfortable after knowing him less than a month, which was a lot more than I could say for anyone I was currently standing with. Why the heck did I find myself caring what these mean girls were doing without me?

The bell rang, interrupting my thoughts, and the Sherpas all seemed to be staring at me. Even Madison.

"Don't think you're off the hook, Sam," Hillary tossed behind her as she sauntered away. "You're not. Not by a long shot." She twisted her head around, giving me the impression of a somewhat less-flexible Regan from *The Exorcist.* "I always know when someone's hiding something."

And the school week had begun.

CHAPTER TWENTY-TWO

Before I left his place Sunday night, Zach had told me he had a busy work week, but he wanted to get together on Friday. I told him about the PSATs Saturday morning and how I thought I should get a good night's sleep. He squinted and cocked his head a bit but then shook it as if he was a dog trying to shake off a sneeze. He immediately said, "Understood. Saturday night then." He gave me his email address and told me to write him when I thought of something I'd like to do. Again, no cell number. Definitely strange.

Monday after school, I couldn't resist calling the number he'd called me from last week. I figured if he didn't mind me emailing, he wouldn't mind me calling. But it was weird; the phone just rang and rang and still never went to voicemail. I shrugged it off. I was 89% sure he wasn't playing me at this point. But that 11% still nagged at me a bit.

I spent the next day going over the Zach date options in my head:

1) Dinner. We already did that, and since this was only our third time hanging out, I didn't want to be repetitive. It seemed too early to get in a rut!

2) A movie. True, we'd rented one Saturday night, but we hadn't actually gone out to a theatre together. It was an option but not one that I was totally excited about.

3) A party. Except none of our friends were in the same circles. And social events with alcohol and drugs had a high potential for drama and disaster. The one in the cornfield was a good example. A month ago at a different blowout the Sherpas held, Madison

caught a gymnast guy she liked making out with this girl in the host's parents' bedroom, and she cried on my shoulder for a half an hour. I realize she was probably on something that night, too. Also, if it was someone from my school's party, Hillary would find out about Zach and me. I was so not ready for that. No way. A party was out.

4) The mall. The mall always made my fingertips itch a little, remembering my kleptomaniac days. I didn't want to be uncomfortable.

5) Rick's Place. I'd gone dancing at this Under 21 club with Madison, and not many kids from my school ever went there. But a lot of guys didn't like to go to clubs, and I wasn't sure if Zach liked to dance. Could be boring for him.

So what else was there to do? I wished I could email him and say, *Hey, for Saturday night, let's just make out more please. But no goofing around pretending you're a vampire and accidentally giving me a hickey! The one you gave me is finally fading away.* But I was not even close to being bold enough to do something like that. By Wednesday, I felt so much pressure to write to him, I thought I'd implode.

That's when I saw it. An ad in the LancasterOnline.com when I was reading a piece about Wilbur Chocolate Factory moving. It was for a new haunted house that had opened up. I'd heard about another local place, "Scream in the Dark," that had been around forever, but people said it took over three hours in line to get in. Zach and I both loved the macabre, so going to a haunted house seemed perfect. And it would give me a great excuse to hold his hand, or maybe his whole arm, if I had enough chutzpah as we walked through it.

This new haunt was on the outskirts of the tiny town of Lititz, the one with the "First Pretzel Factory in America!" When I visited it last spring with Simon, we had more fun than we wanted to admit twisting pretzel dough. Lititz also boasted a spring that people in the 1800s believed had miraculous healing powers but now just seemed to draw more stoners than a Grateful

Dead cover band. When we'd first moved to Lancaster, my mom told me Lititz had lots of cool festivals, but she'd never brought me to any of them. Typical.

The first draft of my email looked like this:

Hi Zach!
Do you want to go to a haunted house with me on Saturday? I found a cool looking one! It's called "Hell House." You could pick me up and we could go together or I could pick you up. Do you have a car? If not, I totally don't care! I'm not one of those superficial girls who judges people by their cars. Or lack of a car. Or maybe you lost your license to a DUI and that's why you don't drink now?

Ugh. How horrible. I tried again.

Hey there Zach,
You're a hard guy to know what to do with! Maybe we should just make out?!! Haha! Just kidding. No, seriously, how about we go somewhere first and then we make out after.

Oh God. Even worse. I sounded like some weird nympho. I tried once more.

Hi Zach!
I hope your work isn't killing you this week. ☺ I have a surprise for you for Saturday. I'll pick you up at your place at 7 pm. Hint: Come prepared to run from the un-dead if necessary!

Best,
Sam

PS How are the kittens and mama cat?

I debated how I should sign it. "Sincerely" seemed too formal. "Love" seemed presumptuous and scary. So I settled on "Best" because Mrs. Long, my favourite middle-school teacher, used it in all her emails, and I'd always thought it sounded sophisticated.

Within a few hours, I got a reply.

Hi Sam!

Great news—my landlord says the cats can stay as long as I take care of them. When they get older, I will try to find them good homes. He hinted that I might even be able to keep one or two myself.

I can't wait until Saturday! This sounds like so much fun. I've never had anyone try to surprise me before. I've been thinking of you a lot. Whatever we do, I know we will laugh together! Even getting my brains eaten would be enjoyable as long as I was with you.

Yours,
Zach

He signed it, "Yours."
MINE?!!
Seriously?
Wow.

I was sitting on my bed reading this off my laptop, and I couldn't help myself. I tightly hugged my favourite stuffed bunny from childhood, Sweetie, and rocked back and forth with a derpy smile on my face and a heart bursting with bliss.

CHAPTER TWENTY-THREE

Zach was waiting outside his place for me with a wide grin when I pulled up at 6:50 p.m. I guess we were both eager to get this date started! He wore jeans, sneakers, and a bright blue tee with the Coachella Music Festival logo on it. The blue of the shirt made his hazel eyes seem almost gold, but what I couldn't stop staring at were his arms and chest. I think the flannel shirts he'd always sported hid them before. Wow. This guy put in some serious hours at the gym. Zach was lean but cut; he had the body of a Marvel superhero. Then I remembered how he signed his emails: "Yours." I got a warm feeling, and my stomach flittered a bit thinking about him being "mine."

During the car ride, he asked how the PSATs went. I'd told him they were pretty soporific, that I'd spent a lot of time sitting around after I'd finished each section, unable to move on to the next section. He nodded. That's exactly the kind of thing I couldn't tell my friends, because one of them would make me feel like a nerdulent dork because standardized tests always came easily to me. They could talk about how many guys hit on them or how excited they were to win a cheering competition, and that was ok, but kicking butt academically and feeling stoked about it, well, that was just plain bragging and very uncool.

"There was this one math problem that you had to find the digits of a locker number using clues in variable equations. Pretty fun!"

"You're smart," he stated, not like it was a bad thing but in the same way that I watched guys act when Madison slammed a shot of tequila. He made me so happy, I thought I'd burst.

"Also, I knew every word on the reading section except one: 'avuncular.' But after my test, I looked it up and I'd gotten it right."

"It's like an older mentor who takes a rookie and affectionately teaches him the ways of the world," Zach said, sitting forward a bit.

"Geez, yeah! Aren't you 1337!" When he didn't respond, I snuck a glance at his slightly crinkled nose. "Oh, that's text-speak for impressive. Just heard it myself recently from my friends."

"I guess I read more Charles Dickens than I do text messages." We both laughed. It made me feel a little better about him still not giving me his cell number.

"Well, you're going to ace the reading section when you take the test. I can't believe your teachers didn't encourage you to take it last year," I told him as we pulled into the dirt parking lot of the Hell House.

He nodded tentatively. Why wouldn't his teachers be supportive of trying to help him get college scholarships? Before I got to ask him what his high school was like, he was out of the car and opening my door for me. Now I was the flustered one.

When we got to the side of the the Hell House, we saw a line snaking from the front door reaching a good four hundred feet to the dirt field a parking lot. This was a more popular attraction than I'd thought it would be. But it was too late to turn back. I hoped if I kept my head down, I wouldn't see anyone I knew. I saw quite a few groups of kids wearing nametags; they looked like they were in elementary school, waiting with adult chaperons like they were on a field trip or something. Seemed a bit young, and I'd never heard of any schools sponsoring field trips to haunted houses.

"Look, Zach, it must be a ghoul school!" I pointed at the kids with the matching red shirts. He smiled but seemed distracted. Ugh. When you make a bad joke on a date, it's worse than trying to catch a burp in a butterfly net.

The staff at the door in witch costumes seemed to be taking a pretty large group in every ten minutes or so. The line moved in spurts. We were going to be waiting a while.

In front of us, I heard a mom snipe at her daughter, "Get off your stupid phone. It's like you can only see the world through social media and YouTube videos."

The young teen rolled her eyes. "I'm not freakin' Amish, Mom. We all use our phones. It's boring to just stand here."

Zach coughed a little, like you do when you swallow and breath at the same time. In the car, he'd found out everything about my week, but I hadn't asked him anything about his. He probably thought I was so self-centred.

"So was your week as stressful as you'd thought it was going to be?"

"Yeah, it was busy. I'm just happy to be here with you now, though!"

"Me, too."

"So we talked about silly low-budget horror movies, but what's your all-time favourite studio-produced horror film?"

Was he purposely changing the subject? Why didn't he ever want to talk about his life?

"Hmmm… for 'truly scary,' 'best idea,' or 'funny?'" I dug my toe in the dirt.

"Let's say 'truly scary' to start."

"Ok, probably either the first *Nightmare on Elm Street* or *Halloween 2*."

"Both of those films had iconic scary villains in them, too. Those series and *Friday the 13th*… and maybe *Texas Chainsaw Massacre*, too, even though it wasn't a series." I could tell he'd been binge-watching older horror films since our last talk. It made me smile to myself. "How about most original concept?"

"That's easy, *Cabin in the Woods*. Not that scary but an innovative idea."

"That's one of my favourites, too. I like Joss Whedon."

"Did you ever see *Buffy the Vampire Slayer*, not the movie, though that wasn't as bad as some people say, but the TV show?" I asked. Zach's left eye twitched, then he shook his head slowly. "Oh, well, it aired years ago, so I figured you hadn't seen it when it aired because of the whole family 'no TV' thing, but I caught all the episodes on Netflix one summer. That and *Angel* were awesome shows. There's this actor I like, Christian Kane, who played Lindsey on *Angel...*" Zach seemed to be digging to the Earth's core in the dirt now, but with his heel instead of his toe. Maybe I shouldn't talk about actors I had crushes on. "So... yeah, I watch almost everything now on my laptop with Netflix or Hulu. You can catch up on your computer..."

I took a breath, but before I could continue, Zach did something a little out of character—he cut me off. "So what did you think of *Halloween 3*?"

I blinked at his non sequitur but then rebooted and went with it like he did with mine. "You can't seriously be asking me that!" We both laughed. The awkward moment seemed to have passed. "The worst!"

"Yeah, Michael Myers replaced by a weird cult making deathly masks." His eyes crinkled so adorably when he laughed that it almost made me forget how my calves were starting to cramp up standing in this ridiculously long line.

"One of the stupidest plots to destroy the world ever, so the mask melts on the kid, killing him or her, then bugs and snakes come out to attack the parents, but this is only going to affect maybe one third of the houses in the United States, right? And not every country celebrates Halloween by trick or treating, so all those people would be ok. And what about the fact that the kids had to be in front of TV watching a 'special commercial' for the mask to work? Not a lot of kids are going to stop trick or treating early to do that! Good job, evil cult people!" I ranted.

"Maybe that's why I avoid TV; I don't want bugs coming out of my melted head." I loved Zach messing with me like this. He seemed to be moving in closer, maybe to put his arm around me or to kiss me? Who knows? I'd never find out because of what I did next. I don't know what came over me, but I took a step back, lowered my chin, and looked him in the eyes.

"But why do you keep avoiding telling me stuff about yourself? Details. I feel like you're purposely hiding something from me," I blurted, destroying all the fun, because I can't seem to help being the murderer of the mirth.

According to my mother, I'd always been phenomenal at ruining a good time.

CHAPTER TWENTY-FOUR

've heard the expression "Like a deer caught in headlights" used to capture the look of someone who is surprised, confused, and scared all at once. But I think it would be more accurate to describe the way Zach looked at me as "a cow caught in headlights," because there was something sweet and sad and not at all wild mixed in with the surprise and confusion in his eyes. I felt like a low rent Cersei Lannister.

"I... I didn't mean to... I'm sorry. What do you want to ask me?" he asked.

Part of me felt I should apologize for my totally rude behaviour. But I didn't. Instead, I took the opportunity to plunge ahead.

"What exactly do you do at work? Either at the factory or for your cousin. You never tell me any specifics." If I was going to be rude, I might as well go for it a hundred percent

"Um, ok... well, at the factory, I just work on the assembly lines sorting tiles. Not very exciting to tell you about. When I work for my cousin, it's a little more interesting. He has a new beekeeping business. He sells honey and handmade soaps and lotions. It started out as a booth at the farmer's market downtown, but we're expanding. We are selling wholesale to different stores locally, but are also in the process of trying to get out-of-state contracts. We just hired a firm to handle the marketing, but I'm trying to learn as much as I can about it. Since I have been with the company from the beginning, helping my cousin Abe transport and sell his products, I might quit the factory soon and work for him full-time."

"Wow, that's pretty impressive." Zach's job wasn't at all shady. He worked in the grown-up world. I felt a twinge of *why the heck would this cool guy want to be hanging out with me* doubt. "It sounds like you're doing great without needing to go to college."

Two girls with giant gold crosses around their necks walked by. Probably Twi-hards. Those tweens who love passive aggressive, sparkly, stalkerish vampires were everywhere. Ugh.

"Others have said that to me about skipping college." Zach grimaced. "But I guess it's not about what I *need* to do. It's more about what I want to do. There is so much out in the world to learn about and explore. I am just not content to do what I've always known, what I've always done. Do you think that's wrong?"

"Gosh, no! I'm the same way. I have no idea what I'll major in at college. When people ask me about that, I never know what to say. I want to learn more about quantum physics. I love statistics. I want to take a class to learn about surrealism, both in art and literature. I…" Crap. I was doing it again, making our conversation all about me. "How about you? What classes do you want to take?"

"I love history. I know some about American history, but I want to know more. And I want to hear about the history of other nations and cultures."

"I love world religions! Would you want to take a course in that?"

"Definitely. And I want to study film! Even though I know maybe that's not the most sensible course…" There was a bit of an awkward pause. The line felt like it hadn't moved in a long time.

Zach dove back in. "I also want to travel. I've only ever been out of Lancaster County twice. Once a few years ago to go to Ohio to attend a family wedding, and then recently I took the train to Philadelphia."

"Oh, funny! We might've walked by each other in Philly."

He looked up and to the left. "I don't think so." I guess he was right. The chances were slim.

"Right, probably not." My neck was at a weird angle talking to him while standing in line, and it started aching. "So, you've never been to New

York City? We should go!" *Um, did I just invite a guy to go to New York City with me?*

"I would love to go to New York City—you've been?"

"Oh sure, lots of times." My one trip had been with my dad years ago. It wasn't like my mom wanted to take me there after the whole shoplifting scandal.

I pointed to a big sign near the entrance. "Hey, look at that sign."

No Fee

Optional donations will be accepted if you LIVE THROUGH

The Hell House!!!

"No wonder this is so popular. It's free? Geez. I've never seen that before."

"Me neither," Zach said. "I'm hoping it won't be too much longer that we'll be in limbo, waiting."

We finally moved up a few feet, getting closer to the entrance, but I still couldn't see where people were leaving. Maybe the house was swallowing them up?!! It was a funny idea, but before I could share it with Zach, he made a proposal.

"We will have to make a plan soon to go to New York, then." Zach smiled. I wondered if he meant an overnight trip. My toes tingled at the thought. "Would your mom be ok with that?"

I flushed red. "Yeah, she doesn't care what I do..." Then I tried to make a joke. "How about your parents? Will they be ok with you going with me into the city?"

His answer was not what I expected.

"No, they probably would not." He sighed and shook his head slightly. "But since I have not talked with them in months and probably never will again, I guess I won't know."

Never would again? Huh? Never? WTF did that mean? He couldn't be serious, could he?

Then, before I could respond, we moved again, and we were waved into the Hell House.

CHAPTER TWENTY-FIVE

The Reaper escorted the twelve of us into the first room by grunting and gesturing with his scythe that wiggled way too much for it to be metal. The first room had exactly twelve seats. We sat. I'd never been to a haunted house like this, and I'd been to quite a few over the years. It appeared we'd be seeing a play of some sort instead of the typical experience, running from room to room with monsters chasing us and jumping out.

Zach and I picked two seats in the front row centre. I warmed when he reached over to hold my hand. I couldn't imagine this act of touching would ever get old for me. I loved the feel of every rough and soft spot of his hand. The lights lowered on our side of the room but stayed bright in the "staging" area.

A doctor entered. We knew he was a doctor because he had a stethoscope hanging from around his neck, wore a lab coat, and carried a clipboard. The front of his white coat was splattered with blood, but other than that, he looked pretty normal. He was followed by a nurse carrying giant salad tongs dripping blood onto the floor. Clasped in the tongs was some kind of raw meat. Yuck. Then they both stopped and started laughing maniacally. *Maybe they were escaped patients doing lobotomies on doctors?*

"Is that thirty babies we've killed already today?" the Nutso Nurse cackled.

"At least forty, I think!" Demented Doctor crowed and grabbed a nearby bucket from a shelf. "The blood of innocents!" He ran over to the audience to show us the contents, a red, viscous liquid with arms and legs from a plastic doll floating in the goo. For a second I panicked that he was going to dump the gunk on us.

"This will keep us looking young! It's even better than Botox or plastic surgery," Nutso Nurse screamed. Funny and scary. That's always a good combo.

"Abortion is awesome! We are doing Satan's bidding!"

Say what? What the heck did the doctor dude just say? Weird.

"We are Disciples of Evil!" The nurse rolled her eyes back in her head. Nice trick.

"The blood of the innocents!" Then the Doctor dumped the bucket of blood over his own head, cackling. The lights went out. I heard a few people scream. The lights came back on. The doctor was gone, and the Reaper was centre stage.

"Next room," he growled, standing between us and the puddle of blood, gesturing to his left, where a door mysteriously opened. "Up! Or your souls are surely damned!"

Zach and I giggled nervously and stood, keeping our hands clasped. But I noticed his lips were tight, thinner than usual. At the same time, the Nutso Nurse started throwing little white candies up in the air while dancing and chanting, "Birth control means no more babies! Hahaha!"

Was Zach scared, or just a little confused like I was? I started feeling like the creator of this Hell House might have some political agenda, which is always more unpleasant than scary.

The next room had no chairs, so we stood up against a wall. A red velvet curtain cut the room in half. As everyone filed in, I took note of the wide demographics of our group: a girl who looked about eight years old with her dad caught my attention first. I was far from conservative when it came to horror stuff, but she seemed too young for this. There was a dark-haired couple that looked like they were college age, a group of four blonde guys with very square jaws, just a little younger than me, and two middle-aged women wearing prairie dresses and big barrettes in their Nashville-looking hair.

When the curtain dropped without any warning, we were treated to the sight of a man strapped into what looked like a very real electric chair. This was better. It seemed like classic scare-fare, more familiar than the stuff going on in that last little skit. The guy looked just like the killer from Wes Craven's *Shocked*, giant, bald, buggy-eyed and sporting a malicious grin. Two prison guards entered.

"Yeah, he's gonna fry tonight!" the shorter, ginger-haired guy snickered.

"Cool, I love to see their skin turn brown and flaky and their eyes pop out!" The taller, older one nodded.

"Yeah, playing God is fun!" they said in unison. *Um, ok. There was definitely something odd about the dialogue of the actors in these scenes.*

"So what did he do? Murder? Rape?" asked short guard. Boy, Daniel Day-Lewis would never have to worry about losing an Oscar to this guy. His delivery was so robotic.

"No, nothing so mild! This deviant professed Jesus Christ as his Lord and Savior to a small peaceful congregation of people!" tall guard solemnly replied.

"Oh, no! How horrible! This is a country that forbids religion. You can't do something so disrespectful to our great government and exalted leaders as that! We worship men, not God!" This couldn't be serious. I scanned the crowd to see if anyone else was going to start laughing. Only the dark-haired couple looked as surprised as I felt. Zach was looking at something on the floor near his feet.

"Exactly! So let's watch him BURN!"

Then the giant bald dude looked up at the ceiling and boomed, "God, I am not scared, because I HAVE FAITH THAT I WILL SOON BE COMING HOME TO YOU AND YOUR ONLY BEGOTTEN SON, JESUS CHRIST, IN HEAVEN!"

Huh. The actor seemed to enjoy chomping the scenery like it was funnel cake at the Ephrata Fair. After some flickering of the lights, a loud, recorded sound of electricity, ZZZZT! and a scream, the lights came back on. The man in the chair was slumped over, presumably dead. The Reaper returned.

"Weep not for him! His body is but a shell!" the Reaper addressed us, and I could see his mask was slipping a bit and some red hair was poking out.

Maybe he was the brother of the short guard? "His soul has gone to Heaven for all eternity. But the real question for you is, where will YOURS go?"

Wow. I finally got that this was not your normal, garden-variety haunted house, though there hadn't been any warnings or disclaimers on any of the ads or signs to let unsuspecting visitors know. This was some sort of crazy religious-themed haunted house. How the heck could they get away with that? I was pissed. It didn't seem like this kind of false advertising could be legal.

I finally made eye contact with Zach. He looked sickly green. His skin colour would've been perfect if he was playing an alien in a REAL haunted house, but it just made me feel horrible that Zach felt so disturbed by this.

"I swear, when I suggested this I had no idea that it would be… that this was…" I stammered.

"I wonder if we could just leave," Zach whispered, desperately scanning the room. But everyone was quickly herded into the next room through the only open door, and neither of us was bold enough to fight the against moving pack. We were like the only two lemmings who wanted to back out of the cliff dive but lacked the gumption to physically rebel.

The door out of this room led to a long hallway, no chairs. Instead of the play format we'd been "treated" to before, we had to walk through this scenario. My eyes adjusted to the darker environment, and I made out people who looked like caricatures of demons and devils scurrying around. Several gathered around two shackled men. The man on the left being poked mercilessly with a plastic pitchfork had a pencil moustache literally pencilled in. The man on the right wore a purple suit and had bright red lips. *Was that supposed to be blood?* Lipstick. It was garishly applied lipstick.

"You aren't feeling so GAY now, are you?" one demon cackled.

The two men attempted to hold hands, and a demon lady wearing a shiny black latex unitard that looked like it belonged in the front window of a porn shop poked their hands with a spear.

"It's blasphemy to lie with another man! Disgusting! Procreation is divine and should exist only between a married man and his wife."

My stomach soured then flipped. Zach held my hand firmly, and we both moved as quickly as we could, weaving through the other people to get out of this nightmare.

Gobsmacked by the hatred festering in this exhibition can't even begin to describe the disgust I was feeling.

The next room was flooded with bright lights that made me squint, immediately setting off a minor headache. Three large crosses had three bloody men hanging from them. The one in the middle looked like and a scraggly James Marsters wearing a crown of thorns: and moaning, "Father, why have you forsaken me?" and ad-libbing something about God not really forsaking believers, only sinners.

Yep. No doubt about it. This was definitely some freaky conversion attempt cleverly disguised as a haunted house.

"Hell House" indeed.

CHAPTER TWENTY-SIX

After the speech about all the forsaking, there was about one achingly long silent minute of us looking at the crosses and the actors hanging on them. Finally, mercifully, music was piped into the room. A loud crescendo of lyrics Halleluiah-ing. A girl standing near me was crying. Others were swaying. Some were on their knees. Praying.

Then the Reaper took centre stage. "Your life doesn't have to be like a horror movie in slow motion. You have the power to change it! You can REPENT! You do not need to be doomed for an eternity of suffering in hell. God gave us the precious gift of his SON, and if you believe in Jesus and are BORN AGAIN through Him, you can be SAVED!"

I heard many murmured "Amens." I looked around. *Was everyone else cool with this except me?* I felt like I'd entered *The Twilight Zone*.

"Now is your chance to REPENT and to ask Jesus to be your personal LORD and SAVIOR. You will be washed clean by his BLOOD! You can start down the path away from death and SIN and be promised ETERNAL LIFE!" There was some applause.

As the Reaper droned on, I checked out. Making a list served as the only way I could cope with this.

Ways This Hell House Mirrored an Actual Haunted House
1. Vampirism at its finest: the fixation with blood as a "drink" and a purifier and achieving the goal of "living forever."
2. Zombies also rose from the dead. But they were a lot crankier than Jesus, who usually epitomized gentleness. Interesting side note: some people claim there's evidence Jesus was a vegetarian.

3.   Fear of witches originated because men worried about women's power, especially feeling anxiety about their sexuality, which led to the broomsticks and naked dancing rumours. Women having birth control access has historically loosened patriarchal control... scary for some men.

4.   Archetypical villains like Jason, Freddy, poltergeists, Lady Gaga in *AHS:Hotel,* all use trickery and lies. Wasn't the hallmark of Satan his deception of Eve in the Garden? So whose side did these Hell House people think they were on?

Then the door behind the fake messiah opened, and we were led into a room that looked like the Time Share real estate office that my mom worked in when I was a kid. There were tables, each manned by a shiny young person, obviously eager to counsel us. I thought I recognized one or two of the "prayer counsellors" from outside when I was in line. Wasn't that one of the square-jawed dudes I saw walking in a pack a few minutes ago, now at the table to my right?

This Hell House must have a heck of a lot of people working to keep it going, mopping up the copious amounts of blood between shows. It also required several different actors playing the crazy dude who dumped blood over his head, because there was no way he could clean up so quickly between "shows." A giant congregation of people had to have been involved in this elaborate fabrication.

After we filed in, we were guided to a table in a group of at least twenty other tables, all occupied by people in intense conversations. I sat where I was directed. Zach stood next to me, shifting from foot to foot. A woman in her late twenties with teeth so white they looked like they'd glow in black light began bombarding us with questions. "Are you Christians? Do you have a 'Home Church'? Are you aware that if you aren't born again, Satan will get you and torture you?" We both gaped at her, not responding. Then, I started to get my "sea legs" for this and responded.

"So... where in the Bible does it advocate subterfuge to coerce people into converting?" I mumbled.

She just smiled at me in a patronizingly pitying way and shook her head. I hated her superior act. It reminded me of Hillary's. It only made me get louder. "And that homophobia stuff was gross."

"Let me guess, you're not yet saved as a Christian." She shook her head as if I was a naughty three-year-old.

"I tell you what, I know so many cool Christians who wouldn't think this sabotage thing was a good idea. In fact, they'd be as appalled as I am," I said, thinking of my friend Tracy from elementary school who took me to a free weeklong Bible camp with puppet shows and yarn crafts one summer. And Mrs. Taylor, our neighbour in King of Prussia who had a collection of gorgeous nativity scenes from around the world that she proudly displayed on her shelves all year long.

"Some people claim to be Christians but aren't carefully reading their Bibles." The woman across from me clicked her tongue against the roof of her mouth.

"Oh, yeah? Find me the verse where Christ says, 'Use trickery if you have to, whatever it takes, just get people to become Christians,'" I challenged.

"The end justifies the means," she replied smugly.

"Yeah, ok, that's not even from the Bible. Not at all. That quote is from Machiavelli, who was, for your edification, denounced by Church leaders of his time as an apostle of the devil." I'd hit my mark. She looked flustered but tried to recover by taking off her little granny glasses and fake cleaning them on the sleeve of her white Peter Pan-collared shirt.

She looked at Zach. "So, are you are also fine with burning in agonizing pain for all eternity in Hell?" Her sweet tone juxtaposed with the threatening words she'd used had a creepy effect similar to that of the weird blonde kids in *Children of the Damned*.

"I believe in God's grace now and am not obsessed with the laws," Zach murmured.

"Have you *read* your Bible?" she challenged.

"'Whoever says, I know Him but does not keep His commandments is a liar and the truth is not in him.' 1 John: 24," Zach stated a little louder. I did a double-take when I saw his determined face. "Your deceit makes you not very reputable as a representative of His word." Zach calmly stared her down. Wow. I hadn't expected that from him.

"Yeah!" I pumped my fist a little, seriously proud of Zach. "Anyway, this is stupid, whether it's legal chicanery or not. What if I go on my vlog, Snapchat, Facebook, Instagram, and Twitter pages and let everyone know what kind of deplorable trick you guys are pulling here?"

I didn't have any of those accounts except my Facebook page, which had a potential status update that less than a hundred people would see.

"Nobody watches vlogs anymore," she said, unimpressed. She looked away and made a hand gesture at a dark window to someone that I couldn't see. Then an older man appeared beside me and gently but firmly placed his hand on my elbow. Other people in the room were starting to stare at us.

"It's fine. I've got this," the man told her as he attempted to manoeuvre me to standing.

"No. Now, you need to let off her arm immediately, jah?" Zach's voice was no longer steady. It was angry. "Remember your Matthew 26:52?."

Who replaced Zach with this Bible-Bot? And what the heck was a "jah?"

The man was clearly shaken. He let go of me quickly. "Whoa, wait, I... ah, I wasn't trying to hurt her. I..." I actually felt a little bad for him. He seemed like a more flustered version of my gym teacher, Mr. Kreider, who was pretty high-strung himself.

"No. We're done. We'll see ourselves out," Zach said firmly and put his arm around my shoulders, protectively stepping between us. I didn't want him to think I needed a "defender" or anything. I could take care of myself. But I also couldn't deny this made me a bit mushy.

"You're garbage people," I said, not very eloquently, but it was all I had in the moment. The man continued to glare at me.

Before he started walking away, Zach made eye contact with the man. "Shame on you for violating the most basic concepts of the Bible. If you do not speak and act with love, you are not following Jesus. Read your Corinthians." Ok, Zach's parting shot was a little more effective than mine, because the man's head jerked back a bit.

We walked away. Zach kept him arm around me. "Are you all right?"

I nodded and smiled up at him. He felt so warm up against me.

My heart swelled. I'd never felt so safe before. Yet in the back of my mind, that little voice nagged me. *How the heck does Zach know so much Bible stuff?*

CHAPTER TWENTY-SEVEN

When we got out of the Hell House, I wanted to run up and down the line of people still waiting to get in, warning them about what they were about to stumble into. I wanted to nullify the "religious blindsiding" they were about to get. I figured at least some of them were in the same boat we'd been in. They just wanted to go to a good old-fashioned haunted house, a normal one with ghosts, vampires, and serial killers. Odd how benign those icons seemed to me now. It was all a matter of perspective, I guess. The hidden agenda of the zealots running the sham scare disturbed me more than imaginary monsters could.

In retrospect, I realized the people I'd seen while standing in line, the girls with the big crosses, the buses of younger kids with chaperones, etc., these were all people in the know, church groups and believers. And though probably not everyone would be of that ilk, I just didn't have the moxie to go address a bunch of strangers in a loud voice about this deceitful Hell House. Part of me wished I did have that confidence and spunk. If Madison had been with me, she would have. But I couldn't. And then there was the matter of Zach. After his impressive thwarting of the nutjobs' attempts to "convert" us, he'd been pretty quiet. He was upset, but I got the feeling it was not merely because he was angered at the fright house fraud.

We got to the car without saying a word to each other. I put the key into the ignition, but then I stopped. I didn't know where we were going. It was only 8 p.m., and I certainly didn't want the night to be over.

"Hey, thanks for that back there," I said, "when you got that guy to lay off me. I appreciated it. I probably shouldn't have said what I did about them being garbage people, but I was so mad."

"No man should ever act threateningly to a woman like that." Zach seemed more appalled than angry.

"Well, no *person* should ever threaten another person," I corrected.

Zach nodded. "Yes, of course. Sorry. You're right. I'm too old-fashioned sometimes. I apologize."

Now I felt like I'd done a blurtful thing again. Great.

"Not that I didn't appreciate you having my back in there," I said. "I'm sure he was just trying to get us to shut up and leave. I don't think he was going to hurt me or anything. But still, I'm grateful you made him take his hand off me."

"I just reacted too quickly, sorry." Zach smiled shyly at me. "But I'd never let anyone hurt you. I mean, not because you're a *girl* I like. You're a *person* I like. I mean…"

I was enjoying his sweet contrition but decided to go for it and tell Zach my real feelings. "Look, nobody has ever taken my side like that. Back when my parents split up, I felt like my mom got stuck with me, and I've never had a friend that I've trusted a hundred percent so I, well, I…" I wanted to tell him I thought I was falling in love with him, but the words stuck in my throat.

Zach was silent but kept eye contact with me. Maybe his words were stuck, too? I hoped that was it and that I hadn't freaked him out by my gushing.

"So, you sure know a lot of Bible verses!" Probably not the best way to break the silence, but I had a knack for making the awkward more awkward. He dropped his eyes.

"I… um… hope you don't mind me asking. If so, just say, but I was wondering if you have ever read the Bible?" Zach asked, studying me.

"Uh, parts of it. I think if you want to understand modern literature, you're at a disadvantage if you don't understand the allusions. So many titles come from the Biblical references: *The Sound and the Fury*, *Of Mice and Men*, *Song of Solomon*…"

"But not for church?" he asked.

"No, I never went to church. Did you?"

"Every Sunday. Almost all day long."

"Whoa! Are you Catholic or something?"

"No, not Catholic," he replied with a small smile.

I knew I shouldn't push it but couldn't help it. "So your parents were super-religious? Is that why you're not talking to them anymore?"

"It is a major part of why…"

"They're not in a cult or something, are they?" I felt so bad for Zach. His face was much paler than normal; this was obviously hard for him.

"How would you define a cult?"

"I dunno," I said. "I guess a group of people that separated themselves from others and had beliefs that were outside established norms. They do unconventional things. I think of them usually with a leader at the top who thinks he's a messiah or something."

"I think the group I grew up in falls under some of those descriptions. But there's no one leader making the rules. Vanity and ego are strictly forbidden."

"Well, then who calls the shots? I mean who says everyone has to follow all the weird rules or they will be banned?"

"Everyone agrees, I guess." He rubbed the back of his neck like a bee had stung him hard.

"Oh…" I couldn't think of anything else to say. "Anyway, I'm sorry." I tried to lighten the mood. "Wow, that Hell House was a pretty crappy choice for a third date. My bad. We're definitely going to have to do a better job for our fourth!"

"I'm not sure you'll want a fourth date with me. I haven't been honest with you, Sam." Red rimmed Zach's eyes, and he got all thick in the voice. "I think I'm as bad as the deceivers in the Hell House in a way."

My esophagus felt like I'd swallowed the contents of a whole jar of peanut butter. And then washed it down with a V8.

"Ok, so what haven't you told me?" I locked eyes with Zach.

"I was raised Amish," he said.

"Oh," I said.

I so hadn't seen that coming.

CHAPTER TWENTY-EIGHT

When I got home, I replayed in my mind the conversation I'd had with Zach in my car. Sitting on my bed, eating a strawberry Pop-Tart and listening to this old band from the '80s called Yaz play "Only You" over and over again on my laptop. I was like an old-school photo lab; sometimes it took days for things to fully develop.

After Zach told me he was Amish, all I could think of to say was, "Amish, huh? I knew a girl when I lived in King of Prussia whose grandparents were Mormon." Even as I said it, I'd known it was stupid. It was like saying, "Oh, you're Hindu? Cool! I know this other person who's Buddhist!"

Zach then said he wasn't sure if people outside of his community would call him "Amish" now that he'd left. He told me that by now he should have been baptized by choice as an adult, but he hadn't been. He said his Rumspringa never ended. I didn't understand that word, but from what I could gather, it was a rite of passage of some kind before you got baptized. I guess after you went through it, you became a member of the church. However, it was unclear to Zach what happened if you were never actually baptized Amish and chose not to make that commitment. He studied this variance during Rumspringa and thought it meant he wouldn't be formally "shunned" if you left the church. But his hopes were dashed, because even though there was no "official" edict, his parents and siblings were refusing to talk with him now.

I didn't know what to say in response. So I picked my cuticle until it bled.

Silence ensued for two minutes, but it felt like two days before he broke it.

"I am really sorry... I hadn't expected to talk to you about this tonight. I mean, to tell you about my Amish upbringing. I knew soon I must. Hiding this from you... horrible it is. If I am honest, I did not want you to know until you got to know me first. Selfish, I suppose." He'd said all this very quickly, even with the weird speech pattern of emphasizing each word without any contractions and speaking his sentences backward like Yoda.

"No, it's ok, I understand," I said, playing with the car keys, not sure whether to put them in the ignition and start the car or not. I knew I didn't want to have this discussion while driving. But I also knew I was making things worse by not contributing to the conversation, or empathizing, or whatever the heck was the appropriate thing for me to do.

"Well, I mean, I don't exactly understand, but I don't want you to feel like you have to... uh..." I stopped. He nodded. More uncomfortable silence. I decided to put the keys in the ignition, and I swear I heard Zach breath a sigh of relief.

On the ride back to his apartment, he looked out the window. I tried to talk about the unseasonably warm weather we'd been having for October and whether it meant we'd have a harsher or milder winter.

When I feel all my assumptions shatter like bone china, I guess my conversational skills mirror those of a vapid meteorologist. Nice to know.

When we got to his apartment, Zach finally looked at me before getting out of my car. "I am sorry again. Can I call please tomorrow to talk?"

I wanted to say, *No, let's talk now! Time apart will only make us more tongue-tied and weird!* but instead, I nodded mutely. He didn't try to kiss me or anything. He hung his head and patted my shoulder. I felt like hugging him, but my body had turned to granite, and I couldn't budge. So instead I pulled away and bared my teeth in what I hoped looked more like a smile than the threat of a rabid dog.

And he got out of my car and walked away. A part of me thought, *That's the last time you'll ever see him again. Men don't like it when things get complicated. Look at your dad.*

I thought about making a list of why "Alone Is Better than Trying" but instead I made this:

10 Things I Know About the Amish From the Internet and Gossip

1) They don't have TVs, so they can't watch *The Librarians*, my and Madison's favourite show. Also, they aren't supposed to go to the movies (especially horror movies, I'd imagine!).

2) They make nice quilts, shoo fly pie, and gazebos.

3) Amish refer to themselves as "Plain People" with pride. Buttons are considered too fancy, so they use hook and eye closures instead (learned this from my Home Ec teacher last year).

4) I'd heard Hillary's mom caught a group swiping stuff again. Pretty sure they do it because they don't have money, not for the thrill, like yours truly used to.

5) They don't go to school past the eighth grade and are discouraged from reading things other than the Bible. Yikes.

6) They believe in handling wrongdoings within their community and generously granting mercy. When someone does something unfathomable like that waste-of-skin guy did in 2006 when he murdered five Amish girls for no reason, the families of the girls were expected to forgive him. They did.

7) The dolls have no facial features, which is supposed to show their lack of vanity but just makes the dolls look creepy to me.

8) They can't date or marry non-Amish people, who the Amish call "English," even though they're not British but American or Canadian. (There are no Amish communities in Europe any more.)

9) Only about 40% are full-time farmers now, but about fifty years ago, 95% were. (This guy named Kraybill writes tons of stuff about the Amish. But I bet he's never dated one.)

10) I *had* been dating an Amish guy… without a clue that I was.

CHAPTER TWENTY-NINE

When I hadn't heard from Zach by 4 p.m. Saturday afternoon, I called Madison.

"Holy fart butler! *Amish*? You've got to be kidding me!" Madison laughed hard. "Wow, that cornfield party makes so much more sense now! I knew some of those people had to be on Rumspringa but had no idea Zach was a buggy driver."

"Madison, it's not funny. And don't tell anybody." I knew Madison could sometimes be a little immature, but I was hoping to get the kinder Madison I'd been talking to about Zach lately and not her rude twin. But then I realized she'd been hanging out with almost exclusively with Hillary lately, and Hill's 'tude was probably rubbing off on her.

"Right. Of course it isn't funny. But I mean, it's not something you hear about every day. Now I get it why his friends had such good drugs! I've always heard Amish kids have the wildest parties with the best drugs when they're on Rumspringa. This might be our lucky day as far as connections go, Sam!"

"I STILL don't do drugs, Mad," I said, getting irked. But there was that word again: Rumspringa. I kicked myself for forgetting to Google that. "So what does that mean, Rumspringa?"

"Oh, the Amish kids aren't confirmed to the church until they're baptized, so they get this period to sow their wild oats. It's only supposed to last a year or two. Starts when they're about sixteen. They're allowed to be bad and out in the real world, and their parents pretend not to notice," Madison explained a little pedantically. I think she liked knowing something I didn't for once. "I bet Zach was liking the freedom so much, he didn't want to go back!"

I felt a pang of jealousy. Was she implying he was a player? As confused as I'd been by his revealing he was Amish, a part of me had been a bit relieved. But now Madison's words had reawakened my nagging insecurity that he'd been seeing other girls. Why wouldn't he be? We weren't exclusive or anything. What if the reason he didn't want to go back to his Amish life was because he was into dating non-Amish girls? What if I was merely one of the "perks" of his new lifestyle?

Madison kept chuckling. "Gosh, I mean, I was totally not expecting this, and I have serious Plain-dar!"

"What's 'Plain-dar'?" I paced, wondering how Madison changed the focus of our conversation to herself so quickly.

"Like gay-dar but for Amish." Madison laughed again.

"Ri-i-ight," I said, rolling my eyes, because I knew she couldn't see me. "I think I need to go…"

"Oh, Sam, stop acting like such a big baby. Don't go." I almost hung up on her but was glad I hadn't, because then Madison paused and said softly, "I'm sorry. Look, I'm just trying to lighten the mood with dumb jokes."

I was taken aback. I'd never heard Madison be so self-aware and honest before. "No. You're right. I am being a big baby. I'm sorry, too. I have a capricious temper right now because I didn't sleep at all last night…"

"Want to come over and get smashed? That might help." I didn't know if this was another dumb joke until she started laughing.

I felt the sobs welling up in my throat, and I tried to squeeze them back down. "I'm upset. I like him." I was surprised at how ragged my voice sounded.

"Well, look, he didn't break up with you or anything, right? So don't let this crazy revelation get in the way of your fun. He's seriously hot. Just tell him you don't care about the Amish thing and don't want to talk about it anymore. Then pretend last night never happened," Madison said.

"But I think his being Amish, or not being Amish now, or whatever is going on with him, matters a lot… to him, anyway. And the idea of us not ever talking about it, wouldn't that be putting a big wall between us if we ignore it?" I pushed thumbtacks into the corkboard by my desk one by one and then took them back out in the same order as I considered this.

"You're not talking about getting married. He's just your first crush. Maybe he's even your first love. But trust me on this, there will be so, so many more guys. So enjoy the kissing and whatever else and don't sweat the details."

"But maybe he'll be my first… you know." I was grateful we weren't Skyping, so she couldn't see me blush.

"Yeah, about that." Madison laughed. "Maybe you should sleep with someone else for your Plan P. Two virgins fumbling around, that's not going to be fun for either of you!" I winced. That seemed like a dig.

"I don't think I can… I mean… I'm not like you," I blurted. I was pissed she wasn't taking my problems seriously.

"NOT like me? What do you mean by that?" In retrospect, I should have pulled back when I heard the edge in her voice.

"I don't make out with just anyone." My voice rose a bit. "He's special to me, not one of many hook-ups."

"What? Are you saying I'm a slut? Wow, Sam. I'd expect that from other people, not you." Madison's tone sounded genuinely wounded, but this turn of the conversation pissed me off. Why were we talking about her again? I was the one who was hurting, and she kept turning this around to be about her.

"Look, we are different people, sure…" I decided to try her tactic and joke my way out of this. "I don't drink and do drugs, because I'm the uptight one. And I don't sleep with guys when I don't know their last names, because I'm the picky one. But I also don't make other people's problems all about me because I don't have low self-esteem. So, yeah, that makes me a prissy Saint Sam, and I guess you're the wild slut." I tried to pull off a laugh so she'd know I was joking, but it came out sounding weird.

Then the dial tone in my ear told me my "joke" hadn't gone over very well at all.

CHAPTER THIRTY

Five minutes after Madison hung up on me, my emotions were a messy jumble like a Black-and-White milkshake. I was still a little irked at her, but replaying the conversation, I think I probably got too defensive. I definitely shouldn't have gone off on her like I did, joke or no joke. Then my cell rang. It was a blocked number. I figured it was Madison, but I couldn't help but to hope it was Zach. Either way, I wanted to make things right, so I hastily accepted the call. It wasn't Zach or Madison. Instead it was my mother.

"So I have this big problem," she cooed, slurring a bit.

"Hello to you, too."

"Awwww… Sammy, don't be that way." I hated when she called me "Sammy." I also hated it when she called me when she was schlitzy.

"Ok, what?" After a big fight with my best friend and worrying that Zach might never call me again, I really didn't need the tension of another confrontation with my mom. So I resolved to try to be noncombative.

"Well, I know you don't date much. Yeah, ok, whatever. But I mean, you prolly read about that kinda stuff a lot, right? And I can't reach any of my friends, so you can help your mom out, right? I need your advice." I was silent. She plowed on anyway, ignoring this. "Now, imagine if you had the studly-hot captain of the football team and the richest kid in school fighting over you. Which would you pick?" I hated when she did these hypotheticals.

"Neither. They are both tools. Carter Burger, the captain of our football team, is a misogynist pig, and Cooper Smith is a snob who once dated Delia," I replied.

"No, no, no! You're being too literal!" I heard her take a breath. "So scratch that, ok? So here's the deal, I've been seeing this guy, John. He's an investment banker who'd make wonderful second husband material, right? He's got a penthouse in this amazing building with a view to die for in Philly, and I plan to move back to civilization again after I get you off to college and stuff. Then he's ALSO got a McMansion in Boca Raton. You've heard me talk about John, remember? He's the one who bought me that five-thousand-dollar necklace. I showed you that, right?" She could go off on tangents like nobody's business when she was drinking.

"I don't know what the problem is, Mom. He sounds great. Go for it." I wanted to end the conversation, but she kept going.

"Well, I'm getting to that if you'd stop interrupting me. Sheesh." She paused for a big gulp of whatever her current poison was.

"Aren't you working today?"

"No, I closed a giant deal this morning on this home owned by a Mafia boss reality TV star guy, so I'm celebrating this afternoon. Totally legit. But see, here's my problem. I have a date with John tonight, but then there's this massage therapist who I've been seeing for my tennis elbow… his name is Karma, and he's so freakin' sexy! He's only twenty-eight and so cut he looks like a Roman sculpture of like, Zeus, or something…"

"If it was a Roman sculpture, then it'd be Jupiter. Zeus was the Greek version," I said, trying to be helpful.

"Oh, whatever. Who cares? God, you're such a little know-it-all sometimes." I heard another gulp. "Anyway, I didn't think I had a shot with him. I'm twenty years older than he is, for Chrissakes, but last time, I was pretty sure he was purposefully being all sexy when he was working on my muscles, and he couldn't take his eyes off my cleavage. And now he jus' called to ask me over tonight for a date! And I'm not sure what to do… I mean, I want to jump all over Karma, but what if John finds out?"

"Oh gross, I think I just threw up in my mouth a little bit," I said, unable to help myself. This was obviously a bad thing to say, because my mother went off on me. She told me I was too judgmental, just like her parents had been. This surprised me, because she rarely talked about my

grandparents. Then she reminded me of all the sacrifices she'd made for me. I told her I NEVER asked her to do ANYTHING for me.

And then I said … and I knew I shouldn't have as soon as I heard it come out of my mouth, "I can understand why your parents were disappointed in you. You make lousy choices in men!"

I heard a sharp intake of breath.

"Well, if your dad hadn't been such a loser, we wouldn't be having this conversation," she slurred. "Besides, you're not as perfect as you pretend. Remember, I was the one who bailed you out when you decided to start stealing!"

I finally told her to leave me alone. Then she hung up on me. Wow. So I was two for two with the hang-ups today.

When my phone rang again, I almost didn't answer it. But I of course I did. I'm a masochist that way, I guess.

"Hi." It was Zach. "Sorry I didn't call earlier. I guess I've been nervous to talk with you. But I apologize that I took so long."

"Oh. Well, that's ok," I said. "But why are you nervous?"

"I, um, I do not think I was very kind to you last night. And I feel bad. I tell you this surprisingly bizarre thing about myself, that I am, or was anyway, Amish, and then refuse to talk with you anymore about it. That seems like not a very nice thing."

"Well, it's not like you told me you're a vampire or a zombie!" A long pause plopped into our conversation like a seagull dropping.

I should stop trying to make jokes. I'm obviously not very good at it.

"If I were a zombie, I think you'd know, and I wouldn't have to tell you. Zombies aren't exactly known for their ability to blend in." We both laughed. "So I was wondering, could you meet me? Talking on the phone, not seeing you when speaking of serious matters, this is hard for me."

"Sure," I replied, knowing Skyping or FaceTime weren't options. "Where? When?"

"How about in two hours at House of Pizza?"

The place where we first met and first talked.

"Ok, sure, sounds good," I said. We said goodbye. I noticed he waited for me to hang up first. Not getting hung up on by yet another person felt good.

I went into the bathroom, ran a comb through my hair, and put on some lip gloss, blush, and mascara. As I was trying to decide whether to wear a pullover sweater with a Japanese anime character or a colour-blocked cardigan with my jeans, my cell buzzed again. This time it was a text from Madison.

So glad U finally let me know how U really feel. Sorry Im a druggie slut and not a megabrain like U.

Ugh. I so didn't want to continue this fight by text. Especially now. I was hoping we could work this out quickly and laugh about it. I knew it wasn't smart to do, but I texted back:

It was supposed to be a joke. You and Hillary do it all the time to each other. Why is that ok and this isn't?

I knew I probably shouldn't bring up Hillary and Madison's friendship, because it sounded petty and jealous of me. But it had been something I'd been thinking about for a while.

Then I got this back: **Yeah, right. Whatever. It's all good.**

I had a feeling it wasn't "all good," but I decided to stop texting. This would get us nowhere. After the thing with my mom, I figured if Madison and I kept going, we'd just make everything worse, too. So I typed a few things in return like:

Fine! Can't even.

You're my friend, please don't be upset.

You're so narcissistic. Can't talk now. I'm busy.

I'm sorry. I want to work this out…

But I deleted each one. Instead of sending her any of these replies, I put my phone into my purse.

I told myself that I'd call her later to work it out. But it seemed like Zach wanted to make up, and all Madison wanted to do was escalate. I could only handle one drama at a time.

And sorry, Madison, but this was Zach's afternoon.

CHAPTER THIRTY-ONE

When I arrived at House of Pizza, Zach was already there, sitting in the first booth near the door, smiling. This seemed to be a good sign. I sat down and returned his smile.

"I know you don't go to church, but may I ask, do you believe in God?" he asked.

Oh, crud. I didn't know what I'd expected him to say to me right off the bat, but it wasn't that. Maybe I should've agreed to meet up with Madison instead. Couldn't he have just complimented my Agatha Ruiz De La Prada jumper or something?

I stood up quickly. "Wow. Um… so, to go get a soda. You want one?" Maybe my mom was right. Maybe I was like my dad. He always avoided hard situations, and it looked like that was my M.O. right now, too. "Or were you going to eat?"

"No, but I'll have a root beer, thank you. But please, let me pay for them both." Zach fumbled for his wallet.

"No, I've got it this time." I practically sprinted to the counter and ordered a regular Coke for myself and the root beer for Zach. It didn't surprise me that neither of us had the stomach to eat, despite both being such pizza fiends.

When I got back to the table, I set the drinks on the table, sat down, and concentrated intently on removing the paper from my straw in one long, unbroken piece.

"I am sorry. I think maybe that question I asked you was a rude way to start," Zach started.

My phone starting vibrating in my front pocket.

"Just a minute," I told Zach and looked at it. It was Madison.

Do U rlly have such a sugar honey iced tea opinion of me? R U perfect, Saint Sam?

Oh, geez. I had the feeling she was buzzed texting me, but I didn't want to try to explain this to Zach in the middle of a conversation with him about religion. Besides, I genuinely had no idea what a "Sugar Honey Iced Tea Opinion" was.

I texted her back:

Can't talk now. Phone battery low.

Then I shut my phone off.

"Sorry, about my belief in God. No, no, it's fine you asked me that. I don't mind talking about profound esoteric stuff," I replied, trying to seem casual. "I'd say I'm polytheistic because I've always loved Greek, Norse, and Hindu mythology. Why do we have to have only one god when you can have a whole pantheon of them?" I attempted a chuckle, but I could see by the way Zach looked at me, he wasn't sure if he should take me seriously.

"Ok, no more jokes." I continued. "My dad is half Jewish and half Catholic, and my mom was raised Christian Scientist, and she won't talk much about it. She hates all religion. So I never regularly went to any place of worship. My dad's mom took me to the Catholic Church with her a few times before she died. I remember feeling bored but liking the colourful windows a lot. Pretty much all of what I know about religion, other than a week-long summer Bible camp when I was in the second grade, which had fantastic colouring pages that I could use to design Joseph's amazing coat, comes from books. Both fiction and nonfiction."

He continued quietly studying me. He was starting to unnerve me like that kid in *The Omen*. I knew I was babbling but couldn't stop.

"There's this one book I read that says we're hardwired to believe in God, so when we pray, meditate, or worship in groups, we activate certain parts of the brain, making the participant happy and peaceful. It seems if there's this provable physiological component to faith, we should give it some consideration."

"So, um, you do believe in God, then?" Zach hadn't touched his root beer.

"I think so. I like the idea of God. Maybe I'm Agnostic? Or Unitarian? Is there even a difference? I mean, can you be both at the same time? I believe in the possibility and validity of everything, I guess." Zach cocked his head pensively. I realized I probably wasn't making much sense. I'd honestly never thought much about my spiritual beliefs. "So... do *you* believe in God?" I ventured.

"Yes. I definitely do. I've been thinking about this a lot. But it is a very different God than the God of my parents and community. Their God is all about rules and following a very strict code. Their God doesn't seem to value love. Only sacrifice and punishment."

"Wow, that sounds a lot like those people running that haunted house, huh?" I refrained from the calling the haunted house people "crazies" or "whackjobs." *See, I can be tactful at times!*

"No, my family and neighbours would see the Hell House people as liberal sinners." He smiled ruefully and stabbed his straw into his drink lid. "Unlike the Amish, the Hell House religious recruiters wore buttons, the women didn't cover their heads, and they use electricity."

"Oh, wow." Inadequate response, but I couldn't think of anything else to say. We both sipped our drinks. After a minute or two of this, I looked up at Zach. "So you mentioned punishments. Were you spanked a lot as a kid?"

He shook his head. "Whipped. Usually with a belt. Sometimes with a horsewhip. All my brothers and sisters were beaten. Even Mose, and he was born lame in one leg. My sisters mostly got a hand or a wooden spoon." He pushed his lips together. "There's an Amish saying that 'you must bend a branch when it's young.'"

"Yikes, I knew a girl in Philly who told me her parents used to spank her, too." I was trying to be fair. The Amish weren't the only ones who believed in spanking. "She told me they always hugged her and told her they loved her after but just wanted to teach her to behave."

"I never, ever remember, not one time, being hugged by either of my parents." Zach sounded not accusatory but sad.

All my memories of my dad snuggling me on the couch, watching *Scooby-Doo* and *SpongeBob*, came flooding back to me. And for all her faults, my mom had hugged and kissed me when I was younger. Poor Zach. I struggled to find the right words but couldn't.

"I still love my mother and father," he said softly. "They do not know any other way. This is how their parents raised them."

"Yeah, but that still doesn't make it right. You're the oldest, right? What about getting your younger brothers and sisters out of there? Can you call Child Services or something?"

Zach looked shocked. "No, I could never... I mean, I still hope one day my brothers and sisters will talk to me again. We will never eat a meal together or spend much time together unless they choose to leave too, but then that choice is theirs to make." His wistfulness killed me, and I decided not to push. For now anyway.

"So what are the rules of shunning? It's 'limited contact' but not 'no contact'?"

"Ah, this is hard to answer. Truthfully, different groups have varying levels of strictness for those violating Ordnung. Some groups are not as strict about those in the Bann, like me."

So I got that "Ordnung" must be the code, the rules, and "in the Bann" must refer to outcasts, but I was still confused. "But the Bible doesn't say to do this shunning thing, does it? So why do the Amish do it?"

"Not explicitly," Zach said. Just then the song "Stairway to Heaven" came on the jukebox. My inappropriate giggles bubbling up threatened to derail our conversation, but I fought them. "The verses that are cited as support are Romans 16:17, 'Now I beseech you, brethren, mark them which cause divisions and offences contrary to the doctrine which ye have learned; and avoid them.' And 2 Thessalonians 3:14, 'And if any man obey not our word by this epistle, note that man, and have no company with him, that he may be ashamed.'" He seemed to intuit my confusion, so he explained more. "The shunning is used to make the deviant change his ways; it works like a fence keeping the sheep from the fox. It is also used by the Amish to show commitment to the church."

"Um, calling yourself a 'deviant' seems a bit extreme," I said, chewing on a piece of ice, eyeing a bunch of mutton-chopped dudes I recognized from my school, hipsters who always reeked of weed and booze, sitting in one of the back booths. "It's kinda hard to think of *you* as a deviant."

"I was visited by the leader of my church after I'd been on Rumspringa for a while. I was asked to stop flaunting church rules, to turn my back on my sinful ways," Zach said.

"Um, what exactly were your sins?" I asked. "I mean, what did they think you were doing wrong?"

"The bishop was most upset by my reading novels. I'd stopped hiding the fact I was reading when I was on Rumspringa, so my family must have noticed and told him. And he didn't like that I wanted to go to college. Amish are supposed to stop their education after what you'd call middle school. I was told I must consider my arrogance and to repent and stop reading so many secular books."

"That sounds like how the people in the nineteenth century reacted to Flaubert's *Madame Bovary*. Books are corrupting influences, right?"

"The Apostle Paul seemed to think so. How did that work out for Flaubert?"

"Attempts at censorship made him more popular than ever." I happily noted Zach's ghost of a smile.

"Our bishop has one of the strictest rules regarding Meidung in all of Lancaster County, I think. So my family and friends in our community were encouraged to shun me even as I was still living in my parents' barn. They started by not talking to me or acknowledging me but then decided to try something more drastic. At eight months, I had not agreed to stop pursuing knowledge, so the bishop told my parents they must try to change my mind with stronger methods. Because I'd never been baptized, I couldn't actually be excommunicated. That's when I had to move out, and I got my apartment."

"How long ago was that?" I asked.

"Only a couple of weeks before we met," he answered. Now the no-voicemail thing made sense. He'd probably used a payphone to call me. "Luckily, my cousin's family is in a more liberal Amish community with

a different bishop, so I could work for them at Central Market. They also helped me find my apartment."

"This no-education rule is nuts to me." I shook my head. "I admire you. You're a real-life autodidact!"

"What is that?" Zach smiled and raised his eyebrows. His curiosity was so awesome.

"Someone who learns in a self-directed way, mainly by reading." I was happy to be teaching him something, because he'd taught me so much. But the thing with his parents spurning him still bugged me, so I couldn't drop it. "So how long have they not been talking to you?"

"It will be one year this December 24th."

"Christmas Eve? They started shunning you on Christmas Eve?" I heard my voice rise, and saw a few people turn to look.

Zach lowered his voice self-consciously. "Well, our celebration of Christmas is different from those who aren't Amish. A few families do small gift exchanges. But most, like mine, don't. There is no Santa Claus or trees. It's about worship." He smiled then, remembering. "We did have a program in school, though. I did love those. We'd sing and do little plays."

He felt nostalgic about parts of growing up Amish, and his pain was palpable. His eyes looked like those of a dog you see in an animal shelter. I grasped for something to make him feel better. "That sounds like a good memory."

"It is. But sad it makes me, too," he said. I figured that was my cue to change the subject.

"So, this is a complete non sequitur, but what's up with all the Christmas-themed horror movies? You need to see the original *Black Christmas*! That was pretty good. Also, *Christmas Evil*. But then there are some exceptionally bad ones, too. Like all the sequels to *Silent Night, Deadly Night*. Though the first one was pretty good." I could see he wasn't listening. His attention seemed fixed on a map of the New York subway system above the booth across from us that seemed ubiquitous in every pizza joint. "Sorry, that was impolite that I changed the subject."

"No, it's my fault. I'm not very good at explaining all of this." In that moment, I could see what Zach must have looked like at four and what he might look like at seventy. He looked so innocent and confused. So lost. I just wanted to hold him tightly in my arms.

"Hey, it sucks. I mean, I get the family drama. My dad hasn't been around at all for the last two years, and it hurts so bad when I think of him, sometimes I can't stand it. It rips me apart." Zach reached his hand out to hold mine. I couldn't believe those words had come tumbling out of my mouth. I'd never admitted to another living soul how hurt I was by my dad. I hadn't ever admitted it to myself. But now I had. It was out there.

"I'm so sorry. I've been selfish, brutzing so much about my problems. What happened for you? I guess I still do not understand why you do not see your father." Zach gently squeezed my hand before sitting back and cocking his head.

"Brutzing?" I asked, eyebrows uplifted. Zach laughed. I loved his laugh.

"Jah, it is Pennsylvania Dutch. I've been trying so hard to talk like an Englischer so you wouldn't guess I was Amish, but I guess the cat's out of the bag and now that you know, I can use a few Dutch words in conversation if you don't mind. Brutzing means complaining." He seemed so much more relaxed now. I hated that he felt he'd had to hide something from me. But no wonder my radar had gone up when I met him. Turns out I wasn't just nervous about Plan P… I actually could read people and sense their secrets better than I'd thought I could.

"I had a friend in Philly who used to say 'kvetching' for complaining. Brutzing. That's a great word," I said, happy we'd gotten off the subject of my dad.

"If you don't want to talk to me about your father yet, it's fine," Zach said. "But it surprises me that you are in a similar situation with one of your parents and can understand what I'm feeling. I did not expect that."

"Well, the religious stuff, the rules and community shunning stuff, I don't totally understand. But the feeling of abandonment, wondering why your parents' love for you isn't more important to them than anything else... yeah, that I get," I said. I hoped I wasn't making his problem all about me.

"I'd be happy to listen anytime you wanted to talk about it." Zach reached across the table and took my hand in his again. That did it. Big tears rolled down my cheeks, and I didn't know how to stop them. We sat that way for about three minutes. Then I took a long draw off of my Coke. Nobody in the pizza place seemed to notice my crying, or if they did, at least they were kind enough not to stare.

"It just seems that your father is, in a way, more selfish than my parents," Zach said tentatively. "I think my parents truly believe that shunning me will help bring my soul back to God. I mean, what is this life's temporary pleasure and pain compared with the unspeakable joy of heaven in the afterlife? I guess that's their justification." He looked down at my left hand, still in his on the table. "But what's your father's reason?"

"I don't know, but I like it that you feel so protective of me." I smiled at our joined hands. Then I continued. "But listen, I don't blame him 100%. I know he hates my mom, and their divorce was rough. She cheated on him right after she got her real estate license and started making a boatload of money. She got this shark lawyer, so my dad never got a cent of 'her' money. I imagine he still struggles. But then again. I also think he's a jerk-fink because he could try to put up with her to visit me. I wasn't the one who betrayed him."

Zach nodded. "I agree."

"But I guess he just can't deal with her. Look, at times I can't deal with her. So I guess losing his relationship with me was a sacrifice he was willing to make to get her out of his life. I was just acceptable collateral damage." I saw his head tilt at that last phrase. I was starting to get when he didn't understand something I'd said. "Acceptable collateral damage— that's a war term for something you don't mean to destroy when you are aiming at a target, but you are willing to if it helps you achieve your objective."

"Ah, divorce and war. Both are things I do not know much about. We do not have divorce in the Amish community. Nor do I understand why people do wars. Amish are pacifists. It is one of the philosophies that I will

keep, even if I am not Amish." He seemed so serious and sad. When he said "do wars," all of his odd ways of talking finally made sense. *Amish.*

"Right? And do you think horror movies are pacifistic?" I just couldn't help myself. Luckily, Zach laughed. It made me happy that I'd inspired two hearty laughs in under a half hour!

"But the horror movies with vampires and monsters, they are just for pretend."

I couldn't help but notice when he lapsed into his more Amish way of speaking, his "just" sounded like "chust" and his "Gott" was "God."

"I know these films are not based on anything real, so that makes them fun," he countered. "Also, I was never allowed to feel the emotion of anger as a child. We are to always forgive everything and not get upset. And the Amish also believe 'fear' is a wasted emotion. We are told to always trust in God. But with scary movies, I can experience these things through others, yes? I don't need to repress my feelings so much. I can see pretend versions of violence, vengefulness, fear, and anger manifested, and for some reason, after watching, I feel calmer. Like I can safely experience these feelings without actually having them in my real life." He paused a bit, as if remembering something. "Wait, I'm not sure if I'm saying this right. Does this make me sound like a monster, myself?" He grinned. *Wow. He was telling a joke!* That was the first time I'd ever seen him do that.

"Yeah, you're the first Amish psychopath!" I grinned back.

"Well, maybe I'm not the first…" A cloud came over his eyes. "Amish are not allowed to report if they know another is breaking the law or sinning. Everything must be dealt with in our own community. Many Englischers think the only Amish law violators are those who refuse to put reflector lights on their buggies. But that's not the case." He paused, seeming to consider whether to continue or not. "My parents always told me, 'It is about the Law of God, not the Law of Men.'"

"Right, I read a bit about this. Amish are all about forgiving, not pressing charges." After I said that, I got a little embarrassed that I'd just admitted I'd been researching the Amish like some sort of Amish Fan-Girl. But Zach didn't seem bothered.

"Well, yes. But it can be a little darker than that. Amish regularly ignore child labour laws. Kids lose limbs and die in farm accidents all the time. And you saw the drugs at the party we went to. I know of two different marijuana patches in Amish cornfields." He hesitated again before plowing ahead. "We sometimes have abductions, assaults, rape, and incest that get covered up."

"That's crazy! Forgiving sins is one thing, but to not even acknowledge them? To ignore them? Why don't those people get punished by shunning? I mean, look what they're spurning you just because you want to live a different lifestyle that's not hurting anyone! You just want to go to college! Where's the logic there?" I kept my voice low so as not to draw attention from the other customers, but I was pretty fired up.

"Most times, the bishop gets involved in knowing about any of these trespasses. But if the sinner confesses and repents and stays in the fold, the general outcome is that he or she is forgiven. Of course, there are some things that get hidden from the bishop, too. People can be very secretive in our community. We are told from our childhoods to obey and not to question others. *Gelassenheit*, it is called. Sometimes this can make it easy for an older person to abuse a younger person."

"That's horrible!" I had to ask, though I wasn't sure I wanted to hear the answer. "Did you know anyone who..."

"Yes, maybe. I suspected my friend Mary's brother, who was fifteen years older than her, was not behaving correctly toward her. But I was only eleven and did not know who to tell. Then her family moved away. I never knew where they went. I had no way to contact her again."

"Oh my gosh. That makes me sick," I said.

"And me as well," he said. "My dream is that I will be able use my education somehow to help these girls, Amish and English, who need help. I would very much like to spend my life doing that."

That's when I knew it for sure. I was in love with Zach Stoltzfus.

CHAPTER THIRTY-TWO

Last night, I slept with Zach.

Well, to be specific, I stayed overnight at his place all night Saturday, and we *did* sleep together in his bed. But when I make up with Madison and tell her the details, she'll be disappointed. We hardly kissed. He just held me in his arms until we fell asleep.

I'd gone over to his apartment to hang out and watch *The People Under the Stairs* after our long talk. But when it got to be after eleven, I could barely keep my eyes open, and he was yawning a lot.

"I'd better get home so you can go to sleep," I said, dreading the drive back to my place.

"I think you're too tired to drive. I'd be worried for you," Zach said, reading my mind. "And no buggy here, so me driving you is verruckt." We both laughed. I assumed that "verruckt" meant "nuts."

"Well, I can't stay here... can I?" I said.

"You said your mother is never home on the weekend, so if you want to stay in my bed, I can stay on the couch," Zach said.

"Yeah, I know for a fact she won't be home tonight." I shuddered a bit at the reminder of our gross phone call. "But I don't want to make you have to sleep on the couch."

"Well... there is another option..." Zach tilted his head and looked up and to the right.

Oh, boy. Was he saying what I thought he was saying? After finding out he was Amish, I didn't think I'd have to worry about the sex thing. In fact, if anything, I was worried that at some point I'd want to, and he wouldn't.

Maybe he had been with some other girls before on Rumspringa. Now he'd find out what a loser I was.

"Oh no! I didn't mean… what I think you're thinking." Zach blushed a bit. "The Amish have this practice, well, some Amish do anyway, called bundling. My cousin Josh told me about it."

"Wait, Josh, the guy I met when I first met you? He's your cousin?" I practically fell off my chair. "And he's Amish too?" Zach looked a little scared. I resolved to lower my voice.

"Yes, he's my second cousin, once-removed. But he is no longer Amish. His family left when he was a boy, and they moved to Ohio. I think they might go to a Mennonite church now. He comes back sometimes to our community to visit. And some agree to meet with him. Outside of their houses."

"How about Scowly… I mean, that other guy who was with you in the pizza place? Is he Amish, too?" I asked.

"Zebediah? Yah, he is on Rumspringa but is very unhappy. I think he will soon return to the church and be baptized. He is not much talking to me any more."

"Oh, wow. Ok. Good to know," I said, not sure why knowing all of this was actually good for me to know in any way. But maybe we were getting closer by getting any secrets out in the open. "So anyway, what's this 'bundling' thing?"

"When two people are courting, they can sleep over with each other. The woman sleeps under the sheets, the man on top of the sheets. But you can… you know, cuddle."

"Oh, really? That's an Amish thing? Huh," I said. The whole idea seemed so weird to me, but then I thought about how my private day school in Philly wouldn't allow jeans. Yet in Lancaster, in public school, we could wear jeans but not shorts, like I could in Philly. So I guess different groups have distinct things they're afraid of. In some ways, bundling is probably not as likely to lead to lascivious outcomes as making out in a car might. Although in both cases, it would depend on the intentions of the participants.

And I wasn't sure we were totally chaste in our motivations.

Zach must have sensed my hesitation. "Or I could drive with you to your place as a passenger to keep you awake and make sure you are safe, and then just sleep in your car. You can bring me back tomorrow," he offered earnestly. I laughed at this and yawned at the same time, which was weird.

"No, no, that's silly. Let's try this bundling thing!"

So we did.

At first it was odd. We stood by the opposite sides of the bed and each wrapped soft quilts around ourselves. It felt so silly; I repressed the urge to snigger. Instead of undressing for bed like I usually do, I was putting more on.

"We probably shouldn't start kissing again when we lie down because..." Zach smiled sheepishly.

"No, agreed!" I interrupted.

But I after I got in bed, I did wiggle my way closer to him, feeling a bit like a caterpillar. We giggled.

He smelled good, like baby powder and a slight whiff of oranges.

It felt great to fall asleep with my head in the spot where his arm met his chest. Although muscular, it was surprisingly soft.

The most awkward part of staying overnight at Zach's came in the morning when I woke up. I felt self-conscious with my morning breath, smeared mascara, and rumpled clothes. But Zach didn't seem to mind. He got up and made me eggs with lots of yummy melted cheddar cheese. He also spread the best honey I've ever had on thick slices of homemade bread. His work at the farmer's market obviously came with some perks. I was happy to let him share with me.

"I feel weird that I didn't brush my teeth," I admitted sheepishly.

"Did you know some Amish have all their teeth pulled out by the time they're nineteen?" Zach scooped up some eggs with his fork.

"What the heck... wait, are you pulling my leg?" I asked.

"Nope, if some Amish get cavities, they often choose to get their teeth all pulled to get dentures so they can avoid the cost of ongoing dental work. Others just get all their teeth pulled at eighteen because they are proving they aren't vain." Zach lifted his eyes to me and could see my raised eyebrows. "I'm not joshing!"

"Good, gosh! That's worse than torture horror!" I exclaimed. He nodded solemnly. "Well, I'm glad you didn't do that."

Zach pulled his lips over his teeth. "You wouldn't kiss me if I looked like this?" he asked, and we dissolved into giggles.

After breakfast, we went down and checked on the kittens. I'd missed them. Their small eyes were starting to open, but they weren't walking yet. Zach said he was building a little gate to put around them to keep them safe when that happened. He told me I needed to choose names for them soon. I said I'd think about it.

I went back to my place and quickly showered and changed. I couldn't wait to get back to Zach. I wasn't in such a hurry, though, that I forgot to brush my teeth. For the first time in my life I thought about how grateful I was to have them as I gently ran my tongue over them.

Then I thought about how grateful I was to have Zach, too.

CHAPTER THIRTY-THREE

We spent most of the day in Long's Park, feeding the ducks with bits of cracked corn. It was one of those perfect sunny and crisp fall days. Everything felt so romantic; I decided not to bring up my initial reluctance to feed wild animals because it's not so good for them to get dependent on humans for food. Anyway, there were so many little kids feeding white bread scraps to the ducks, I figured we were doing the ducks a service with our corn option.

At noon, I saw on my phone that Madison had called me twice Saturday night and three times Sunday morning. I hadn't picked up or called her back. I felt a little guilty, but I just didn't want to have another fight with her now when things were going so great with Zach. Besides, I knew she'd gotten mad at Britt and Delia for worse things before, like when Britt made out with a guy Madison was dating and when Delia ran against her for student council and won. Their fights always blew over quickly, so I told myself it would be like that for us, too. It was just our turn to have a little spat. I think I actually convinced myself of it. Our minds can accept what's convenient pretty easily.

Zach and I hiked to a remote part of the park and spread out a blanket over some fallen leaves, still soft, not yet crunchy. Zach had packed a picnic of fruits, veggies, red beet eggs, a sweet macaroni salad that was to die for, and sticky buns with walnuts, all of which we devoured while we admired the fire-coloured trees surrounding us. I was chuffed by how sensitive he'd been to the fact I didn't eat meat.

Around three, we went back to his place. I used my phone to search "duck horror films," and we found one we could view for free online. It was challenging for us to both try to watch it on my phone's small screen, but we didn't mind the excuse to get close to each other. The short, this creepy yet hilarious low-budget film called *The Hunt*, was about two first-time duck hunters who follow the advice of a peculiar bearded dude named Doyle who tells them to go to a remote area for the best hunting.

"No one should ever take the advice of a peculiar bearded dude when guns are involved!" I screamed in mock alarm at the little screen.

Of course, the evil monster-dog rips the hunters both apart in particularly gory ways. Because it was only about ten minutes long, Zach and I watched it several times, laughing more each time, and agreed it was pretty well done for a low-budget film.

"It's based on that dumb video game, *Duck Hunt*," I told Zach, but of course, he'd never heard of that.

"I started reading books before I went on Rumspringa, but movies I am first viewing now, since I left home. Still no games for the video, though."

I loved it when he slipped into that distinctive Amish way of talking, because it reminded me how peculiarly extraordinary he was. It also meant he didn't feel like he needed to pretend he was anything he wasn't.

"Lately, I've watched a lot of TV, especially reruns of that show you told me about, *Buffy the Vampire Slayer*. It still plays late at night on the USA network!" Zach remembered that I'd recommended he watch that series on our first date. I smiled, touched he was trying so hard to impress me.

"Wait until you get to *Once More With Feeling*. That's a great one in season six." I thought about how that episode was all about secrets, too.

He pointed to an old TV in the corner. "Got it at a yard sale for twenty-five dollars, and my landlord gives me the cable for free."

We started joking about other seemingly innocuous things that we could randomly search for that might have horror films connected to them. For example, there's this film called *Scary Dairy Tales* that comes up when you put "milk horror film" into the search line. I put that in my Netflix queue on my phone. It's about two people turning into deformed monsters after drinking tainted milk. I knew we'd get *Children of the Corn* when we tried "corn horror film," but we also got a bizarre film called *The Corn Mole* that had just been released on DirectTV. When I looked at the site, I was surprised to see on the cast list that Hillary's sister, Teagan, had a small role in it! Before I had a chance to put that on my Netflix list, my phone was buzzing again.

I saw a text from Madison on my cell.

Why R U not calling me back??? Call me. Now!!!

"Wow, somebody wants to get a hold of you, yes?" Zach said. "It is fine if you need to call them."

"No, it's nothing important." I shut down the power on my phone. I told Zach the battery was at ten percent, but the truth was I just didn't want him to hear any more message pings. And to be totally candid, I still didn't want to deal with that situation. I figured I'd just tell her I'd forgotten my phone when I went out on Sunday. Lame, I know, but I heard people use that excuse all the time. Besides, she was being so bossy. Like I didn't have anything better to do than call her.

"Perhaps it is the Hell House people still trying to recruit you..." Zach raised an eyebrow. I loved it when he made a joke, but his tentative delivery clued me in on the fact that this kind of banter was still pretty new for him. I laughed and then grabbed a pillow and hit him lightly on the shoulder. But what I really wanted to do was to kiss him. I took a breath and leaned on him a bit.

"So, hey, if you don't have a computer in your apartment, how did you email me?" I asked, leaning back on his couch and hooking my left leg under me. My neck hurt a bit from hunching over my phone so long.

"The public library has one, and I can walk there. Also, my cousin has one at work, but I try not to use that one except for business," he said. "I'm going to make some microwave popcorn. I love having a microwave to make popcorn! Want some?" He jumped up and ran into the kitchen.

I was a little disappointed that he hadn't read my physical cue, but he was *so darn cute*. So even though I wasn't that hungry, I said "Sure!"

Well, the lack of computer explained why he wasn't on Facebook and also provided an excuse for all the delays he had getting back to me. *I wonder if I'm the first girl who suspected my boyfriend was a player but then discovered, no, he's not a lothario, he's just Amish.*

"Would you ever get a computer?" I asked Zach when he came back.

"Of course! I have electricity and a TV, so why wouldn't I?" He laughed.

"What about a phone? Why didn't you get one of those?" I remembered the number that had showed up on my cell the first time he called.

"The ring startles me. I don't like it when I am enjoying the quiet," he mused. "That's the one 'modern convenience' I would like to avoid." He sighed. "But I suppose I will eventually get one of those portable ones and just keep it turned off. I do not like that texts and calls might always be interrupting me."

I could certainly relate to that right now, with Madison blowing up my phone with her excessive overdramatic texts.

"Yeah, I'm sorry about all the ones I get," I smiled ruefully. "They can be a pain for sure."

"No, I didn't mean to imply…" Zach stammered.

"No worries!" Wanting to get him back talking about himself, I asked, "So do you think you'll get a computer before you get a phone?"

"I'm actually saving up for one right now and am close." He seemed both proud and conspiratorial.

"So you don't think computers are sinful?" I teased, popping a few fluffy kernels in my mouth, enjoying the fake butter taste, which I prefer to real butter.

"Well, there was that one episode of *Buffy the Vampire Slayer* where Moloch takes over Willow's computer. THAT'S one evil computer…" He pretended to be considering it.

"Oh, good one!" I laughed. "Seriously, why do the Amish not have computers, TVs, microwaves, and stuff anyway?"

"Well, nothing is inherently sinful to Amish, if that's what you're asking. It's just that some things can be used in bad ways, or seem wasteful, or can inspire envy, which are some of the reasons Amish don't own many man-made comforts, including any new technology." He grabbed another handful of popcorn. "But in my opinion, your faith in God should help you resist temptations, or it's not a very good faith." He ate his popcorn, chewing slowly, considering. "The whole idea that Amish don't feel envy or get prideful anyway isn't true. Many have pride in their large farms, good cooking, big families, many cows, the list goes on and on. There's even an Amish hierarchy; the *gut oh tzene*, meaning the 'well-regarded,' are the highest on it, and there are also 'Low Amish,' the uncouth drinkers and smokers like at the Geauga settlement."

"Wow, maybe we should make our own horror movie about the Low Amish," I joked.

"But what would we call it?" His eyes twinkled mischievously.

"*Something Amish This Way Comes?*"

"Very funny! How about *Rosemary's Bonnet* or *Night of the Living Plain People?*"

"Or *Barnraiser 2: Dutchbound!*"

We were laughing so hard, we were crying.

"I love this! We're making a list together! I love lists…" Then we were kissing. After a little while, I pulled away to try to calm my hyper hormones a bit and put my cheek on Zach's chest.

"So if we make a movie, I want you to be my leading lady." Zach played with my hair.

"Oh, that's not a very good idea, not if you want a blockbuster anyway. I'm not pretty enough to be an actress."

Zach pulled away a bit and studied me. "Are you touched in the head? You're gorgeous!"

"Please." I shook my head, blushing. "We all know Hillary is the beautiful one who's going to be an actress like her sister, Teagan." I thought about the Sherpas and felt a little shiver go through me. "Truthfully, all of them, Britt, Delia, and Madison are pretty, too."

"None of them is prettier than you. You took my breath away the moment I saw you." Zach cocked his head. "I think your friends are fine but very common-looking. You are special; you're radiant."

"Agree to disagree!" I was flustered. He actually seemed sincere. I couldn't process this. I attempted to change the conversation. "So, none of your family could come see your big blockbuster movie if you made it? That doesn't seem fair."

"Denying technology instead of using it wisely just seems lobbich, um, that means silly."

"I love learning Pennsylvania Dutch words and expressions," I told him, leaning into him again, even closer, if that was possible.

"Oh you do, do you? Well, how about these then." His voice took on an accent and sing-songy tone I'd never heard from him before. "I see your bowl of popcorn is all. There's more back! But don't eat yourself too full, onest!"

We both laughed. Then we kissed again.

"Schmeck," he murmured.

"What's that?"

"It has two meanings. It means a kiss, but it also means 'tastes good,'" he said.

"Schmeck," I repeated.

It had been the best day of my life.

And tomorrow, Monday, would be one of the worst.

CHAPTER THIRTY-FOUR

The first time I tried to make peace, I approached Madison at the tree in front of the school. Probably not the best plan, because she was flanked by Hillary and the other Sherpas. But I'd already put this off too long, and I felt bad about it. So if that meant I was going to have to grovel a bit for forgiveness in front of everyone, then so be it.

"Hi." I smiled at them all, feigning a casual attitude to Madison, a *let's ignore that phone call and pretend it never happened* kinda thing. I tried to make eye contact with her, but she avoided my eyes, so I ended up scanning her from head to toe.

"I like your boots, are they new?"

This "compliment as implied apology" strategy worked sometimes on TV, but Madison wasn't going to give me an inch. However, she did finally make eye contact: she shot invisible hate lasers at me.

It was Hillary who responded instead. "Hi, Sam. Did you have a nice weekend?" Her overly enthusiastic tone bordered on sinister.

I blinked twice, and I took a deep breath, trying not to show panic. "It was ok, I guess. Not great." I hesitated. "You know... ups and downs." I'd never felt comfortable with Hillary since the Sherpas had let me hang with them, but this was definitely the most freaked out I'd ever felt by her.

"Mmm..." Hillary said in an unsympathetic way, letting her eyes drift away from mine, slowly and deliberately. She then engaged Delia in a conversation about whether berets were geeky or retro-cool. Madison just kept glaring at me. So I tried again with something I thought everyone would enjoy talking about.

"Hey, Hillary," I said, extra loud to get her attention again, with a big smile. "I was watching some films online and saw that your sister, Teagan, has been getting some work! That's cool." Hillary whipped around and gave me the worst look that I've ever seen, much worse than shooting invisible hate lasers, more like stabbing me with the Damascus death sword. Or did she? It passed over her face so quickly. *Didn't anyone else see it?* Was she jealous of Teagan?

"Yeah, right, she's doing just fine, thanks." Hillary's tone was like a mother telling her kid to knock it off, settle down, and shut up. Weird. Then she turned her back on me. Madison and Britt also subtly turned their backs to me as they discussed the fact Peter Atwell had been seen amateurish on his girlfriend with some girl from a private school and how all the girls that went to Country Day School were soooo stuck up.

Since I was frozen out of the conversation, I pulled deep inside myself, like I used to do all the time in middle school. My mind went to how my mom had looked at Country Day School for me when we first moved to Lancaster, but she'd decided the atmosphere there would be bad for me regarding "temptations triggering my desire to shoplift." A lot of girls there carried Kate Spade, Reed, or even Prada purses. The fact that my mom worried about upscale labels only revealed her inattention to the types of things I took. I'd steal from Target as well as from Nordstrom or Saks. It wasn't about things I coveted that I couldn't afford. It was the thrill of the chase, reading the salespeople, timing the moment to hide the object close to my skin and to turn to walk out. IMHO, hiding the object in your purse or bag was cheating. It gave plausible deniability: *Oh, I meant to pay for that but just forgot as I was walking around.*

My mind snapped back from this disturbing meditation on shoplifting. Why was I thinking about stealing again so much lately? It made me feel shame, but it also calmed me in a way. What was more disturbing was that I yearned to do it again. It was as if I was romanticizing an old boyfriend, purposely forgetting all the negatives. Not that I had any experience with ex-boyfriends, but I imagined it was the same feeling of nostalgia.

I looked at my phone. Only three minutes until the bell would ring. I touched Madison's shoulder.

"Can we talk?" I asked in a low voice. There was a beat. No response from Madison. "Look, I'm sorry I couldn't call you back when you called yesterday." Hillary, Britt, and Delia stared at us like Drama Vultures, desperately hungry for blood to be drawn.

"No biggie, it wasn't important." Madison shrugged and pursed her lips.

"I hoped it was about... Saturday," I ventured, realizing I probably wouldn't be able to get Madison to step away with me for a private conversation.

She faked confusion. "Uh, no. It was about that project for art studio. Just wanted to know if we could do a collage of materials or if it had to be free-hand." This was a blatant lie. She'd already done the project. She'd shown it to me last week.

"Oh, ok. Yeah, a collage is allowed." I backed away. "Well... I'm going to hit the bathroom before the bell rings." *Any excuse to leave ASAP.* I only got a few feet away before the bell actually rang, but at least I didn't have to awkwardly walk to the school door with the Sherpas after my epic fail trying to talk to Madison.

At lunch I made my second attempt with her. I hadn't been able to concentrate in my morning classes, wondering if Madison had told the Sherpas about our fight. When I arrived at "our" table, I was surprised to see my seat was occupied. I stopped, confused. *What is Elli Weiss doing in my place?* Elli was a new girl with whom I had a few classes. She seemed quiet but nice. I think she was on the stage crew for the school play Hillary was in. Maybe she didn't know she was in my seat? Two of Hillary's cast mates, Amy and Gina, sat in the other "temporary" spots. There was no room for me.

"Hi, Sam." Britt smiled her wide, sarcastic smile usually reserved for teachers and ex-boyfriends. "Sorry! We seem to be full up today! Guess we weren't sure you'd be eating lunch." After a fake laugh, she plunged the knife in, and using a saccharine tone said, "Figured you'd be on a di-et, trying to impress the new boy-friend."

My mind blanked. What did she know? How much had Madison told them? I tried to assess Madison's level of anger toward me, but she seemed to be having a grand old time chatting with Elli.

I took a deep breath. "Hey, Madison, wanna join me?"

"Nope, I'm good here, thanks." Madison looked at me briefly and then at Hillary.

"I see you got the veggie stir-fry." Hillary arched her eyebrow. "Good choice. The spaghetti sauce is super-watery today." Then I noticed Madison pushing her hair behind her ear with her right pinky, a favourite move of Hillary's that I'd never seen Madison do before.

"Oh, yeah, thanks," I mumbled and shuffled away. I walked straight to the trash can at the far corner of the cafeteria, where I hoped they couldn't see me. But I didn't look back to see if they could. I quickly dumped my tray. I knew I wouldn't be able to eat even a little bit of my food because a giant knot had taken up residence in my stomach. I left the cafeteria and sat in a stall in the girl's restroom for fifteen minutes.

What could I do? I was angry at Madison for her betrayal, and also worried about what Hillary, Britt, and Delia knew, but even more scared considering what they might do with the knowledge. My insides hurt. I'd thought they were my friends. Yes, I'd seen them laugh at others, but didn't we share a bond? How could I have been so stupid? I'd seen what they'd done to one of our "temp Sherpas," Annelisa, when she'd merely corrected Hillary's assertion that Dan Link starred in a movie when it was actually Dan Rockaway. The next day a rumour started in school that Annelisa had been fighting a losing battle with chronic lice. I remember feeling bad for Annelisa. But I couldn't prove that Hillary started the rumour. I reassured myself: *Madison's different. She's your friend. This is temporary. She wouldn't let them do anything to really hurt you.*

That afternoon in my American History class, we were discussing the first Union General, McClellan and his ineffectuality. Any other day, I would have enjoyed actively participating in the class discussion, gleefully submitting evidence of his pomposity from the primary source reading we'd been assigned. His letters to Lincoln showed his out-of-control hubris.

I also would have brought up his penchant for having people take pictures of him and his avoidance of actual combat. But today I merely nodded mutely as Simon defended McClellan as a great trainer of soldiers and a judicious general who cared about the well-being of his soldiers and held back from wanton bloodshed accordingly. And Susan Scarfo took up my slack, bringing up McClellan's insubordination. I tried to smile at Delia several times during class, but she avoided looking at me.

As I was leaving at the end of class, Mr. Kohn, the teacher, asked me if I was feeling ok and told me I looked pale. I assured him I was fine and practically sprinted away, hoping he'd mistake my speed for vigour.

The third time I tried with Madison was more of an accident than a planned approach. But it was my first opportunity to talk with her alone. My last period was a study hall, so I got a pass to go to the library. Madison's English Lit class was also in the library, doing research on their papers for *A Separate Peace*. I was researching the PTSD found in kids in war zones for my honours elective on Current Events. She and I found ourselves face-to-face, just the two of us, in the shelves containing books on child psychology.

"Oh!" She froze when she saw she was unable to avoid me because I was standing a few feet in front of her.

"Hey," I said, scrambling for the words I'd been wanting to say to her this morning and at lunch. "Look, I saw you called Sunday, a few times actually." I shifted from foot to foot. "And I know it wasn't about art class." I took a breath. "I'm sorry I couldn't pick up, and I'm also sorry I didn't text or call you back."

"So you admit you made a choice not to talk to me, huh?" Her eyes flashed dangerously. I'd seen her mad at her sister or mom in the past, but this seemed different. I felt like a garter snake cornered by a mongoose.

"Well, I was with... I mean, I wanted to talk but..." Great. I was blowing it. Again.

"Oh, listen, I understand. I'm just a druggie and a slut, right?" She cocked her head defiantly.

"No! That's not what I meant..."

"What DID you mean, Sam? Do you think I've slept with too many guys? That I party too much? That instead I should be a goody-goody like you? You knew who I was when we became friends. So now YOU want to judge ME?" Her voice was getting kind of loud, especially for a library.

I didn't know which question to answer first. "I don't care what you do!" was the brilliant response that tumbled out of my mouth. I didn't mean it as a jab. I meant to say, "I like you and am happy to be your friend and I don't judge you for anything. Your choices are your own business." It wasn't received that way.

"Well, screw you very much. I don't care what YOU do either anymore! I can't believe I tried to help you. Whatever. Go have fun with your Amish boyfriend. You're perfect for each other. I'm sure you'll love wearing a black bonnet and churning butter." She turned and walked away.

I knew if Madison hadn't told Hillary and the others everything she knew about Zach, including his being Amish, she sure as hell would now.

In total, I'd tried three times to apologize to Madison. It's weird how many times the number "three" comes up in the Bible: the Holy Trinity, Peter's three betrayals of Christ, the three temptations from Satan, and of course, Jesus died and then rose from the dead after three days. I was thinking more about religion lately than I ever had before in my life. But then again, going to a Hell House and realizing you're dating a guy who had been raised Amish will do that to you.

CHAPTER THIRTY-FIVE

After that brutal school day, I wanted to do something that would wipe the whole crapfest from my mind. As I sat at my desk in my room tapping my Vampire Angel bobblehead, trying to think of what I wanted to write to Zach, I remembered the first time that I really became aware of the Amish. It was then I saw how some tourists thought of them as the equivalent of a circus sideshow attraction.

My mother and I were scouting out our move to Lancaster right after "my shoplifting crime." It was fall of tenth grade. My mom took me to an odd little old-fashioned amusement park called Dutch Wonderland. It would have been awesome if I'd been six years old. But riding on the Turtle Whirl or the Dragon's Lair log boat at fifteen just wasn't my thing. My mom didn't care and kept shushing me and motioning me away with her hand when I attempted to complain, because I was disturbing her texting or phone calls. The worst part of the experience was when I got dragged up onstage at "Duke's Dance Party." My mom took a picture and posted it to her Facebook page to show her clients and boyfriends what an awesome mom she was, spending a fun day with her daughter. I immediately unfriended her and blocked her on Facebook that afternoon. She didn't even notice.

Out in the parking lot, after the humiliation had finally ended and we were leaving Dutch Wonderland, a big black Mercedes pulled up. I'm sure my mom was disappointed when the driver rolled his window down and she saw that he was not alone and was not stopping to ask for her phone number.

"Where are all the Aim-ish?" a hairy man with a thick accent demanded. His wife in the passenger seat smiled weakly at us, the kind of gesture that long-suffering spouses of schmucks like him get accustomed to regularly sharing with strangers.

"Well, they're all around here." My mom shrugged. "Just keep your eyes open."

"We saw one up the road on the way here this morning," I offered to the wife.

"Where? Where EXACTLY?" the man demanded in a frustrated pique.

"Well, near the furniture shop on Route 30, but that was, like, six hours ago." I looked at my mom. Her eyes were down on her cell; she was texting again. This man wasn't dateable or looking to buy real estate, so my mother was done with him.

"Give me an ADDRESS! Why can no one give me an EXACT ADDRESS for my GPS?" The angry man pounded on his steering wheel.

"Well, they do move around during the day," I said. What I wanted to say was, "The Amish aren't caged exotic animals, performing tricks for your camera." But of course, I didn't.

"Thank to you for trying to help," his hazy-eyed wife called to me before Angry Man slammed his car into gear and squealed out of the parking lot. In hot pursuit of the elusive Amish, no doubt.

"Some people are so stupid." My mom rolled her eyes.

"Yeah." I was surprised and pleased that my mom acknowledged this guy's insensitivity.

"It's so funny to me that people are so obsessed with the Amish lately!" She snorted. "The Amish are just a bunch of whackjobs driving around in their anachronistic buggies, tying up traffic while their horses poop all over the streets."

Of course. Now that's what I'd expect from my mother.

As I came back from spacing out, I looked at the blank email in front of me, and my mind was still empty. There was still so much I didn't understand about the culture Zach had grown up in. But I wasn't even sure what the questions were that I should be asking.

I knew he'd told me that he'd be checking in on a computer more this week, hoping to get emails from me, and I didn't want to disappoint him. It was weird for me because I was more used to texting people or getting a quick reply by phone to a short email.

I decided to just plunge in. I wrote to Zach about my bad day at school with Madison without going into any of the specific details, the A I'd gotten on my Physics test, and the rumour I'd heard online that Joss Whedon was going to direct another horror movie. Of course, I asked how the kittens were doing.

I also told him about the incident with Angry Man in the parking lot that I'd remembered. I asked him how often things like that had happened to him when he was growing up as an Amish kid—was it common that obnoxious tourists tried to take pictures of him and his siblings while they were playing in a red wagon or walking to school or helping at a barn raising?

Then, as a PS, I told him I missed him.

I received his reply later that night.

Dear Samantha,

I am excited to hear you received a good mark on your exam! You are very smart and work hard. These are two qualities I so admire about you. I must say I do not understand why your friend Madison is now so mean to you. Maybe you can explain it more to me? Though I admit, she has always confused me, so I cannot promise I will ever be able to understand. I will try, though! Her friendship is obviously important to you. And anything important to you is important to me now also.

I did like Madison better than your other friends when I met them. (I hope it is not upsetting for you for me to say this.) I watched many people I knew, not friends but people I had grown up with, abuse Rumspringa with their use of drugs, alcohol, and sex. So it does not shock me that Madison seems to do this, too. Unfortunately, trouble is easier to get in than to get out of. (Yes, another Amish proverb.)

I believe that Madison cares about you deep down. I am sure there are also admirable qualities that the other Sherpas, as you call them, possess for you to hold them in such high esteem. It wonders me but I will keep trying to comprehend this.

As for your questions about tourists, my family's farm is in a more isolated area out near the town of Intercourse, on a not very well-travelled road. So we did not have much problems with intruding schniclefritzes (this means "troublemakers.") However, I do remember one time when I was age 13—I had snuck out to a nearby Mennonite bookstore, and some tourists asked me to pose for a photo with their four-year-old son. They were very nice about it, though, not like the angry man you met. And I wanted to be nice, too, so I did pose with him, though the taking of photographs is not encouraged in the Amish community. As Amish, we are discouraged from feeling any personal vanity, and it is believed that photographs emphasize the outside and not the inside of a person, (which is more important), so they are to be avoided. The Amish avoiding photos is not because of silly misconception that I hear sometimes about Amish believing that a camera can steal a soul. But I do love how the camera captures a brief period of time and keeps it forever. A story that can be as versatile as each viewer.

I will tell you a secret. One of the first things I did on my Rumspringa was to go to a photo booth in the shopping mall and have my picture taken in one of those strips of four black and white photos. It is an interesting thing to see your image frozen on a piece of paper. Quite different from looking in a mirror. One day maybe we can take pictures of ourselves together. I would like that very much.

The kittens have started wobbly-walking. I have put the gate up. Mama cat seems very proud. They are still awaiting their names.

Yours,

Zach

PS I cannot wait to see you, too! I miss you.

I read his email over and over. Nobody wrote long emails like that. I felt like we were writing letters like the characters in some schmaltzy historical romance novel.

Curiously, I thought he sounded even more Amish in his writing than his talking. Was it that he hadn't done much writing since eighth grade, when he'd been made to stop school? Or maybe he was just feeling more comfortable with me now. I felt like I could handle anything now because he was in my life. It wasn't about any stupid Plan P anymore. I just wanted to be with him because of who he was. I wrote back:

Hi Zach!

I have ideas for names for the cats! As an homage to *Buffy the Vampire Slayer,* and because they like to bite each other, how about naming them all after little vampires: Darla for the mom, Angel for the little black one with the white patch on the head, Spike for the all white one, Dru for the all black one, and Harmony for the white one with black feet. I think those would be perfect names!

How about you and I make a horror movie about a Soul-Stealing Camera? I think that'd be a great plot.

I can't wait to see you this weekend and we can take selfies!

Yours,

Sam

Dear Sam,

Let's not wait! How about we meet tomorrow after school? Could you pick me up? We could go to a pumpkin patch I heard about and get ourselves some pumpkins! I've always wanted to have Halloween pumpkins.

Yours,

Zach

The last email was so short. I felt a pang because it was so much like a normal email and not Zach's usual verbose style. But I couldn't brood. This would be our first midweek date! So I told him that sounded great. It was something to look forward to if everyone was cold to me again tomorrow. Which they were. Bitterly. Freezing. Cold.

CHAPTER THIRTY-SIX

"Do you like them tall and skinny or shorter and rounder?" I asked as a battered green tractor pulled our very full wagon decorated with witches and skeletons up to its stopping point next to a giant pirate flag on a pole.

Zach quickly jumped off the side first and made a big gesture to hold out his hand for me to get off. I heard a little girl giggling behind me. I purposely didn't take his hand. *Why does everyone think it's cool to make fun of me? Even little kids?* My toe caught a bit, and I thought I was about to face-plant. But Zach caught me. I thought for a second that my clumsiness was working for me when I fell forward onto his chest.

I soon realized that this situation differs from how it looks when it happens in the movies. Instead of sinking into his warm, manly embrace, I jerked back a bit as we made contact. My left cheek felt smooshed up against my eyeball when my face connected with his shoulder, while my hand smacked his ear. Then I heard more kids snickering as I disentangled myself.

"Oh geez, sorry." I was flustered, but the mocking had died down as the rugrats found a new distraction.

"It's fine. You ok?"

"Yeah, yeah, just not very graceful." I snorted. Zach had a way of not making me feel like a giant dork the way other people did. "There's a reason my mom stopped paying for my dance classes."

"I've never danced. Maybe you can teach me sometime." There. He did it again. Instead of hearing my self-effacement, he saw me as something better than I saw myself.

"You got it." I beamed.

As we walked into the field, Zach said, "So the tall versus short thing, you were talking about pumpkins, right?"

"What if I was talking about girls?" I tried to make my voice sound like I was playfully teasing, but to my ear it sounded more like a *Hocus Pocus* witch's shrill, cackling query.

"If you are asking that, maybe you need to read more Naomi Wolf," his eyes twinkled, "and stop thinking of girls as merely shapes."

"Wha... *The Beauty Myth*. You read that?" Boy, this guy might be newly not Amish, but I didn't know anyone who read more than him.

"You'd be surprised what you can find in a used bookstore run by Mennonites."

"I thought the Mennonites were just like the Amish. Kinda Amish-Lite."

"Some are conservative-leaning, they're both from the Anabaptist movement. But some Mennonites are politically liberal, even progressive, and focus on peace and social justice more than strict Biblical interpretation, just as many Quakers do. Some even ordain gay pastors."

"Huh." I was so distracted thinking about this that I tripped a bit on a dead corn stalk. Zach immediately reached out to catch me. Again.

"Ok, so I've got to bring this up, because you started it. You leapt out of the cart so quickly to help me. And at the Hell House you jumped in to defend me. Don't get me wrong, it's all so sweet, and I guess I've proved I'm clumsy, but it is kind of old-fashioned, and SOME people might think it's a wee bit sexist." Zach was quiet. *Great, there I go pushing people away, criticizing instead of just going with the flow.* I hated proving my mom right.

"Just forget it. That was dumb of me," I said.

"Not at all. It's a struggle for me sometimes to separate what is being kind and what could be interpreted as old-fashioned and patronizing. In the Amish culture, women are not treated as equals. Their job is to marry, submit to their husband, and bear children."

"To be fair, how guys should act toward a girl is up for debate in the non-Amish culture, too. Some girls love to have doors opened for them, and some like having the guy pay for meals. And many women choose to be stay-at-home moms." I brushed a fly off my arm. "Anyway, maybe all this conversation about deep stuff is boring. Madison's always telling me to keep it light."

"How is everything with Madison?" Zach asked.

Oh, great. I didn't want to ruin our date talking about how she turned her nose up at me, as if I stank of sewer scum, while Hillary kept making eye contact and grinning like Pennywise at me every chance she got.

"Fine, I guess..." I was hoping he'd sense that I didn't want to talk about it.

He did.

"I think I'd like being a stay-at-home dad," Zach said without even a trace of a sarcastic lilt in his voice. "That sounds fun and is something you don't see in the Amish culture. Few Amish women have jobs, maybe less than five percent. But I'm just estimating."

His earnestness made my heart beat harder. I wished he had a fly on his arm so I could lightly stroke it under the guise of brushing the insect off. But since he didn't, I babbled on instead.

"I do think most women agree that they resent the idea that only boys want to play with trucks or footballs. And I personally hate the t-shirts that are made for little girls that say, 'Math is Hard.'" I felt like smashing the nearest pumpkin just thinking about the t-shirt thing.

"You're waaaay better at math than I am." He raised his eyebrows, and for a second he looked like the scarecrow from *The Wizard of Oz*. Very apropos for the surroundings.

I dissolved in laughter. Then we looked at each other, and I wanted to kiss him right there. I knew he was thinking the same thing. My whole body flushed, as if I'd just eaten some Chinese food loaded with MSG or something. But it wasn't an unpleasant sensation, just overwhelming. He inhaled, looked away, and shifted his weight a bit.

I pointed to a cat stretched out lazily on a haystack. "That cat's got a nice life, huh?" *Brilliant comment. Ugh. Why was hanging out with guy I liked so embarrassing and confusing?*

A hayride train putted by us, carrying a group of kids. I noticed a few adults in the train with their little ones, but every one of the parents was distracted by texting or scrolling down social media, looking at various functions of the fitness devices on their wrists or touching up their lipstick.

I turned back to Zach. "You know, there are also lots of relationships that the couple pretends to be equal, but one is really more powerful and manipulates the other." My mouth really just didn't know when to quit. "Like my mom was much stronger-willed than my dad was."

Zach slowly picked up a pumpkin and tested it a bit, as if weighing it with his hands. "So you said your dad doesn't call or write. But now you sound like you feel bad for him a little?"

"I guess. I mean, I know my mom bossed him around and made him feel bad that he wasn't more ambitious. But I still think he's a coward for just leaving like he did. I mean, he left me too. Not just her."

"Yeah. I can't understand that."

"Me either. I know they were young and that my mom's parents disowned her for the marriage. They always told her that he was born poor and would stay poor. I think she came to believe they were right about him being a loser."

Zach set the pumpkin down.

"They died, and I never met them." I shrugged. "But I bet they wouldn't have liked me anyway." I felt that hot sting in my eyes that I hated. "Look, a white pumpkin. That's pretty cool."

"Well, I think that anyone who wouldn't like you is touched in the head... I like you a lot." Zach met my eyes, and we both smiled. "Oh, and that's called a 'Casper' pumpkin. Let's get one of those for sure."

We found three more pumpkins, one with a funky twisted stem, one that looked like it had a good shape to make the head of The Master from *Buffy* on it, and another we thought we could use to paint the face of Sally from *The Nightmare Before Christmas*.

As we drove back to Zach's place, silence fell over us. I thought about how easily families outside of the Amish community fractured, how I was used to everyone giving up on relationships, so easily. Both romantic and parental. How, in the non-Amish world, everything and everyone was regarded as replaceable and disposable. And how the Amish community would do anything, including keeping secrets of abuse, to keep families and friends together.

I didn't know which choice was worse.

CHAPTER THIRTY-SEVEN

I didn't post much on Facebook compared to my friends who loved to Vaguebook things like "Stupid jerk, I hate his assface!" or "Crushed it!" They also liked to tag people with inside jokes at least a few times a week. Snapchat and Instagram confused me even more, so I generally posted pictures me making funny faces to Madison or pics of clothes I liked to small groups. I did make sure to like every post a Sherpa made.

My latest Facebook status updates had been: "I love Halloween! Keep it scary!" and a link to a hilarious rant Aasif Mandvi from *The Daily Show* did about NYC taxi drivers. Two weeks before that, I'd posted a cool photo of a pair of Fluevog boots I wanted. I only had 92 friends on it, and I felt like I didn't know most of them. I couldn't understand how Hillary could have 4,353 friends on her page. Did everyone she'd ever met in her life, from the checkout guy at the Turkey Hill Mart to the lady who does her mani-pedi, friend her?

I will admit, I checked my page at least ten times a day, though. I tried not to, but I couldn't help it. Madison caught me doing it once and told me I was a "lurker" because I pretended I didn't care but actually I clearly cared too much. I smiled with my lips pressed tightly together because I chafed a little at that label.

Imagine my surprise when I got a friend request on Facebook from myself.

At first when I saw the notice that "Samantha Stonesong" wanted to friend me, I figured it was someone who'd put their own name into the search engine to see who'd pop up, and then this name sharer wanted to take it a bit further to learn about other people around the world who also had her moniker, so she tried to add them to her Friends. I tried to view her info and other pics, but her page was restricted unless I accepted the friend request. I almost deleted it. But there was something about the tiny profile picture that seemed a little too familiar… When I clicked on it, I saw it was a not-very-good, blurry picture of myself. My chin was down, my hair was over my right eye a bit, and it looked like I was chewing my bottom lip. On closer inspection, I could see it was from last year's Spring Gala, because I recognized the dress I was wearing. It was teal, kinda slinky. I'd only worn it that once. Madison had taken me shopping and had convinced me to buy it, right after we'd started regularly hanging out.

My mom had been over the moon when she saw me in the snug frock. She made me model it and said, "It shows off your nice waist. Now, put on some mascara to bring out those tiny little eyes of yours, and you'll have a date for the *next* formal dance for sure!"

I was blissful to attend my first formal with Madison. She had lots of guys who'd asked her to go with them, but she said she didn't like any of them and would rather go with me, her new friend. I wasn't a Sherpa yet, but Madison was already strategizing about how to make me one. Going to the dance with her was a good first step, she'd said.

The picture accompanying the friend request looked like it'd been cropped from a random group shot I'd never seen before. It was a little grainy, but on closer inspection, I could see Madison's arm and purse. And a bit of the magnificent embroidered gold dress Hillary had worn.

I looked uncomfortable in the picture, but I remember having a pretty good time at the dance until Madison started doing shots of peach schnapps and making out with John Hampler, who'd smuggled in a flask. Then Madison booted all over a toilet in the girl's bathroom, and we'd found her semi-conscious on the floor. Delia and I had to sneak her out past the chaperones by draping her arms over our shoulders and scooting out the door to Sasha's waiting car. I hated it when Madison did things like that to herself, but the next day, I just laughed about it with the other Sherpas.

I pulled myself back to the present and closed my Facebook page without accepting the friend request. I had a bad feeling but wanted to take some time to process what could be going on. In retrospect, I realize I was just in denial and prolonging knowing for sure what was happening. I tried to tell myself it was probably some weird virus. I hoped I'd have an email from someone about "a new Doppleganger virus" on Facebook, so I opened my inbox. Nothing like that appeared, but what I saw made me smile to myself in my empty bedroom. There was a new email from Zach. But my smile soon faded.

Dear Samantha,

I wish I was talking to you in person instead of writing to you. I tried to call and will try again when I can. I just found out my father has advanced cancer of the mouth. He has been sick most of August and September. And now one of my brothers fell from the barn loft and broke his thighbone so is bed-ridden as well. My sister, Hannah, just visited me in my apartment and begged me to come home to help. My family is far behind where they should be in the harvesting of the tobacco crop. My mother has finally taken my father to The Amish House of Pomerene in Millersville. My sister does not think my father is long for this world. I am saddened by this more than I can express.

I hope you will understand. I need to return to help them. The neighbours have been pitching in, but the closest ones have a new baby, and the other farm owners near them are quite elderly. I do not know if my parents have let others in their church know how dire things are. So I will not see you for a while. I feel very bad about this because I know you are having some problems with your friends. Although, I am hopeful that you've "worked it out" by now, as you predicted in your last letter to me.

I am also sad because the time I've spent with you these last few weeks has been the happiest in my life. I'm sorry I won't get to see you this weekend. Of course, I look forward to more special times with you in the future. I just feel I have a chance to help my family right now. That they are willing to let me do so means the world to me. I do not want to jeopardize this fragile trust by violating their rules about technology or make them think they are not my priority right now. I hope you understand. God willing, it will not be long before I can see you again.

Mir leid. (This is PA Dutch for "I am sorry.")

I will think of you much. I have strong feelings for you.

Yours,

Zach

PS Do not worry. I will take the kittens and the Mama cat with me. Darla, Angel, Spike, Dru, and Harmony will miss you, too.

The last part was hard to read; it was all blurry because I was crying. All I could think was *I am totally and completely alone.* Everyone had deserted me so easily. First my father, then my friends, and now, most heart-wrenchingly, the boy I loved. And sure, Zach said he'd be back, but my father had made similar promises to me. Once Zach was back with his family on the farm, he'd probably go back to the Amish and forget all about me. I'd worried about that, and now it was coming true.

I couldn't imagine how things could get worse.

Then a random fact I'd read a while ago popped into my mind: Albert Einstein was a giant kleptomaniac, totally shunned by the vaudeville community he was trying to fit in with, partially because they discovered him hoarding his fellow performers' props. So he started pursuing other interests. And he found some pretty cool alternate paths, studied Physics at the Fashion Institute of Technology, and changed the world with his brilliance. But after I'd finished the article, I doubted that he ever totally gave up his compulsion to take things. *Maybe a little indulging wouldn't be so bad...*

So to distract myself from over-thinking Zach's letter and to resist the pull of shoplifting, I went back on Facebook and accepted the strange friend request from myself.

Silly me. Things can always get worse.

CHAPTER THIRTY-EIGHT

After I accepted the friend request from this "other" Samantha Stonesong, my feelings of trepidation bloomed into a full-fledged rupture in my core. According to her info page, she shared my whole life. We lived in the same place, attended the same high school, and had the same birthday. For a brief moment it crossed my mind: *What if this is not just a ringer but literally me in an alternate reality?* That would have been cool. But no such luck. This was obviously a fake page set up by someone who knew me. Someone who wanted to make fun of me. The following is a list of posts made as status updates to this dummy account and the times they were posted:

I hate the boys at my school—give me some Amish loving! (October 23 at 4:16pm)

I'm sad I can't find anyone else at Lancaster Township HS who likes to churn butter and go to quilting bees with me. (October 23 at 4:45pm)

The smell of horse manure turns me on! (October 23 at 4:56pm)

Barn raisings and parties in cornfields are my kind of fun! (October 24 at 7:30am)

I wanted to unfriend this page. It was obviously created to torment me. But I can only compare my morbid curiosity to keep opening this page and peeking at it to the people who slow down in their cars to look at a horrible accident that they know they will be traumatized by seeing. You know you'll regret it. You'll be disgusted. It will make you upset. But you do it anyway. Is it human nature to be perversely masochistic? I don't know. I was devastated but passively watched this tiny tormentor turn into a malicious monster.

Within twenty-four hours, the fake Samantha page had double the friends I did on my real page. By the following day, there were over four hundred people on it. There weren't many comments to the posts other than an LOL or LMAO every now and then. After the first couple of hours, the status updates slowed in frequency. I couldn't help but to hope the joke had been played out after the first two days. But people at school were still sniggering when I walked by them, and someone stuck an "Amish Crossing" sticker from a tourist-trap souvenir shop on my locker.

On Wednesday, in the hallway at school, I made eye contact with Simon, my first buddy when I'd first moved to Lancaster, before I joined the Sherpas. I smiled weakly at him. Good old Simon. He'd be above all this. He stopped. I thought he was going to say something. Then he just shook his head, dropping his eyes. His mouth turned down in a way that made him look like he'd just read an op-ed piece espousing the theory that the dinosaurs weren't real, just a hoax. He walked quickly by me. I wondered if he had disdain for me because of what he'd heard about me recently; maybe he too harboured prejudices about the Amish. After all, he was a science and technology guy, and they rejected most of that stuff in their day-to-day life…

Then it hit me. *Didn't I swear to call him a couple of weeks ago? But I never kept that promise.* Simon was probably just disgusted that I hadn't talked to him much since befriending Hillary and the Sherpas. I was a pretty horrible person to have abandoned all my first friends, including him, once I got in with the popular girls. I couldn't blame them for not wanting to be kind to the pariah that I was now. I'd been the one to blow off our friendship, and I couldn't expect him to just welcome me back now that the popular crowd had dumped me. I was just as bad as they were. Maybe I deserved

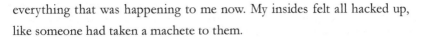

everything that was happening to me now. My insides felt all hacked up, like someone had taken a machete to them.

During a study hall, I made a list:

Top 6 Things I Want to Yell at the Other Sherpas but Don't Dare

1) How could you all be so mean?

2) You all wanted me to get a boyfriend. And I did. But obviously I'm still not cool enough.

3) You suck! Why do you even care that I'm going out with an Amish guy?!! Why is it okay to be so prejudiced against Amish?

4) Most of you have secrets, too—drinking, drugs, dating older guys your parents don't know about. How would you like it if I told everyone things you wanted to keep private?

5) I wish I'd never become friends with you. I never want to be a Sherpa again. I should've stayed friends with Simon.

6) I hope some crazed zombie tears each of you apart, rips out your squishy brains, and feasts on your medulla oblongatas, frontal lobes, and cerebral cortexes tonight!

Not my most inspired list, but it'd have to do.

I wanted to write Zach and tell him I needed him, but I didn't even know if my email would get to him, so I didn't. I wanted to confront Madison to find out her involvement and to beg her to make it stop, but I was afraid she'd just laugh at me. I wanted to send some kind of note to The Powers That Be on Facebook to tell them I was being cyberbullied by a fraudulent page, but I didn't know how to do that and was afraid that they'd contact my torturers, and then things at school would get worse. So I did none of those things.

Most of all, I wanted to go to a store, find some precious object to make mine, and to steal it.

CHAPTER THIRTY-NINE

It was my seventeenth birthday. And Zach had obviously forgotten all about it. I should know by now, Amish guys don't call.

It had been a week since I'd heard from Zach. He'd sent me one more brief email. He'd told me he was enjoying his visit more than he could have imagined. Seeing his brothers and sisters, taking care of the animals, running into old friends, it was a lot more fun than he recalled. He'd written, "Maybe I was just remembering the things I didn't like because it was easier to let that life go by doing that, I don't know…"

I wondered if now he was thinking of all my bad qualities so it'd be easier to let me go and return to his Amish life. But when I wrote him back, I didn't ask him if that was true. Instead, I assured him I was fine and that I understood that he needed to be with his family and that I was ok not talking with him for a while. It was, of course, horsecrap. But he bought it. Probably because it was what he wanted to hear. I would have been so happily surprised if Zach had been able to telepathically sense that everything in my life was falling apart since I'd found out about my fake Facebook page. But of course he didn't.

So I had no friends and no boyfriend to wish me a happy birthday. Of course, I still had my mom, though. Not that my birthday was a high priority for her.

"Look, Sam, happy birthday," my mom said, breezing into the dining room, arms loaded with flyers. "But I figured you were too old to want a lame-o birthday party, right?" She started sorting papers on one end of the dining room table while I ate breakfast on the other. I didn't look up, feigning interest in the *Lancaster New Era*'s story about a new play opening at The Fulton Opera House.

"I know last year we went out to that theme park Dutch Wonderland to celebrate, but I'm super-busy right now. I've got three houses closing in four days this week." She handed me two hundred-dollar bills from her pocket. "Get yourself something that you've been lusting after."

I looked down at the money and shook my head. I rolled my eyes, too. I thought I'd done it after she'd turned her back, but I guess she caught me out of the corner of her eye.

"Really? That's your idea of a 'thank you'?" She slammed down the papers she'd been sorting. "You are seriously the most negative person. You get that from your father, not me."

"Don't worry, I'll be gone soon enough," I replied, shovelling honey-flavoured Greek yogurt with Grape Nuts into my mouth. "I graduate next year."

"Oh, Sam, that seems like an eternity." She made a dramatic fake sigh. "I'm so tired of this. It's not fair; your deadbeat dad should be taking some of this responsibility!" She shook her head and walked out of the kitchen.

"Good luck with that," I muttered, knowing that if my dad hadn't shown any interest in me for the last few years, it wasn't like he was going to start now.

After school the next day, I drove over to the local mall, Park City. Truth be told, I was in a bit of a daze. When I parked, I found myself walking aimlessly around the sprawling, starfish-shaped building.

I didn't know what I'd take or where I'd filch it, but I knew the pressure that had built up inside me could only be relieved by a good old-fashioned shoplifting. If you had a painful boil, you'd lance it, right? That's all I was doing. I needed this. I deserved this. With all I'd gone through, this was owed me.

I waited until the precious object called to me. That was the secret, you see. The precious object was already mine. It was *meant* to be mine. I browsed H&M. Nothing. I went into bebe but left quickly. Salespeople were way too pushy and nosey there. They seemed to be watching my every move. I was out of practice and likely to be clumsy. I was too weak to fight my temptations any more, but I wasn't stupid. Then I saw it and knew. Victoria's Secret. It was a surprise to me that this particular store called to me. I always bought my underwear at Kohl's. I figured why pay a lot for clothes nobody would ever see? But as soon as I walked in Victoria's Secret, I could see the appeal. There was a gorgeous green-and-purple bra. I loved that colour combination. And a silky dusty rose nightgown that looked like it could have been worn by Marilyn Monroe. And big piles of soft cotton underwear, so easy to hide away. And none of those pesky security tags. They were easy enough to take off, just freeze the ink in them and smash them with a hammer, but they added another level of complication when leaving a store. And as I said, I was a little rusty.

There was only one salesgirl working. She was only a little older than me but went to a different school because I didn't recognize her. She was sitting in the back at the cash register, alternately reading a copy of *People* and typing on her phone. She didn't bother to look up at me when I came in. Perfect.

I got more and more excited as I hid each item. The bra went down the front of my pants. I tucked the nightgown into my shirt. A few pairs of underwear fit nicely deep in the pockets of my cargo pants that I'd worn for that exact purpose. Walking out of the store undisturbed gave me an additional rush. And when I left the mall, the feeling ramped up higher. I loved that I hadn't touched the two crisp hundred-dollar bills I'd gotten from my mom this morning currently in my wallet.

I was superior to everyone. I did not need anyone. Clearly Zach didn't want to date me anymore now that he was back with the Amish. Madison probably never really cared about me. And my own mother and father obviously wished I hadn't been born. Screw them all. Being alone was great. Alone. Alone was the best. I sat in my room at the computer listening to The Weepies "The World Spins Madly On" and Edie Brickell's "Circle" and laughed at how stupid everyone was and then cried until I had no more tears left.

Happy birthday to me.

CHAPTER FORTY

B efore, when I'd nick things, I could recreate and relive some of the thrill I'd felt taking them by doing a little ritual. For the next few days, I'd take my wins out, look at them and touch them, replaying the experience. When the tingle faded from doing that, I often felt a new rush wearing my precious items out in public. Then, when that no longer did it for me, I'd lift new things and start over.

The underwear, bra, and nightgown I'd filched from Victoria's Secret were spread out on my bedspread, as well as a Tangerine Dreams lipstick and violet mascara I'd pocketed at a drug store the day after my mall escapade. But looking at everything just made me feel sick. It was as if my shame had taken actual physical weight and space, like a large rock, and it was lodged tightly under my ribcage.

What would Zach think of me if he knew what I did? Would he hate me? Think I was evil? Could he ever forgive me? It was all I could do not to break down sobbing. And then there was still another small voice inside me, insisting I'd feel better if I just took something else, something more. I was reminded of the cartoon characters that had an angel version and a devil version of themselves, each perched on a shoulder, offering conflicting opinions and dubious advice. Yet as much as the creators of my faux Facebook page wanted to make my other classmates believe I was a laughable, two-dimensional caricature, I knew I was not.

"Sam, could you come down here?" my mom called up to my bedroom.

"Sure." I stuffed all my goods into a bag, which I shoved into a box and buried in the back of my closet. My mom hadn't done a "shoplifting room check" in months, so I felt relatively safe with my barely marginal hiding spot.

My mom sat at the kitchen table, wearing one of my sweaters that pulled too tightly across her chest. She had a policy that if it wasn't on my back, she could wear it, if she washed it. She offered that I could borrow her clothes anytime, too. As if. I sighed. Another ruined piece of clothing for me.

"We need to talk."

I sat across from my mother and studied the painting on the wall behind her like I hadn't seen it every day for the past eight months. It was a blurry, pastel-coloured rendering of a lady in a rowboat on a placid lake, holding a fancy umbrella over her head to shield her from the sun, or maybe to hide her delicate self from rude, peering eyes.

I knew my mom had been irritated with me last night. She'd asked me to pick up some candy on my way home from school for the Halloween trick-or-treaters, but I'd forgotten because I'd gotten distracted by stealing the makeup. Then, at dinner, when she tried to tell me something about some friend of hers getting an extreme face peel that made her look like a tomato frittata, I just stood up, interrupting her, and told her I wasn't hungry anymore because stories about old people trying to look young were nauseating. She'd slammed her drink down and told me that was fine with her, because I was a little brat.

I should have known this confrontation was brewing.

"What the heck is going on with you? Frankly, you're a real acid-tongued bitch lately, and I'm about at the end of my rope." My mom tapped the table with her nail extensions, zebra-print embellished fake fingernails. I stayed silent.

"Is it that boy you've been seeing? Did he break up with you? Look, boys come and go. Especially at your age. Plenty of fish in the sea." I just shook my head. "Trust me, I wish I'd dated a lot more, then maybe I wouldn't have messed up so bad by picking your father." She continued to thrum her ghastly nails on the table. "So... is that it? Or is it something even more silly, like you got an A- instead of an A or something?"

She waited to see my reaction. I gave her the dead fisheye stare, wishing I could make her head explode with telekinesis. I couldn't, so she continued.

"Well, look, I don't know what the hell it is, and you're not telling me, so there's nothing I can do. I wash my hands of it." She threw her palms up in the air dramatically. "But I'll say this, young lady, you'd better not be starting up any of that nonsense you pulled before that made us have to leave Philly. Because if you do and get caught again, I'm going to tell them to lock you up and throw away the key this time. Don't smirk. I'm totally serious. I'm not going through THAT again. Do you understand?" Her voice had reached an uncomfortable screechy pitch near the end of her rant.

I didn't know what expression she'd thought she saw on my face, but I certainly hadn't smirked.

"Yes, I do. I understand." I looked down at my clasped fingers, knuckles white, and then back at her. I decided I needed to tell her a partial truth to get her off my back. I wasn't the natural actress Hillary was, so I knew I wouldn't be able to pull off a complete lie. I just bit the bullet and offered up my confession. "Look, I'm going through a rough patch. I just had a big fight with Madison."

My mom exhaled loudly. "Oh well, that's it, huh? Oh, that makes total sense!" She laughed, relieved. "Yeah, girls your age can be so catty. I remember how jealous some of the girls got of me at school, and they used to say horrible things. That's all it is, you know. Just stupid teenage stuff. Don't worry. It'll blow over. These things always do. You'll see."

"Yeah, you're probably right." I forced a small smile, though my throat burned like I'd been crying.

"Sure I am!" She got up, grabbed a banana nut muffin from the breadbox on the counter, and put it down in front of me. "Just picked up some of these at the new café that opened on Queen Street. They're made by the Amish or something. They're delicious, try one!"

I started to tell her I wasn't very hungry but then thought better of it. I took a big bite. "Mmmm… yummy."

"Yeah, right? Ok. Well, then, good talk! I'm going to run some errands. See you tonight. Glad we got that cleared up!" And with that, she was gone.

Alone, I had time to think. I'd learned three very important things that morning:

1. My mother wasn't completely clueless and devoid of all mothering instincts. She'd realized something was wrong. This was both impressive and scary at the same time. But I had to give props to her.

2. It was a priority to find a much better hiding place for my most recent precious items in case she started snooping again.

3. I needed to find something more special, more specific, *more personal* to take. To fill this hole. To take back my power.

CHAPTER FORTY-ONE

I figured out why I felt so dissatisfied by my recent lifts, even though they'd been successes. I'd been too cowardly; I hadn't aimed high enough. That's why I felt empty. I'd been purging old makeup from a drawer in my bathroom when it hit me: I knew what to take next.

This thing called out to me stronger than anything had before. And it would be tougher to take than anything else had ever been. But this truly belonged to me. My mom had sold her engagement ring a few months ago, because she'd thought it was hers. But it wasn't. It was rightfully mine. It would have been, anyway, if my parents hadn't divorced, and it wasn't my fault they divorced, so why should I suffer for it? Luckily, I knew right where my new target was.

Last spring my mom made a big deal about all the "spring cleaning" she was doing. She took out all of the jewellery my dad had ever given her and sold everything. Try as I might, I couldn't help but look every time I walked by Now and Forever.

The fact that Hillary's mom owned this store was just the icing on the cupcake I was about to devour.

I knew stealing the ring would be tricky. The shop was made up of two rooms and a storage area. It'd once been a narrow railroad apartment, so each room led back into the other in a long vertical configuration. But the good news was that the front display window had a barely perceptible opening, just big enough to fit a hand through. One of the first times I'd been in the store, my then-dormant "shoplifting brain" had noticed the hole, partially hidden behind a rack of clothing. Maybe I'd always known deep down that I'd be boosting again some day.

Of course, there was also the risk that someone walking by on the street would see me grabbing the precious item, so I'd have to be quick. And Hillary's mom knew who I was, so I'd have to pick a time she wouldn't be there. Or maybe I'd wear a disguise. I decided to do both. Better safe than sorry.

Right before closing seemed like the best time. The street would be the least crowded and, hopefully, whoever was working there would be in such a hurry to close, she might not notice the missing items from the window.

I stopped riffling through my makeup when it hit me.

I knew our school play had its opening night performance this Friday, and Hillary would be performing the lead. Hillary could make even a school play seem cool, so almost all the kids at school and their parents would be there. I was counting on the fact that Hillary's mom would be watching her daughter, which would mean someone else, hopefully an inexperienced stranger, would be watching the shop.

Because opening night was so soon, I wouldn't be able to do much planning, but that added risk. Just thinking about this plot gave me a super thrilling buzz. I'd been so irritated with Madison for chasing this kind of feeling with drugs and alcohol. Maybe we were more alike than I'd realized? Then I thought, *Screw Madison!* and laughed out loud and went back to throwing out all my pink lipsticks and blushes.

I whistled in the shower and smiled at random people on the street. I almost didn't care that I hadn't heard from Zach.

The next day at school, I walked right up to my old lunch table at school and stood my ground until Hillary and the Sherpas noticed me. I took a long deep breath in, preparing. The lunch room always smelled like over-cooked mystery meat, rising dough, and industrial cleaners. I felt a hush come over the whole cafeteria, but that could have been just my imagination. Madison looked at me like she was seeing a ghost. Appropriate since this was October 31, Halloween.

"Hey, Hillary, just wanted to wish you luck tomorrow night for your big acting debut. I'm sure you'll be fantastic. I think you're a born actress."

Hillary's eyes narrowed for a millisecond. I'd surprised her. People never got the best of her. But she recovered quickly with a big fake smile.

"Well, gee, thanks, Sam. Isn't that sweet?" She glanced over at the Sherpas, then back at me. "I sure hope you're gonna be there. You *can* still go to plays, right? I know watching TV is probably forbidden for you now with your new lifestyle choices, dating Zach and all."

Wow, she was ballsy. She just practically admitted to my face that she'd created that fake Facebook page. But she was not going to win today. I had my mojo back now. There was a new bitch in town.

"Oh, yeah, I could go to your little play… I mean, if I wanted to. But I don't know if I want to." I casually grabbed and then popped one of the new girl's tater tots in my mouth. "I mean, does the world really need another mediocre high-school performance of *Grease*? Teens today trying to emulate a movie that featured adults from the 1970s trying to play teens from the 1950s. Just sad, really!" I laughed. "Wow, who's the anachronism now?"

Hillary blinked. Madison's jaw dropped. Kensie looked like she was about to cry. Delia seemed like she wanted to say something.

Hillary recovered. "Look, Sam, the only reason I ever even let you hang out with us is because Madison said your mom was never around, so we'd be able to party at your place on the weekends. But a LOSER like you doesn't have a clue how to throw a party." She paused before going in for the kill. "I totally get why someone like you would be more comfortable as an Amish girl in a bonnet and apron, hosting an evening prayer meeting by candlelight."

That was the best she had? I'd already guessed long ago that Madison had wheedled my way into the Sherpas with promises of revelries at my place. I wanted to tell Hillary I'd rather hang out with the Amish at a board game night than with her at the hottest party in town.

Before I could respond, it was Britt who spoke next. "So Sam, are you going out trick-or-treating as an Amish person this year?" She was truly pathetic and so easy to grind up into dogmeat.

"Nope, why would I do *that*?" I laughed again, but this time it felt almost genuine. "See, let me explain Halloween, Britt. And I'll go slowly for you... ok, you douchecanoe? Halloween is the time when you dress up as something you're *not*. Since you think I already *am* Amish, it wouldn't be a costume. Duh. Haven't you seen my new Facebook page?" I gave her a mock eye-roll.

The Sherpas were gobsmacked.

Even Hillary looked completely stunned. I wanted to stay and savour the moment. But I more than that, I wanted to get the last word in. So I turned and left before any of them could recover from the blow. Walking away, I felt both lightheaded and grounded at the same time. I think I may have even had swagger.

And tomorrow night, I'd be able to further prove not just how totally over all of them I was, but how *superior* I was. Not that they'd ever comprehend the magnitude of my awesomeness. But I'd know, and that's all that mattered. Soon I'd have the ring. Sure, if I got caught, it'd be a third-degree felony. But that wouldn't happen, because nobody ever really saw me anyway. I was invisible. And invisible meant invincible.

After I pulled this off, I'd be totally in control. I'd turn as hard as the two-carat diamond I'd finally possess.

And nobody would ever be able to hurt me again.

CHAPTER FORTY-TWO

As my hand made contact with my treasure, the engagement ring in the front window, the second it became mine, a quiver of thrill raced up my arm. But that rush was quickly quelled by the weight of a hand on my shoulder.

Rejected Reasons Explaining Why My Hand Was on the Ring

1. I didn't want to disturb an employee, so I was pulling it out myself to try on.

WON'T WORK BECAUSE: Most overused, suspicious reason ever.

2. I noticed a problem with the ring display and needed to examine it.

WON'T WORK BECAUSE: The Grinch That Stole Christmas defense, "I'm just taking it back to my workshop to fix it, Cindy Lou Who..."

3. I have a muscle spasm problem that causes my arms to flail out.

WON'T WORK BECAUSE: What if she asks for a doctor's note? Also, stupid.

4. I think I'm "Birdo" from Super Mario Brothers, and this is my ring!

WON'T WORK BECAUSE: She actually might think I'm delusional, but that'd be problematic in another way because I might be sent to some home for the insane like Arkham.

5. I'm working for an extremist group, kind of like PETA, that protests diamonds, so I was going to damage this to prove a point.

WON'T WORK BECAUSE: Again, it might, but I'd still be committing a crime.

    6.   My arm is nefariously controlled by an evil witch doctor.

WON'T WORK BECAUSE: *The Voodoo Curse Defense* might make a good title for a horror movie but won't convince most policemen.

CHAPTER FORTY-THREE

B ut I should back up a bit...
The night before the heist, All Hallow's Eve, I'd handed out candy to the trick-or-treaters, checked my email at least twenty times to see if Zach had written, which he hadn't, and then I flicked on the remote to watch the Halloween movie marathon. But after not hearing from Zach, my heart just wasn't into the horror films. So I turned them off and turned in before midnight. This hadn't happened on a Halloween night since I was eight. I cursed that part of me that still ached for Zach. I tried to convince myself it was only an infatuation, that there were plenty of other guys out there. Guys that weren't so complicated, so... Amish. But then I realized I was saying the same things to myself now that my mom and Madison both said to me earlier about Zach, that there were plenty of fish in the sea. I got mad at them and at myself. I hated my stupid life. But only I could make things better so it was time to stop being depressed and all victim-y.

My mom left early the following Friday morning for her normal weekend residence, far away from me. I purposely stayed up in my room so I wouldn't have to see her before she left. When I came finally downstairs, there was a note on the kitchen table from her that read, *Don't let the losers bring you down!*

Classic Mom. Always with the trite clichés. But up until now, I'd been the "loser." And that was changing.

In my Politics and World Religions class, I got a paper back marked B-. Odd because it was a cake class. Mr. Lambert had written *SEE ME!* in bright red marker next to the grade. But I didn't.

At one point I caught Simon's eye in class, but he quickly looked away. He had every right not to like me after the way I'd thrown away our friendship, but I was irked about him staring at me like I was a freak. Delia was hanging out near my locker at the end of the day like she wanted to talk to me, but I quickly changed my path to avoid her.

After school, I went home and ate a couple of handfuls of leftover Halloween candy. At six, I put on the shiny, coal-black wig I'd had from a few Halloweens ago when I dressed up as a vampire. I applied a fake mole to my left cheek and put on an old pair of glasses. I also wore one of my mom's low-cut dresses that I normally wouldn't be caught dead in.

Walking to Hillary's mom's shop, I thought of how Hillary would often point to a piece of clothing she was wearing and brag, "When my mom went on her buying trip to New York, she only got ONE of these and put it aside for me so nobody else in Lancaster would have one like it." We, her ever-faithful Sherpas, would oooh and aaah over whatever it was in an appropriately admiring way.

A few blocks from the store, I saw a woman only about five years older than me with a stroller walking along the same sidewalk. She stopped every few feet or so to sing to her baby or to make sure the baby's blanket was tucked around her in a cozy way or to check that her daughter's pacifier was within her reach. My stomach began to pinch. I'd been trying to keep my head clear and focused to help me concentrate on the mission. I didn't want to get emotional and blow it. I'd never stolen anything so intensely personal. But now I couldn't help but to think of my mom and how she got rid of that ring like it meant nothing to her.

I didn't know what to think of the fact nobody had bought my mom's ring, even though it had been in the front window of the store for a while. My mom had just laughed and said she didn't care; she was just glad it was out of her house. It was the most beautiful ring I'd ever seen. The band of the engagement ring was a rose gold that had been painstakingly hand-engraved with roses and featured a two-carat radiant-cut diamond. It broke my heart when, months before the divorce was officially finalized, my mom had stopped wearing it. She'd kept it in a mahogany box on her vanity along with all the other jewellery my dad had given her. Sometimes I'd sneak into her room and gaze at the ring, even try it on my too-small fingers, fantasizing about the day she'd give it to me. Maybe for my birthday? She wasn't wearing it any more. Not that she'd ever promised she would. I guess I just assumed. But that's what good mothers did, right, pass their beautiful things on to their grateful daughters? *Yeah, I know.*

That's where I went wrong—making the assumption back then that I had a "good" mother. After the divorce, I started to realize that nobody ever *gives* you anything. If you want something, you needed to take it. Her selling the ring just reinforced that maxim.

Walking up to Now and Forever, I noted it was 6:45, fifteen minutes before the store was scheduled to close. A pile of colourful leaves on the sidewalk that someone had meticulously raked to the corner of their lawn made me smile. The dead leaves were more beautiful with their fiery colours than they'd ever been when alive.

I surreptitiously gave my wig a little tug before entering.

I was surprised to see Simon's mom standing behind the counter. She looked the same as always, her long wavy brown hair streaked with some shiny white streaks and her beautiful skin rosy without any makeup.

I didn't know she was working here now. I guess I wouldn't be aware of that, since I hadn't been inside the store in months. Last spring I'd bought a top here, just as Madison and I were starting to become friends. I was still in a "trial phase" with the Sherpas. When Hillary saw my shirt, she snorted. "Wow! My mom was *right* that someone would buy that shirt! I told her with all the colours in it, it looked positively clown-ish, and nobody would ever want it. Guess you proved me wrong!" And then after a pause, "But it suits you, Sam! Good call!" Typical Hillary; no compliment was ever without an insult. She was like the crazy lady you heard about who gave out apples at Halloween with razor blades hidden inside.

Simon's mom came around the counter and smiled at me. "Can I help you find something?" I was relieved. She showed no sign that she recognized me from the two times we'd met last spring.

"Maybe. I'm just seeing what you have, as it's my first time here," I said in a fake British accent. My plan was if she didn't leave me alone to browse in a minute or two, I'd ask her for a size not currently on the floor for some piece of clothing so she'd have to go into the back room. Then I planned to quickly grab my ring and run.

Luckily, just as I was about to ask her to go look for a size 27 pair of Citizen jeans, she said, "If you need anything, I'll just be in the back doing a bit of inventory until we close in a few minutes. Feel free to try anything on. I can stay open a little later if you need."

"Sure." I feigned intense interest in a rack of Romeo and Juliet Couture dresses. After waiting a minute and listening carefully, I moved to the window. I gave one last glance to the door behind me that led to the other room. Open but empty.

My hand closed around my precious item. The ring was mine.

How Simon's mom had managed to sneak up on me so fast, I'll never know. That lady must have had Black Cat DNA or something. When her hand softly but firmly clamped down on my shoulder, I panicked, of course, and reviewed my excuse list as I stood frozen. But then, just a few seconds after that, an unusual sensation washed over me.

I felt relief.

CHAPTER FORTY-FOUR

Three seconds after I felt Simon's mom's hand on my shoulder, my paralysis abated, and I snatched my hand back as if I'd accidentally touched Freddy Krueger's hand of blades.

Well, this is it. Jail time. I knew I'd just been caught stealing something worth over two thousand dollars. That's a third-degree felony, punishable by seven years in jail. Sure, under some circumstances my age might've made a judge go a little lighter on me, but there was that issue of my prior. Despite knowing all of this, there was something in me that felt lighter. This would all be over soon.

"Let me lock up the store. Then you and I need to have a long talk in the back, Sam."

Sam? She recognized me in spite of my clever disguise? Oh, great. I stood completely still and watched her calmly twist the sign on the front door to "Closed" and flick the two locks on the door. She also enabled an alarm on the keypad next to the door.

She then turned and smiled at me. It looked genuine. Her sanguine attitude creeped me out. Maybe she was an alien who was about to skin me alive and eat me. She'd then shed her own skin, and identity, and take mine...

"Honey, you're shaking. Come with me, I'm going to make you some tea. And then we are going to talk about why you were trying to steal your mom's ring back."

How the heck did she know so much? But I didn't dare open my mouth to ask. I just nodded and followed her to the back. She wore a flowing purple and pink dress that fanned out lightly behind her as she walked, giving her a blithe, almost angelic quality.

The office in the last room wasn't very big, but it was cozy, decorated with pictures of Simon's family all over the walls. I thought this was odd. Why would Hillary's mom hang up pictures of Simon's family all over instead of ones of her own family?

Simon's mom saw me gaping at the photo of a young Simon jubilantly holding up his car in a Pinewood Derby competition. "I know Simon has missed your friendship very much, too. He's been very worried about you lately."

Simon still talked about me and thought of me in a nice way? And Simon talked to his mom about personal things? And his mom cared? My brain felt like it was about to explode from the overload. So I did the most irrational thing I could: I asked the least important question racing through my mind.

"Why aren't there any pictures of Hillary's family in here? Why does Hillary's mom let you hang all the pictures of your family in her office?"

"Hillary's mom... oh, you mean Anne Markham. Yes, she was originally my partner, but I bought her out about a year ago, and now she's the store manager." Simon's mom took a teabag and dropped it into a china cup on a small antique table next to her desk. *Wait, what?!! Store MANAGER?* Hillary's mom didn't own this store anymore? Simon's mom did? Hillary still referred to this as "my mom's store." I wondered what had happened.

"Oh, I thought... never mind. It doesn't matter." I sank into a chair like my body was a bag of brittle sticks. I watched Simon's mom get a kettle off a hot plate and pour the steamy water into the cup.

"You're right. What matters the most to me right now is how we're going to help you, Sam." She handed me the cup. "Do you like honey or lemon?"

"Help me? Aren't you going to call the police?"

"No, I'm not doing that. I know more about what's going on with you than I think you're aware of. Now, do you take honey or lemon, dear?" She turned and picked up a lemon wedge and a plastic bear containing honey.

"Both, I guess."

"That's good. I like someone who knows what she wants." I wasn't sure if she was being facetious. She took the cup from my still slightly trembling hands, set it on the table next to me, and added both. "Now why don't you take off that dreadful wig and have a few sips of your tea."

"Yes," I mumbled and yanked out the four strategically placed bobby pins that had held my wig in place. I set the wig on my lap and folded my arms over the cleavage that my mom's dress revealed. I left my glasses on because I hadn't put my contacts in.

"Just this afternoon, Simon told me all about the asinine Facebook page that someone, or a group of nasty someones, created to cause you embarrassment. My husband was planning on calling you in to talk about it first thing Monday morning." She sat a few feet from me in her desk chair. There was her tea in a cup, already made, on the desk. Simon's father was one of the school's two guidance counsellors. I'd talked to the other one, Dr. Lowdermilk, as a mandatory thing for all transfers. Dr. Lowdermilk retired last spring and although Mr. Evans seemed nice, we'd never had an official session. But it was a big school, and I didn't know Simon's dad very well. He was overworked, trying to help our school's population, all the potential drop-outs, druggies, cutters, bulimics, and the many kids with serious problems.

"Ok," I said, unsure of what else to say.

"So I understand this is a very stressful time for you. But I need to know, have you stolen things before?" she asked, dropping her voice and looking at me with her piercing blue eyes.

I knew I should lie, that she'd be more likely to forgive me if she thought this was the first time. I could blame the Facebook page and maybe get off scot-free. But I didn't do that. Not so much because I trusted her, but more because I was just so damn tired of lying and pretending. "Yes."

"I figured. Were you ever caught before?"

"Back in Philadelphia." I took a sip of my tea. It warmed my throat.

"Did that have anything to do with why you moved here?"

"Yes." I carefully placed my cup down.

"And since you've been in Lancaster, have you…."

"Twice this week." I twirled the hair of the wig on my lap around my fingers a bit. "But not before that. I swear." I looked up at her to see if she believed me.

"I see." She brought her cup to her lips, making it so I couldn't tell if she doubted me. "Look, I promised, I'm not going to call the police. I'm not. But we also have to make sure you stop stealing things. Will your mom be able to assist us to get you some help?"

I snorted. "If you call her and tell her what I just did, SHE will call the police on me herself. She's already told me so."

"Oh, dear." I felt bad. Simon's mom was too nice a woman to be dealing with the mess that was me. She leaned forward. "How about your dad?"

Hot tears burst from me and wouldn't stop. I started gasping for air. Simon's mom employed her Black Cat DNA once again, and she was standing by me and had me cradled in her arms before I even knew she'd risen from her chair.

"He… he… doesn't care about me… I haven't… haven't seen him… in over two years," I managed to get out.

"Well, crap-sticks! That's just not right!" she exclaimed. The fact she just said "crap-sticks" made me start laughing, but I was still crying, too.

"I'm pissed, Sam. This world has let you down. And that's some serious bullshit. And that is not going to continue. Not on my watch. Not anymore." She continued to hold me as I cried. Then laughed. Then cried some more. And then the weirdest thing of all happened. I felt myself start to trust and believe her.

CHAPTER FORTY-FIVE

I couldn't believe it was almost 10 p.m. We'd been talking for hours. Simon's mom, who told me to call her Bria, was the easiest person to open my heart to that I'd ever met. It made sense, because her husband was a guidance counsellor and all. Probably some of his talent for listening without making people feel guilty had rubbed off on her. She told me she'd been a Deadhead in her teens and had been to almost two hundred Grateful Dead shows. She threw f-bombs and other curses around like they were nothing, but she didn't seem rude or crass at all when she did it.

"The stupid cliché is that if those girls, the Sherpas, were your true friends, they wouldn't be doggish with their cold burns. You see, that's hippie slang for 'acting salty'." I could tell she was trying to lighten the mood when she said things like that. Then she put on her serious face again. "Yet, that's just a simplistic platitude too. Some of them might indeed be little budding psychopaths, but more than likely, most of them are just dealing with their own problems. Look, I'm not justifying their behaviour in any way. But just because they're throwing stones the size of boulders, that doesn't mean they're not living in breakaway glass greenhouses themselves. But I've got a feeling from what you've told me that Hillary is acting out because she's jealous of your friendship with Madison. And obviously Hillary has no problem lying." Then she mumbled (but my hearing is razor sharp), "She's been that way for years."

What? Some adults pay attention to us teens?

"Yeah, that's true." I curled my leg up under myself and leaned in.

"And to be fair, it does sound like you hurt Madison, and that's why she's not accepting your apology. So I think you need to own that."

"Right." I nodded.

"And Delia and Kensie just sound like they're completely unaware of the Female Divinity inside themselves and are giving in to fear... and the Dark Side."

I laughed in spite of myself. What adult talked like this?!!

"Look, that stupid Facebook profile will be down before Monday. I can promise you that. My husband is already on it. But there will be other maelstroms in your life, and you need to get some good tools in your toolbox to learn to deal with things without going all sticky-fingers-crazy when they do happen."

"Yeah. I mean, I thought I was over doing that, though, and then it just came back." I'd cried so much telling her about my parents' divorce, my dad moving out and not wanting to see me, the move, and my friends' betrayal, I felt like my tear ducts were all dried out. I sipped the third cup of jasmine decaf tea she'd made me.

"I know, hon. I know. But when you're in a stressful situation, and you sure as hell are right now, that's when addictions are their most powerful. We need to get you some more help. It sounds like your mom is...." I could see her trying to choose her words carefully, "...overwhelmed. Sometimes people who get married too young feel like they've missed out on a lot, and they try to get some of it back and can be a little selfish." She ran her right pointer finger over her eyebrow. "I think we need to get you back in touch with your dad. Does he pay child support?"

"I don't think so. My mom's parents were loaded. When they died in a car crash, they left her a giant chunk of money about a year before the divorce. I remember my mom and dad fighting about that a lot." I didn't remember the details, but I did remember the shouting.

"'Rather than money, give me truth.' I think it was Thoreau who said that," Bria mused. I could see where Simon got his love of history.

"My mom makes a lot of money now selling houses, too. So no, I don't think my dad sends her anything." I felt like my left foot was falling asleep; it had that pins and needles feeling. I shook it a little.

"And your dad, he hasn't sent you a birthday card, Christmas present, nothing?" she asked.

"Nope, nothing." I shrugged. "I mean, I get it. He's moved on. He might even have a new family or something."

"Hmmm." She pursed her lips. "So he stayed in Philadelphia?"

"No, he moved before we did. He's in Towson, Maryland. He got a job at the university there."

"That's only about an hour and fifteen minutes from here." She cocked her head. "What does he do there?"

"He's an adjunct math professor." I knew he was still there, because every few weeks, I checked the faculty page on the university's website. "But I don't think you calling is a good idea. He doesn't want to see me, or he would've tried by now."

"Sometimes people just need a push." She looked at a picture of her family on the wall. "So your mom has never encouraged you to try to talk to him, but do you think she'd be upset if you did?"

I thought about this a minute before answering. "No, I don't think she would. I mean, she wouldn't want to see him, but I don't think she'd care if I saw him. She pretty much lets me do whatever I want to as long as it doesn't make problems for her."

"Of course you're gonna reap wind when all you sow is ice," Bria muttered, shaking her head, and then remembered I was there and smiled at me. "That wasn't Thoreau. It's a paraphrased lyric from a Grateful Dead song." She twirled a pencil between her fingers like a miniature baton. "Ah well, we all do our best in this bum-trip world. Who am I to criticize. There are so many roads…" She pulled the pencil toward her mouth as if she was going to chew the eraser but stopped herself. "We're calling your dad first thing tomorrow morning. If he's faculty at Towson, he'll be easy to track down. Everyone deserves a second chance to do the right thing."

I felt numb. I didn't know how to react to this, so I just nodded.

"You've been very honest with me. And you can't imagine how much I appreciate that and how honoured I am that you've trusted me enough to share what you have, but… well, here's the thing: I'm a Pisces. Whether it's true or not, I believe I'm more psychic than most people." She smiled slyly. "Like, I always knew which song The Dead were going to play next without hearing the first note. Anyway, I can't help feeling there's something else you're not telling me here." Bria tapped the pencil against her chin. All I could think was *Zach is a Pisces, too.*

"I like Pisces. I'm a Scorpio. Are we psychic, too?" I feigned a smile, but she saw right through my diversionary tactic.

"Why the all Amish references to you on that fake Facebook page?" After throwing out this non sequitur, her eyes probed mine. "Why did the girls pick that to torment you about? You said they called you 'Saint Sam' sometimes, but that's like mixing metaphors. Catholic and Amish don't have a lot in common; it's strange. It doesn't fit."

"Yes, you're right." I pushed the skin around my left fingernails back with my right thumbnail. "There is something else. Something I haven't told you. I was dating this guy, Zach. And he *was*, I dunno, maybe *is*, again, Amish." I noticed a little blood on my cuticle from my picking at it. "See, he was going to leave the Amish because he'd been away on Rumspringa and didn't want to go back because he wants to go to college and stuff. But two weeks ago, he found out his dad was really sick. So he went home to help out. And now I haven't heard from him in a while, which makes me think he's back to being Amish and I'm probably never going to hear from him again. And that sucks because… I think… no… I know… I love him."

It never ceased to amaze me how wrong I could be about things. I did have some tears left after all.

CHAPTER FORTY-SIX

After I told Bria all about Zach, she agreed our relationship was pretty unusual.

"I've lived in Lancaster for almost thirty years, and I've never actually met anyone who left the Amish community," she said.

"I found a site for people who are no longer Amish and want to blog about it. But it seems like a lot of them come from Ohio or other places," I told her. She nodded pensively.

I shared with her that he was my first boyfriend, so I didn't have much with which to compare our experience. I skipped over the part about my and Madison's Plan P and about how I'd decided I needed to change my life by having a best friend and a boyfriend. That just seemed too mortifying to go into.

When she finally drove me home, I slept like Nosferatu. When I woke Saturday morning, everything seemed to be happening so quickly, it felt as if the earth was no longer solid or stable beneath my feet. The fake Facebook page about me being Amish was gone. Vanished into cyberspace. I had a message on my cell from Bria that she'd talked to my dad. He'd agreed to drive up immediately from Baltimore. She'd asked him to come to a 1 p.m. lunch meeting at Issac's Deli. Mr. Evans, Simon's dad, the counsellor, would also be there in an unofficial capacity to support me. I called her back and told her I'd go, but I wanted her to be at the lunch, too. She didn't pause before saying, "Absolutely. Whatever you need."

I went back online, and there was an email from Zach.

Dear Sam,

I'm so sorry I have been out of touch. I know I missed your birthday, and I feel very bad about that. I hope to make it up to you. My father died a few days ago, and we had much to do to get ready for the funeral, which was at our house yesterday. I just could not get away to try to call you.

I saw many friends and relatives I have not seen in years. It felt good to be among them. While Amish see death as a part of life and an individual's death as "God's Will," there is still much shock and sadness under all our stoicism. Real death is so much more complicated than the death in horror films.

I did have the opportunity to see my father in his last days. I hoped he could understand why I left so he could forgive me. Sadly, he did not. But I forgave him for not being able to understand, which I think is ultimately more important for me to have peace.

I'd forgotten how much I love my mom's schnitz pie and how my littlest sister Katie makes me laugh. She's lost so many teeth and grown up so much. Hannah, always the practical one, saved my clothes for me so I'm wearing them now—suspenders and all! My sister Annie has been taking care of all my barn cats. She always knew I'd be back. She wants to take some of my new kittens from the garage, but I said I'd have to ask you first.

I never felt my brother Zeke and I had much in common, but working together in the fields has helped us bond. Mose and I talked about books. He hides some in the barn as I used to. All my littlest siblings have grown so much. I hate that I've missed so many of their "firsts." Seeing my family is the good thing about being back.

Please write to me and let me know what is happening with you. I've replayed your last email in my head many times. I believe something might be wrong, and you are hiding it from me to spare me. That would be just like you, so kind. I feel bad that I was too distracted to notice when I first read it. I hope you are well. The kittens miss you and I do, too.

Yours,

Zach

I read his email three times. Then I quickly and aimlessly walked around my room a bit. Finally, I sat down and tried to catch my breath and assess how I was feeling about the email and everything else that had happened so far this morning. I was relieved the Facebook page was down, terrified about my meeting with my dad in two hours, and a little ashamed I'd been so upset with Zach for not writing me lately. *His father just died—what kind of a selfish bitch am I?*

I knew I didn't deserve him. I was:

1. From a broken family
2. A thief
3. Not sure if I believed in God
4. A liar
5. A loser with no real friends, and I'd never fit in.

Yet boiling under all those emotions was red-hot anger. I felt mad at my friends for betraying me, furious with my dad for deserting me, and even though it was irrational, bitterly resentful of Zach for not knowing I needed him.

I didn't know what to write back to Zach, so I logged off my computer and walked over to the closet to figure out what to wear for lunch.

What does one wear when seeing one's father for the first time in two years?

I looked at a bright pink-and-yellow flowery shirt, too silly. Then I considered one with an anime cat on it, also ridiculous. Why did I have such childish clothes? Maybe Hillary was right; my taste in clothes was totally lame. I finally picked out a pair of black jeans and a soft blue cotton sweater. I remembered that my dad always loved it when I wore blue. I looked at the sweater in my hand for a second before wadding it up into a ball and chucking it on the floor of my closet. I grabbed an oxblood-red faux animal print blouse off a hanger and took it and my black jeans into the bathroom instead.

I took a shower hot enough to drive Pinhead back to Hell. When I got out, I considered wearing a pair of earrings I'd stolen years ago that were still wrapped in tissues at the back of my makeup drawer. But I reconsidered, thinking that wearing illicit bling was probably a bit too trite in its symbolism.

Before leaving, I logged back into my account and wrote to Zach.

Dear Zach,

I'm so sorry to hear about your dad passing away. I'm also sorry that when you talked to him, he couldn't accept you for who you are, because you're a great guy. Isn't it weird how even if we know our dads are wrong, we still want to please them? I guess we can't help it. We put them on pedestals because when we are little kids they seem so powerful. But when it comes down to it, they're just human, too, I guess, and prone to mistakes, hubris, and bad judgment. I'm trying to remember that today. See, I'm leaving right now to see my own dad. It's a long story how this all came about. I'll spare you the boring details. Let's just say I'm not the sweet, kind person you think I am. You shouldn't be in any hurry to get back to me.

I totally get that you need to be with your family right now. Seriously, everything is fine with me. Don't worry about not writing me. I'm glad you've reconnected with your brothers and sisters. I've always been sad I didn't have any siblings. And if you decide your place is with them and that you want to rejoin the Amish community, which it sounds like you do, I understand that, too. Well, maybe "understand" is the wrong word. But I'm fine with it. I actually think it's probably better that I not be dating someone right now. I'm glad to have had the time together that we did.

Sorry.

Take care,

Sam

PS Please give all the kittens to Katie if she wants them.

I pushed "send" without editing the letter, which is very unlike me. I guess I was afraid that reading it would make me cry. Or that I'd chicken out about sending it. I felt like I needed to let Zach go. I knew he'd be so much better off without me.

Ninety-seven percent of me truly believed I'd probably never see or hear from him again.

CHAPTER FORTY-SEVEN

From my dad, I'd expected self-pity: "I was depressed after the divorce, so it's not my fault" stuff. Or blame: "Your mom treated me so horribly, I couldn't stand to see her, so she's at fault here," and that kind of thing. Or excuses like, "I kept meaning to call every week, but my move and my new job kept me too busy…" I didn't expect the things my dad actually said.

When I walked into the restaurant, the hostess pointed me to the back room and said my "party" was waiting for me. Yeah, this was going to be some party, all right. I saw my dad right away. His hair was shorter and greyer, and his beard was gone. The skin on his face seemed saggier, but his light blue eyes were still bright. Maybe brighter than usual, because they were filled with tears. When he saw me, his mouth hung slack. I tentatively walked to the table. I noticed there weren't any other people in this room, but there were three other tables of people seated in the front room. Maybe Mr. Evans had asked for privacy or rented out this room just for us?

My dad stood. Nobody seemed to know who should be the first to speak.

Finally, he decided to cowboy up. "Oh my god. You've grown up so much, Sammy." He rubbed his jawline hard. "I screwed up so badly. I'm so, so sorry,"

I eyed the empty seat they'd saved for me. He was seated to the right of the chair, Bria was on the left, and Mr. Evans was across from me. I didn't know what to reply, so I just nodded.

"I wouldn't blame you if you couldn't ever forgive me, but I love you and regret not seeing you." He started crying. I did, too. "Can I, would it be ok… to hug you?" My dad looked from me to Mr. Evans nervously, and then his eyes darted to Bria and back to me.

I nodded again. He put his arms around me. He smelled the same as I'd remembered, like freshly cut grass. I could only take being close to him for three seconds before I pushed him away.

"I don't want to hug anymore," I whispered.

"Of course." He sank into his chair and took a breath.

"Hey, Sam," Mr. Evans said, "nice to see you. Let's get you a drink. What do you want? Soda? Milk? Tea?" Bria stood up and put her arms around me and then gently guided me to my seat. She continued to hold my hand.

"You have every right to your feelings, Sam, and if you want to end this at any time, that's ok. You're in charge." I expected a follow-up of "But just try to hear him out" or "Don't be so mean." But nobody said anything like that, and I was relieved. I possessed the power here.

"Coke in a bottle," I told Mr. Evans. He got up and walked over to tell the waitress. I gathered they'd all already ordered drinks. My dad couldn't take his eyes off of me, like I was a damn Frankenstein's monster or something. I stared back at him until he dropped his eyes.

"I get that you didn't want to be around Mom after the divorce, but why didn't you even call me or write me or anything?" I figured we might as well cut to the chase.

"I did, Sam." My dad quietly reached into a battered light brown briefcase and brought out three yellow and white composition books. "I just never sent any of them. But not a day has gone by that I didn't think about you and write to you." He laid the notebooks on the table.

"Why the heck didn't you send them, then? What good did it do to write me but not send the letters?" I tried to turn the notebooks to ashes with my glower. Then Mr. Evans returned and smiled at me before sitting down.

"I don't want to make excuses." My father seemed to be choosing his words carefully, but he'd never been a fast talker; I remembered he stuttered a little sometimes. "But I do want to try to explain some things to you, if you want." Mr. Evans nodded. I had a feeling they'd had quite a long phone conversation before my father had left Baltimore this morning.

Just then the waitress appeared with our drinks and to take our orders. She set a cup of warm tea in from of Bria, ice tea in front of Mr. Evans, and then two identical bottles of Coke in front of both my dad and me. Awkward. I'd forgotten we shared a love of Coke in bottles. My mom only ever kept Diet Coke in the house.

We all ordered sandwiches. I got my usual, the Peace Lily with veggies and melted swiss on crisp French bread. My dad got a vegetarian portobello sandwich, the Bird of Paradise, my second fave. The waitress left us again.

"I've been seeing a therapist for the past three months, and I understand a little more about why I've made such bad choices regarding you. None of it is your fault."

"Duh, like I didn't know that already. Now how about cutting some of the psychobabble?" *Wow. Did I just say that?*

"Sam?" Bria cocked her head at me and squeezed my hand. But her tone wasn't so much a "Give him this opportunity" as an "Are you ok?" one. That kindness affected me much more than a reprimand would have.

"Sorry," I mumbled.

"You have nothing to be sorry about," my dad said firmly. "You have every right to hate me. I'm just lucky you're giving me a chance to talk to you." He looked down at his napkin like he was hoping it would come to life and tell him what to say. "When I was growing up, my parents travelled a lot. You never knew them, because they both passed away when you were little, but truthfully, I never knew them that well myself. They just weren't interested in me. I was always aware I was an inconvenience to them. So... I swore when I had a kid, I'd never make him or her feel that way."

I couldn't help but to snort. He smiled ruefully. "I can see you've still got a great sense of irony." Bria and Mr. Evans both laughed a little.

"But in some ways, though, I made all new parenting mistakes," my dad continued. "When I went away to college on a full scholarship, my parents and I rarely spoke. I loved college, the classes, the friends I made and the sense of possibility. But the best thing was meeting your mom. My gosh, she was gorgeous. And witty. And so different from any other girl I'd ever known. I fell head over heels in love with her. We married right after college." He twisted his unused straw a bit and then continued.

"Unfortunately, I wasn't very mature. I was bad with money. I got your mom and me into a lot of debt, and she was always borrowing from her parents. They started to hate me, and I can't blame them." He took a long pull straight from the Coke bottle, ignoring the glass with ice next to it. "They told your mom she had to choose between them and me. She was two months pregnant at the time, and they didn't know. She chose me. I think because she was pregnant. I hated that I was weak and I let her make that choice. I don't know for sure, but I think that's when her resentment of me started."

I looked deep into my Coke bottle. I knew bits and pieces of that time period from my mom's point of view, but she was always so derisive about the relationship. It was weird to think of my parents so in love. I certainly never remembered that. Sure, my dad's story with his parents was sad and all, but I couldn't see how it justified him leaving me. It seems like if anything, he'd never want to hurt me.

"Sam, I'm sure this is hard to understand, and you're probably more confused than before," my dad said.

"Whatever." I shrugged. I didn't like having my mind read. It was my turn to take a long swig of my Coke. The waitress brought our food, which broke up the silence a bit. I noticed I couldn't smell my melted cheese, even though I subtly sniffed the air, trying to.

When she left, my dad leapt in.

"After you were born, I tried to be better with money, but I loved to buy you cool toys, and your mom loved to buy you expensive clothes. And I only had a part-time teaching job and wasn't very motivated to work full-time because I hated the idea of not spending time with you." My dad started playing with his fork as he talked.

"So when you started going to preschool, your mom went back to school for her real estate license. She was a natural. A real people person. But I think her success in her career just made her more bitter about my lack of ambition." As I listened to him, I picked all of the tomatoes out of my sandwich, even though I liked tomatoes.

"We started fighting, and she'd belittle me a lot. I think it felt familiar, like how my mom treated me, so I just dealt with it. The devil you know is... well, comfortable in a twisted way. And I couldn't stand the thought of divorce and being separated from you."

"That sounds NUTS. Do you KNOW how nuts that sounds to me?" I asked, my voice rising to almost a scream. Then I noticed the waitress, standing a little behind me and off to the right, who had probably just come by to ask us how we were enjoying our food. She had frozen and was looking at me with her eyes wide. My face flushed, and I grabbed my phone out my front pocket to distract myself.

You've got to be freaking kidding me! There was a text message from Madison:

Sam, I'm so, so sorry. Can you text me back? Can we please talk soon? I miss you.

Seriously, how much more drama could I take?

CHAPTER FORTY-EIGHT

I decided Madison must have the worst text timing of anyone in the world. But I needed a break from all this drama with my dad, so I excused myself from the table to go to the bathroom. I noticed the quick glance Mr. Evans gave Bria. She offered to come with me to the bathroom, but I declined. My dad's lips looked chapped, and he seemed pale, like he was an acrophobic standing on the precipice of the Grand Canyon.

When I got to the bathroom, I shut myself in a stall and looked at Madison's text again. The last time I'd ignored a text from her, my life had certainly taken a turn for the worse, to put it mildly. But was fear a good reason to text her back? I was still so mad at her.

But truth be told, I missed her, too.

But a small hurt voice inside of me asked, *How can I trust this text? What if Hillary is sitting right next to Madison, and the two of them are laughing at me?*

And with everything going on with my dad at this point, I didn't want to completely short-circuit myself by entering into this territory. I didn't want to get my hopes up or give Madison any other details she could use against me so I just texted back: I miss you, too. We have a lot to talk about, but I can't right now. I'll call you tomorrow.

Within forty-five seconds of sending it, I got back a reply to my message: Of course. I suck as a friend. Sorry. Anything you want.

I was a little overwhelmed by all these apologies today. Was I a horrible person for not accepting them? How do words make pain go away, though?

I left the "bathroom/frying pan" and jumped back into the "lunch meeting/fire" with my dad. When I got back to the table, it didn't look like anyone had eaten much of their sandwiches. I knew for a fact that this ignoring of our food wasn't because the sandwiches weren't delicious. I got them here a lot on the weekends when my mom was in Philly.

At least my dad didn't have Cry Face anymore.

"Sam, do you want to stop talking about this stuff, change the subject for a while?" Mr. Evans asked.

"Maybe you've hit your limit for today?" Bria added.

What else would we talk about? My shoplifting? That stupid Facebook page?

"No, I'm fine," I told Mr. Evans. I turned to Bria, "I just got a text from Madison, who says she wants to make up but I'm not sure if I believe her."

"Well, that's freaky deaky, huh?" Bria hooted. I couldn't help but to smile at her. I took a diminutive bite of my sandwich.

"Yeah… anyway, I told her we'd talk later." I turned to my dad. "Now, where were we? I think you were explaining how you left me because your parents left you?"

"Yeah, I can see how that seems ridiculous." He put down the dill spear he was holding but hadn't taken a bite of yet. "But I didn't think of it that way at the time. I swear, I thought by leaving you with your mom, I'd be doing you a favour. I hated myself so much for not being a good enough husband, for driving your mom away, for messing up all of our lives. I thought going away would be the kindest thing I could do for you. It would be, as my grandmother would've said, a mitzvah, a blessing for you."

I didn't know what to say. I ate another bite of my sandwich, chewing it twenty times more than it needed to be chewed. I remembered the email I'd just sent Zach this morning. I'd written almost the exact same thing to him. And I truly believed when I was writing it that I was doing the noble thing by letting him go. And by giving the kittens to someone else to raise. Because I was sure he and the kittens would be better off without me. Then I thought of something he'd written to me, that forgiving his father was important for him to have peace. Maybe forgiving my father would give me some kind of peace.

"Yeah." I nodded. "I get what you're saying, I think. Mom isn't super-encouraging to me sometimes, either." I pushed a piece of hair back behind my ear.

"Oh, Sam. I never thought she'd..." My dad looked confused. "When you were younger, she was so proud of you, you were the apple of her eye. I guess I just thought... I had no idea you guys weren't getting along..." Uh-oh, now his Cry Face was back.

"Probably because she had you to fight with back then, she didn't need to go after me. But now that you're gone..." I saw the hurt register from the knife I'd just twisted in his solar plexus. *Good.* "Look, it's nothing that bad. Nothing I can't handle most of the time." I said. *Apple of her eye?* That was interesting. I'd always thought I was a big disappointment.

"I think trying to handle everything by yourself is what's stressing you out, Sam," Bria said softly.

"Hey, look, I give it right back to her most of the time. Trust me, I'm no angel." I hated them thinking I was some sort of weak victim.

"We need to figure out how you two can communicate in a better way," Mr. Evans said. "We can talk about some ways to deal with this. Maybe talk with your mom, too."

"No." I wasn't budging on that. I pushed my plate away, even though I had a lot of my sandwich left on it.

"Well, there are obviously some more issues we need to talk about," Mr. Evans said softly. "The stealing and cyberbullying, but we can save them for another time."

"Right on, we can." Bria smiled at her husband. "Sometimes the light's all shining on me, other times... not so much." Mr. Evans smiled at her the way two people do when they know each other well and still like each other. It was sweet.

I looked at my dad to see his reaction to all this. He didn't seem surprised about the shoplifting or the bullying comments that had just been made, like he had been when I said what I did about my mom. I surmised he must have also been briefed on those two things before he came.

"Here's something funny," I said. "You spent money you didn't have," I smiled at my dad, "but I did you one better. I just stole what I wanted without worrying about the silly money part at all." This was my version of an olive branch to him.

"Ah, a chip off the old block." My dad smiled back, accepting my offering. I tentatively stood and then walked a step over to him. He stood and we hugged each other tightly. We both cried. This time the hug lasted for longer than two seconds.

CHAPTER FORTY-NINE

Driving home, I had so much to try to work through in my head. Luckily, some of my calmest realizations came when I was driving.

I knew it wasn't all better with my dad after this one lunch meeting. He wasn't the hero I thought he was when I was a kid. I'd built him more of a sky-high monolith than a pedestal, so watching him fall from it was pretty traumatic. But I couldn't help but to feel hopeful. I reminded myself of my:

Top 10 Favourite Dad Memories

1) How he and I used to run up and down the museum steps pretending to be Rocky.

2) When I first started getting into fashion but we didn't have much money and he'd spend hours with me looking in the store windows at the King of Prussia mall, commenting on clothes, even though all he ever wore was a T-shirt and jeans.

3) Volunteering at the animal shelter with me because my mom didn't like pets.

4) When he, Mom, and I went on picnics in the Philadelphia Zoo when I was little.

5) Drinking chocolate egg creams at Charlie's on South Street.

6) Showing me *Nightmare on Elm Street* on DVD when I was twelve, even though it gave me nightmares for weeks.

7) How he told me it was fine and that "everyone does it at least once" when I puked all over the inside of his car when he came to school to pick me up when I had the flu.

8) Solving my first geometry proofs at the kitchen table in seventh grade with him giving me hints.

9) Our overnight trip to Rehoboth Beach, Delaware, for me to see the ocean for the first time. We couldn't afford a hotel room, so he made a bed for me in the back seat and stayed up all night guarding me.

10) When I was a kid, before the fights started, how he used to look at my mom when he rubbed her shoulders when she was tense. Yes, at the time I thought it was dopey, but in retrospect, I realized it was sweet.

Sure, I could give him another chance. He'd messed up to an exponential degree. Epic Fail didn't even begin to describe it. Colossal Catastrophe, maybe? But I was no stranger to fiascos myself. I'd take it slowly, but I decided I did want to try again with him.

Deciding what to do about Madison's texts wasn't so easy. But before I could begin to think about that, another surprise awaited me.

CHAPTER FIFTY

Zach on my front doorstep when I got home was the last thing I'd expected.

Which is precisely why I shouldn't have been surprised at all by this development. Mercury was probably in retrograde or something. This day was craziness to the nth degree.

After seeing my dad and listening to his whole "I thought you'd be better off without me" spiel, I'd realized that the apple really didn't fall far from the tree. I think we both pushed people away, thinking we weren't worthy and trying to protect ourselves. We'd ended the lunch after our hug. I still had a mostly uneaten sandwich wrapped to go in my purse. My dad was staying overnight in Philly with friends, but we planned to get together to talk more tomorrow, just the two of us.

When I got home, I'd been planning to go right up to my room to send Zach a new email telling him how stupid I'd been and explaining that I didn't actually mean what I'd written in the last one—that the part about not wanting to date anyone right now wasn't true at all. I figured because he had such a limited access to computers and his email right now, I might be lucky. He'd get the first one and this new one back-to-back, so the first wouldn't make such a big impact. But of course, fortune didn't favour my folly, and he obviously happened to be at a library today when I'd sent my last maudlin missive. So here he was, and I had no idea what he was going to say.

"Wow, hi, I, um..." I started, looking at him and trying to read his body language, which made me flash on what it must feel like to confront a yeti, unsure if it was of the bashful or the rampaging variety. Except, thankfully, Zach wasn't anywhere near as hairy as a Sasquatch.

"Sam, I'm so sorry. I feel horrible." He had a too-small-for-him maroon jacket on that I'd never seen, and his hair had been recently cut pretty short. *God, he looks so much more Amish now.* It was endearing but also a little scary. I wondered if I should take this as proof he was going back? But I shook the thought away and concentrated on his clear hazel eyes that were the same as they'd always been.

"No, my gosh, I'm the one who should be apologizing." I glanced off to my right, hoping I'd find the right words to express that I knew what a total tool I'd been. "Look, your dad just died. And I'm so sorry about that. And here I am, a big needy baby, pouting because you're not dropping everything for me. I've been seriously selfish." I wasn't sure if I should hug him or not at this point, so I took two steps forward but then just stopped, hovering.

"Not at all. I think I gave you the wrong impression." He dropped his chin and broke eye contact with me.

OMG. Here it comes. He's going to explain how he never meant to lead me on and that I expected too much from him. That he needs more time with the Amish to see if he wants to go back for good.

"I'm not going back to the Amish community. Ever. That is over for me. I am sure of that," he said slowly, emphatically. "But I would like to be able to visit my family. And after this time with them, I'm pretty hopeful I will be able to. But my life is now here. In the outside world. I want to learn and to travel and to have a different kind of life."

I thought, *Oh, he's not going back to being Amish, but he is dumping me. Why would he want to be limited by me?*

"Sure, I understand..." I fiddled with my purse and fought the tears that threatened to overflow from my eyes. "Why would you want to stay in Lancaster when you've been here all your life?"

"Oh, no Sam, I am making a mess of this! That's not what I mean." Zach reached back and massaged the top of his trapezius muscle under his left ear. "I'm staying in this area. At least for a while. And if you want to keep dating, I sure do, too!"

"Oh," I said, always the font of wit and eloquence.

"Sam, I just need you to know, I decided all this that I was leaving my Amish life before I met you. You are not responsible in any way for my decision. There's no pressure on you that I'm making a change or sacrifice for you, ok?" He reached over to me and touched my arm.

It was like he'd just been sitting with me at lunch hearing my dad's story. I couldn't help but to think of my mom sacrificing her ties with her family for my dad, and how Zach was trying to make sure I knew he'd never resent me, like she had with my dad. How was Zach so wise about all of this? But still, a small part of me wished he were making this choice not to be Amish all for me. That it was my love that changed him. *How screwed up is that?!!* My hubris was remarkably immature.

"Thanks for telling me that." I smiled. "And you should know, that stuff I wrote about not wanting to date you anymore. that wasn't true at all. I'm sorry. It's been a weird couple of days."

"Well, that's a relief." He grinned his big lopsided Zach grin that I'd grown to love so much. "Because Sam, I have feelings for you that I've never had for anyone ever before. I've dated some girls but nobody special like you." He took my hand. "I think… no, I know, I'm falling in love with you."

My heart felt like it had grown too large for my chest, but it wasn't an uncomfortable feeling at all. It was the best feeling in the world. I dropped my purse and threw my arms around his neck and held him close. "I love you, too!" I exclaimed. He started to kiss me.

At that moment, a brand-new gold Jaguar pulled into the driveway. And my mother stepped out of it.

CHAPTER FIFTY-ONE

"Well, Sam, introduce me to your new friend!" my mom said, getting out of her car. The way she emphasized "friend" like she was "in the know" about Zach irritated me. The way her eyes travelled up and down Zach, appraising him, irritated me. The way her lip twitched slightly when he eyes settled on his ill-fitting coat irritated me. That she'd obviously just bought a new car irritated me. The fact she was home when I hadn't been expecting her irritated me. To be brutally honest, I had to admit almost everything about the woman in this moment irritated me. But I didn't know what to do about it.

"Mom, this is Zach. Zach, my mom," I said.

Zach stretched his arm out to shake her hand. "Nice to meet you, Miss Stonesong."

"What nice manners you have! That's unusual in this day and age!" My mom tilted her head, smiled, took Zach's hand and shook it. "I go by my maiden name now, Larreby, but you can just call me by my first name, Lindsey."

"What are you doing home?" I demanded.

"Nice to see you, too, Samantha." My mom sighed. "I spent the morning car-shopping because I didn't have any appointments. I didn't plan on buying anything, but the sales guy offered me such a great deal, I ended up trading in the Lexus for this Jag. Isn't she gorgeous? Do you like cars, Zach?"

"Yes," Zach replied. "But I don't know much about them."

"I thought all boys your age were into cars." My mom betrayed her annoyance with a slight edge in her voice as she found the special side pocket of her purse in which she liked to keep her keys and deposited them there.

"I'm a little different that way, I guess." Zach raised an eyebrow at me slightly, and I suppressed a laugh.

"Well, I didn't want to park the Jag in Philly and get it all scratched, so I thought I'd bring it home and take the Volvo back in."

"So you'll let me drive this one now on the weekends?" Sarcasm was always my "go-to" with my mom.

"You can if you absolutely need to this weekend. But your new car will be here next weekend." My mom smiled. "Kind of ruins your Christmas surprise, but I bet you don't mind. I picked it out for you about a month ago. You'll need your own car when you go away to college in a year and a half anyway."

I was embarrassed. Here Zach was trying to save up enough to buy his first computer, and now we'd have three cars. "Well, I don't know if I'll need a car in New York City—you probably don't remember my first choice is Columbia," I snapped at her. Then caught Zach's eye. He looked a little confused. I realized how ungrateful I must sound. "But thanks, Mom. Really." I felt like I should say something more but didn't know what.

"It's a Prius, so you'll get great gas mileage." She seemed excited by my appreciation, which made me feel even worse. Maybe not all my fights with my mom were her fault. How many times had she meant something to be nice, and I slammed her for it? "I know you're all into stopping global warming and stuff, so you'd like that it's fuel-efficient. And it's a pretty shade of teal, too." My mom turned to Zach. "Are you concerned about the environment, too, Zach?"

"Yes, ma'am. Preserving the ecosystem is very important to me. I love the outdoors," Zach responded. I half-wished he'd point out to my mom how much more fuel-efficient horses and buggies were, just to see her face.

"So what are you kids up to today? What's the fun plan?" My mom looked from me to Zach and back again. When neither of us answered, she said, "Look, just so you know, it's fine with me if Zach stayed here last night. Or if he wants to stay over with you tonight." *Good Lord. She did not just say that. Kill me now.*

Just when I think we've found some common ground...

I had to do something to stop this line of conversation, so I just blurted out the first non sequitur that popped into my mind. "I just saw Dad. We had lunch." It worked! My mom was visibly put off her game. She ran her left pointer finger over the bridge of her nose to try to regain her composure.

"Oh. Ok. Wow. Now there's something I didn't expect," she said then exhaled loudly.

"Should I... uh... leave you alone?" Zach stuttered. "Maybe take a walk or something?" All I could think of was that word Bria had used: crap-sticks.

"No! Please don't!" I gave him a look that I hoped communicated *I need you! Don't leave.*

"No, Zach, Sam's right. You shouldn't go. I think I'm the one who should go. Um... you obviously didn't expect me to be barging in on your weekend plans, and I need to get back to the city, anyway. I have a big showing late this afternoon, a luxury condo on South Street..." My mom fumbled with her coat, trying to tie the sash tighter around herself. She looked so sad, so lost. I couldn't ever remember seeing her like this before. So vulnerable.

"Mom, I would have told you before, but honestly, it all happened so quickly. This morning, actually. I..."

"Sam." She grabbed my hand between hers. Hers felt frail. "It's fine. I just... I just don't want you to be hurt by him again. Be careful, ok? He's fickle and... oh, well, um, it's none of my business. You do what you want. I'm not mad at you, ok. I guess... I just want you to take care." She took her hands back and rummaged in her purse until her hand connected with her keys. I had a epiphany. Maybe she was so "hands-off" with me because she was trying not to be controlling, like her parents had been with her.

"It was nice to meet you, Zach. Sorry it was so short. But you seem great, and I'm happy for you and Sam." My mom nodded a few times at

Zach. "She's a special girl. And boys her age, well, they're kind of idiots for the most part, so it doesn't surprise me it took a different kind of guy like you to appreciate her." My mom opened the garage door by remote and walked over to the Volvo. She got in and was backing it out when she stopped. She rolled the window down and tossed me the new car keys. Of course, I fumbled the catch and they landed at my feet.

"Remember, for emergencies only, ok? Just until you get your car in a few days," she said, seeming to be back to her old self.

"Thanks," I said, dumbfounded by everything that had just happened with her. *She'd been kind to Zach? I was "special?"*

"No problem. And kids, don't do anything I wouldn't do, which leaves you pretty open!" She leaned out and wiggled her eyebrows provocatively at us before backing out of the driveway way too fast, burning a little rubber as she did. At least my mom was back to her usual behaviour: predictably exasperating.

I couldn't help but be impressed that my mom saw that Zach was "different," but what would she think when she found out he was raised Amish? Would she be so approving of us then, or would that be too peculiar? Would I fail to meet her expectations, once again?

CHAPTER FIFTY-TWO

After my mom left, I asked Zach if he wanted to come inside for a little while. I knew my nose was probably turning red from the cold—not my best look.

"I need to get back," he said. "But can I take you out Tuesday? I mean, I know it's a school night, but just for dinner?"

"Yeah, that would be nice." I was wondering if maybe I'd hallucinated the whole "I love you" thing that had happened before my mom interrupted us.

"Great, I can come here to meet you or..."

"Let's meet at the restaurant we went to on our first date." I couldn't help it. I didn't want to chance another meeting between my mom and Zach. It wouldn't take her long to figure out there was something *really* different about Zach, and I had more than enough on my plate right now.

"Ok, good idea," Zach said. "I love my mom's cooking, but I haven't had any Italian in weeks."

"Yeah, well, at least your mom cooks," I teased.

"But your mom works, which is impressive. She seems very intelligent, like you," Zach said. I had no idea how to respond to this. Normally I'd make some snide remark about my mom not wanting to be a *real* mom. But I wasn't feeling that way after our most recent run-in. My world was flipping upside down, and I was motion-sick.

"Maybe after dinner we can go back to my apartment. You won't believe how big the kittens have gotten. They are quite a handful now!"

"You still have them? I mean, I thought Katie..."

"She still wants to take whichever ones she can. And I think my six-year-old cousin wants one too..."

"Zach, I'd love to see them again, but you know which one I want you to keep? The mom, Darla. Sometimes people get so into the cute babies, I think they don't appreciate how hard the mom works." *Was that me sticking up for the mom? Maybe I was beginning to understand how hard that particular job was.*

"I love that idea. But I think I should keep two. Just so they don't get lonely." He smiled. "So you still need to pick one kitten, too."

"Okay, deal! Can I give you a ride back to your family's farm?" I asked. Zach laughed.

"Oh, I don't think my mother is ready for that yet, me stepping out of my girlfriend's car." *Zach just called me his "girlfriend!"* I suppressed an urge to giggle, jump up and down, and clap my hands like a goofball.

"Oh, right, of course." I was smiling so hard, I thought my face would split.

"I'll see you Tuesday." Zach leaned forward and kissed me on my lips. But it wasn't one of the long kisses. This was a short one. Too short. I wanted more, but instead he said, "I missed your beautiful face so much." *Well, it wasn't a kiss, but that was nice, too.*

"Yeah, me too. I mean your face, or um, you. Well, you and your face," I stuttered, smooth as usual.

"I kept thinking of an Amish proverb when I was away from you, 'A happy memory never wears out.'" His eyes had the best crinkles at their corners when he smiled. "Bye, Sam."

He was drop dead gorgeous. And sweet. And he was MY BOYFRIEND.

"Bye, Zach." I watched him walk down the street with his long strides. I figured he must be taking the public bus back, since he was walking toward a stop near my house. When he reached to corner to turn, he looked back at me and waved again. I waved, too, then allowed myself to just be still and feel the happiness that filled me from head to toe in warmth, like I was basking in the sun on a beach in Maui, not standing on the street on a chilly November day in Lancaster, PA.

CHAPTER FIFTY-THREE

Saturday afternoon, I tried to concentrate on my Physics homework. We had a big test coming up, and the last few weeks I hadn't been paying attention very well. The first lessons in September involved applying the formulas for vectors, motion, momentum, etc. Doing them was calming. Formulas lacked ambiguity.

But our most recent chapter on philosophy and quantum mechanics made my head ache. It was all about abstract concepts and probability. I agreed with the famous scientist Richard Feynman, who said that quantum mechanics was impossible to understand. So why was I even trying? How could "all possibilities" be simultaneously occurring? From my experience, you made a choice, and that decision yielded an effect. And there were no do-overs. Sure, sometimes the result to an action wasn't what you hypothesized it would be, both for the good and the bad. While complete do-overs weren't possible, I was learning second chances were. But parallel universes? Places where I might have gone to jail for shoplifting? Places where my mom and dad stayed together? Places where Zach had stayed Amish and we'd never met? Places where Madison hadn't betrayed me to Hillary? Places where Madison and I had never become friends in the first place? Considering every potential was too esoteric.

I knew I was getting distracted and that I needed to call Madison if I was ever going to get any work done. But before I did, I thought about the idea of giving her a second chance. I'd just given one to my dad. Zach had just given one to me. But how many second chances could my universe accommodate before my energy became unstable, gravitationally unbound, and a Big Rip occurred, destroying all matter?

So, I made a list.

Ten Things I Love About Madison

1. Her loud, deep belly laugh when we watched our shows like *Riverdale* and *Veronica Mars* together.

2. Her shrieks when we watched horror films together. That girl had some pipes on her and a hair-trigger response that set off her yelps.

3. She got so excited when she saw Chihuahuas with bows around their little necks. Her mom didn't like pets, just like mine, and she so desperately wanted a fancy little Chihuahua.

4. How when I was stressed about schoolwork, she'd cross her eyes and tell me that I studied too much and my brain would explode if I wasn't careful. Then she'd mime her head blowing up with her hands.

5. Her playfulness. I thought of that sweltering afternoon last summer at the water park area of Hershey Park, frolicking like little kids. We'd gone down all the slides multiple times and had a massive splash battle in the water gun area.

6. Looking at fashion magazines with her in her basement. We'd play a game that involved opening to a page and trying to be the first to slap the picture of the outfit we liked best. Often we'd end up smacking one other's hands and laughing hysterically.

7. She helped me get over stress from my mom. Once I confessed to Madison that my mom wanted to make an appointment for me with her "girl" to get my eyebrows waxed because I looked like an angry South Philly grocer and Madison smiled darkly. Then she took me in the bathroom and used an eyeliner pencil to make my eyebrows darker and thicker, with a Frida Kahlo unibrow. We laughed hysterically. Later, after ice cream, she showed me how to pluck them if I wanted.

8. Her giving me the last piece of gum like it was nothing.

9. Singing Adele songs with her in the car, loudly and off-key.

10. How she believed in me. How she thought I could pull off Plan P, or anything, once I set my mind to it.

I could easily make a list of another 50 things I loved and missed about Madison. So I knew I had to at least give her a chance to explain why she did what she did to me. I texted her.

You want to talk? We can.

She was typing her response within a second.

Yes!!! Now???

I needed a bit of a break. At least a day to mentally prepare.

Tomorrow afternoon?

OK.

After we worked out the details, I slipped in a DVD of old *Twilight Zone* episodes and let myself be transported to parallel universes.

CHAPTER FIFTY-FOUR

"I can understand why you'd never be able to trust me again. I'm a giant twonk." Madison shifted from one foot to the other and wrapped her thin, colour-blocked trench coat tighter around her. She looked like she'd lost a few pounds that she shouldn't have, giving her the effect of a waif from a Dickens novel. The dark circles under her eyes and her pale lips weren't helping to dispel this impression.

We'd decided to meet out in front of the school under "the Sherpa tree" Sunday afternoon. It was sunny but chilly; if the temperature dropped a few more degrees, we could have snow.

This had already been one bizarre weekend. I'd shoplifted, been caught but not sent to juvie, and made a new hippie lady friend named Bria. My father and I reunited after a couple of years, getting together not once but twice and had plans to meet again next weekend. Zach had told me he loved me and had reassured me he wasn't going back to being Amish. And my mom had actually made me feel a little sorry for her.

Now here Madison stood, apologizing for the hell weeks she'd just put me through.

"Yeah, I don't trust you right now." I was glad we were meeting outside, even though it was cold. The fresh air helped me think clearly. She'd suggested talking at The House of Pizza, but I thought of that place as mine and Zach's now, not mine and hers. Also, I didn't like having these encounters in restaurants and having the pressure to eat during them, because I realized the whole confrontation thing made me queasy. Though

I did wish Madison would stop shivering so much. And she did look like she needed to eat a sandwich or something.

"I told Hillary about you and Zach when I was totally high on Molly." She hung her chin to her chest. "It was after school the Monday that we fought. I know that doesn't make it right, but it's the truth. I'm sorry. I'm just glad I didn't tell her about the whole Plan P thing. But then when she used the info to make that Facebook page, I felt so guilty. I didn't think you'd ever be able to forgive me." She rubbed her hands together and looked off in the distance, away from the school. "So I threw myself back into my friendship with her. That was mistake #2. I just didn't want to be alone, and I figured you'd be fine because you were all lovey-dovey with that Amish dude…"

"His name is Zach," I interrupted curtly.

"Yeah, sorry, right. Anyways, then I started drinking and drugging more. Mistake #3. So that's why I wouldn't talk to you. Most of the time I was loaded, even in school." She scratched behind her left ear. I was shocked. I didn't think Madison had ever done that before, come to school messed up. But I tried not to let my surprise or concern show.

"That doesn't explain why you wouldn't give me a chance to explain the Monday after our fight. I'm pretty sure you were sober that day. I tried three times." I refused to forgive her. She didn't deserve it, no matter what she said.

"I know." Madison sighed. "Bad on me. I have no excuse other than I felt so betrayed by you. When the chips were down and I needed you, you weren't there for me." She wiped the back of her hand over her right eye. Was she pushing away a tear?

"Ok, I'll bite. That Sunday I didn't call you back. What was that phone call about?"

Madison bit her lip. "Sam, I thought I was pregnant. I was sure of it… even though I'm on the pill… because I haven't been so great about taking it every day. Anyway, I had no idea what to do. I mean, there were a couple of guys it could have been, but I don't like any of them. I wanted you to go to the store for me to buy a pregnancy test. I was too scared and embarrassed to do it myself, and you're so brave about things like that."

"Oh no. Oh, Madison, I had no idea." I thought of how I'd jokingly called her a slut then disregarded her call when she needed me so badly. *And she thought of me as brave?* "Oh, I'm so sorry." I started crying.

"Hey, it's not your fault. I realize now you had no idea. And I would have eventually gotten that and would've forgiven you, but when I got together with Hillary after we fought at school, she could tell I was all butt-hurt about something. I told her I was mad at you. She used that and got into my head."

"Did she go with you to get the test, then?" I asked quietly.

"No. I didn't tell her what I'd been calling you about in the first place. And she didn't ask. It's weird, she was so focused on you and getting me to give up dirt on you. Jesus, Sam, and I was feeling so lonely." Madison sank to the ground, her back against the tree. I got down and sat on the ground with her. "And truthfully, I didn't trust her to tell her about me and my situation. And yeah, I know how wrong that sounds. Like I'd tell her your secrets but not mine."

"Kind of…" I said, peeling some bark off near the base of the tree.

"Anyway, she was holding, so she gave me what she had, the Molly, and when I started feeling the effects, she played me. She told me how *she'd* always had my back and that you'd come between us and just had used me to get popular. And that she missed our friendship and hated you for taking me away. I just… I was stupid. I told her that it didn't matter now because you didn't have time for me anymore because of Zach. And I also kinda hated Zach. I mean, that's what I was feeling. I was jealous."

I thought of the number of times I'd felt jealous of Madison's friendship with Hillary.

"So then she asked you questions about Zach, and the Amish thing came up?" I peeled some more bark off the tree.

Madison nodded, almost imperceptibly, eyes still cast down. "Yeah. I didn't mean to go and tell her any of the things you told me; it just came out. As soon as it did, a part of me knew I'd made a boneheaded mistake, because Hillary got so excited, so happy. But another part, the one riding the high of Molly, well, that part was happy I'd made Hillary happy, and so

I just kept talking. I'm so, so sorry." Big tears were falling off her face onto the hard, almost frozen ground.

"Well, at least you didn't tell her about my problem with shoplifting stuff. I am glad about that." I paused. "You didn't, right?"

"Oh Sam, no! If I had I'd never be able to forgive myself." Madison looked horrified. "I guess in my mind at the time, I figured you'd be done with Zach soon anyway. I mean, I've never had a boyfriend for more than a month or so. And then the whole thing would blow over. But it just seemed to get worse."

I wanted to put my arms around Madison, tell her it was ok, but I couldn't. I was exhausted. "I want to forgive you. I do. But I can't make any promises." I pulled myself up slowly.

"I understand." Madison looked so small, curled up under the tree.

"Madison, did you… end up getting a pregnancy test or going to the clinic?" I asked. She looked up, finally making eye contact with me.

"Oh, Sam, that's one of the stupidest parts. It was a false alarm. I got my period a couple of days later."

I took a breath. "Well, I'm glad about that. But Madison… and I don't want to upset you. I'm not judging you, but you've gotta lay off the drugs and booze. We need to get you some help."

"We?" Her voice cracked a bit.

"Yes. We." I extended my hand and helped her up.

CHAPTER FIFTY-FIVE

Monday in school, my first encounter with Hillary, if you can call a nasty look an encounter, was in the hallway, navigating the crush, going from my first-period math class to my second-period history class. Our student body had recently been admonished not to take a shortcut through the library between classes, so I was using a new route. When I almost ran smack into Hillary, I think our faces must have been mirror images of one another's, registering surprise and confusion. But after that initial reaction, when I tried to feign detachment, she went from flustered to red-hot angry, her eyes cutting into me as if she could psychically perform Lingchi on me. Then she turned abruptly and walked off in the opposite direction. Was it because she and her parents had been contacted by the school about taking down that fake Facebook page about me? I wasn't sure how that whole thing had been handled or if she'd been reprimanded in some way.

Note to self: Find out about that from Mr. Evans!

The second time we saw each other was in the cafeteria. I braced myself for this one, knowing I'd have to walk by her table as I entered the seating area. What I hadn't been expecting was Madison waiting for me when I exited the food line.

"So where do you want to sit?" Madison smiled at me. "How about over by the window? It's sunny today, and the sunlight always puts me in a good mood. Also, natural light is more flattering, right?" The Sherpas' table was in the dead centre, not near the window.

"Um, sure, I'm good with that." I smiled back at her shyly like it was the 1950s and she'd just invited me to the prom or something.

We walked together, trays defiantly out a few inches from our bodies, heads held high. Hillary fixed her eyes on us like a cat watching mice. It was impossible not to notice the subtle hush that fell over the cafeteria. *Here it comes...* But then Hillary abruptly broke her glare, and seemed preoccupied with her peach cobbler. Knowing Hillary as I did, this pretence of dessert fascination was absurd. After she'd read Gwyneth Paltrow's latest interview in *Charisma* magazine two months ago, Hillary had been treating any kind of processed sugar like it was poison. The noise in the room picked up again, everyone taking their cue from the queen.

Madison and I sat down at the empty table by the window. I'd be lying if I didn't admit it was awkward at first, just the two of us, trying to think of things to talk about. Neither of us were used to leading a discussion without Hillary around. But then we found our old groove.

"Yeah, I know it's unrealistic to expect Jake to confront his alcoholic, waste-of-skin dad," Madison argued, referring to a recent episode of *The Librarians*.

"Look, people can change, of course, I'm not saying that, but I just don't think Isaac wants to." I took a sip of my chocolate milk to wash down the rubbery bite of what was supposed to be eggplant parmesan.

Nice job, Sam. I'd just said I doubted someone would be able to stop drinking to someone who is currently trying to stop drinking and doing drugs.

"Sam, do you honestly think I can change?" Madison dropped her voice to a whisper, and her eyes moistened.

"I do," I said. I decided to go all-in and trust her. I didn't think I'd be able to again so quickly, but she just looked so vulnerable. And she'd stuck her neck out, waiting for me to sit with at lunch. "Look, only two years ago Zach was Amish and miserable. And he changed big-time. He left everything, sacrificing so much for his dream to pursue an education and so he wouldn't feel like such a hypocrite anymore."

"Why did he feel like a hypocrite?" Madison asked.

"Mainly because he knew he didn't fit in with the other Amish people and felt like he was living a lie." I hesitated but continued. "But also because he had a friend, years ago, who was abused, and he felt like his community ignored it, or covered it up, because the Amish are so against involving the police in their business."

"Aw, hell, people ignore things all the time. You don't have to be Amish to do that. Nobody wants to see what goes on with kids. Not really. So the signs that someone is messed up get ignored a lot."

I saw the pain in Madison's eyes. I dropped my fork, put my hands in my lap, and pulled hard on my left thumb with my right hand. It was something I used to do to calm myself when I'd hear my parents fighting. I hadn't done it in years.

"Madison," I tried to keep my voice steady, "did something happen to you? When you were younger?"

"Well, kind of. I mean… not like I was molested or anything. My mom always used to be taking different pills and liquors, Xanax, Adderall, you know. And my parents always left wine and liquor bottles open around the house… and then when I was about nine or ten, I started trying stuff. At first I was all scared that they'd notice, so I'd only take a little, you know, just to see what it did. I was really paranoid about getting caught. But later, I realized they didn't *want* to see anything, or didn't care, so I got bolder."

"Wait, so you were drinking and taking prescription medications at *ten*?" I tried to keep my voice low so nobody could overhear, but I think it made me sound like I was choking. I was swimming in waters way over my head right now. I had no idea of the right thing to do or say.

"Sure." She shrugged, and I got the impression she wished she could take back what she just shared. "But it's no big deal. They never found out or anything, so I didn't get punished."

"Yeah, I think that's odd that nobody caught you." I was trying to be as blasé as she was, but I don't think I was pulling it off.

"Well, me too. A little bit. But I'd only drink and take stuff on weekends, never on a school night. And it made me feel cool to have people over and get loaded. Grown up."

"But you don't usually get high when it's been just you and me hanging out at your place; we just got drunk that one time. Mainly you get wasted at parties, not with me." I blurted.

"Yeah, I know..." Madison seemed to be confused herself. "I've thought about that. I guess I knew you wouldn't be into me being all lit up because you're not even a baby-habit type, so I never brought it up. And after that one time we got a little tipsy last summer and you were so upset the next day, it made me feel bad. Also, I liked that we had something different, that we didn't need a buzz on to have a good time." She'd been looking down but met my eyes when she said, "You liked me even when I wasn't a party girl."

"Actually, I like you much better when you aren't drinking or drugging." I didn't want to sound like an uncool jerkwad, but an even bigger part of me wanted to help Madison. But I didn't know how.

The bell rang signalling the end of lunch. I had one last second to say something. Something impactful. Something supportive. Something useful.

"Madison, listen to me, skip class this period. Go straight to Mr. Evans' office. Trust me on this, he's a good guy. Go talk to him. Tell him what you just told me. Do it before you lose your nerve," I pleaded with her.

"Yeah, maybe I will," she said, picking up her tray of mostly untouched food. "I didn't do the reading for my English class anyway, so it'd be good to avoid that class in case we have a pop quiz or something. He'll write me a pass?"

"Yes, definitely he will." We walked to the exit of the cafeteria, two of the last stragglers out of there, and went in opposite directions down the hall. I'd hoped I'd made an impression on her and that she'd go to Mr. Evans.

That's when I saw Hillary again, standing in front of my locker. *Blocking it?* The hallway was deserted. I felt an eerie feeling like it was High Noon on the Hudson. I was pretty sure she'd consider herself Alexander Hamilton and me Aaron Burr.

Her face was red again, and she practically had smoke coming from her ears like in a *Scooby-Doo* cartoon. "Who the hell do you think you are, Samantha Stonesong? How dare you screw with me? I will annihilate you, crush you."

Then she spat right in my face.

CHAPTER FIFTY-SIX

"She spat? In your face? Are you joshing me?" Zach was as upset as I've ever seen him. Instead of turning red like Hillary did when she got mad, he went pale. It made his light dusting of freckles, barely noticeable before, stand out prominently. "Es gefällt mir nicht. Naett gut."

"Wait... uh, what was that last part?" I stabbed some of my veggie lasagna and brought it up to my mouth. So far our "first-date restaurant" was two for two in the great food category. That evening with Zach seemed so long ago, but it hadn't even been three months since he'd taken me here.

"Sorry, Dutch, er, German. When I get upset, it just comes out. I said that what she did was not right, not acceptable to me." Zach took a sip of his water. I could see he was trying to be calm but was struggling with it.

"Oh, thanks. Yeah, it sucked. Totally gross. I went to the bathroom and washed my face, but then I was late for class. I wanted to go talk to Mr. Evans about it, but I knew I'd just sent Madison there and didn't want to interrupt her time with him, especially if she was telling him something important." I paused. I didn't want to keep anything from Zach, but I also felt like I couldn't tell him what Madison told me. She hadn't sworn me to secrecy or anything, but I just felt her confession about stealing drugs and booze since she was ten was something I should keep private, no matter how compassionate and nonjudgmental I knew Zach would be about it. So instead I just said, "Madison agreed to try to get help to stop drinking and stuff."

"That is very good!" Zach nodded. "But Sam, I think you need to tell someone about this spitting thing. It is very wrong that she did that to you. I do not want her to ever do that again."

"Well, you and me both. She's left me alone after that, though." I was worried that I was shoving the food in my mouth too quickly, but I'd skipped lunch today to talk to my dad about another visit, so I was starving. "Getting a face full of spit kinda reminded me of when that Freddy tongue comes out of the phone and licks Heather's face in *Nightmare on Elm Street*." We both broke up laughing. I was in heaven, sitting here with Zach, feeling like his official girlfriend, knowing he loved me.

"It's weird, but I get the feeling something else is going on, that it's not just that she got in trouble because of that Facebook page." I took a break in my attack on my meal and pulled out my phone. "I can't help it. I keep checking my Facebook page now all the time. I kinda became obsessed with it, like pushing on a cavity even though you know it's gonna hurt. And its weird, Hillary has also shut down her own page. I wonder if her mom made her do that? I know she had to go in to talk to the counsellor, too."

Zach cocked his head. "Maybe her parents realized she was not ready for the responsibility of social media?"

"Yeah, maybe…" I picked up my fork and went to work on the little bit of lasagna I had left. The portions here were huge. I couldn't believe I'd almost killed this one and was still feeling a little peckish. "But because the page they set up was supposedly just a stupid prank, not a tangible threat, nothing really happened to them."

Zach's eyebrows knitted together, but he didn't say anything.

"Her sister shut her Facebook down, too. Now tell me that isn't a bizarre coincidence."

"Does her sister live in Lancaster?"

"No, she's an actress in Los Angeles. Hillary idolizes her, wants to be just like her; both aspire to be giant celebrities." I rolled my eyes, but I, like everyone else at my school, knew deep inside this would probably all happen as Hillary said.

"Well, Hillary does not seem to want for self-esteem," Zach observed.

"That's another strange thing. I thought that before too, but now I'm not so sure. Why the heck would she go after me so hard if I meant nothing to her? If her life's so great, why destroy mine? Why not just freeze me out?"

"I still feel upset that I wasn't able to be supportive of you when that nastiness was happening." Zach shook his head a bit.

"You've barely touched your fettucini alfredo!" I'd just cleaned my plate.

"Do you want some more?" He'd already given me a few bites when we first started eating, because he'd said it was delicious.

I restrained myself. "No, I'm good. Need to save room for dessert, right?"

"I brought some whoopee pies back from my sister's house. They're at my apartment if you want to go there after," Zach said. The way he said it made my body electric. It was a funny double entendre, but I suspected he had no clue about the other meaning of "whoopee."

"Why are they called that anyway?" I asked, enjoying my inside joke with myself.

"I heard they were at first called 'creamy turtles,' but when the Amish men found their wives had put them in their lunchboxes, they'd joyfully yell, 'Whoopee!' so they got renamed."

"I love that story." I smacked the table in delight. Normally, I'd chide myself, *I'm a dork,* after such a display of unmitigated glee. But with Zach I was finally comfortable to let my dork flag fly.

"That 'whoopee' feeling is sort of like how I feel when we're alone." Zach gave me a sexy look.

What?!! Maybe he wasn't so clueless about the double entendre after all.

"So how about we pay and then go back to my place?" he asked.

"Sure, I guess that'd be fun," I said, making one of the greatest understatements of all time.

CHAPTER FIFTY-SEVEN

Zach and I had been kissing for about an hour, though it only felt like ten minutes, before he pulled away and lightly stroked my hair. Then he dropped his hand and looked at me with a wary expression, as if there might be a potentially menacing clown approaching. I almost looked over my shoulder.

"Oh, this is wonderful being with you like this again, but I need to stop." He nodded like he was agreeing with himself.

I should have known that whenever I think things are going well, the other shoe is about to drop.

"Ok..." I said, trying to catch my breath. Zooming from ecstasy to dread in three seconds flat takes a toll on one's respiration.

"I mean, I've never gone farther, um, well, than this, and even though I love you, I'm not sure if we should, you know..." he stammered.

I was dumbstruck. I'd been rehearsing my "I'm a virgin" speech that I'd thought I'd have to make to him. I hadn't expected this. After learning he grew up Amish, I figured there was a chance he'd never had sex either. But I also knew he'd been on Rumspringa, so he could've sowed those oats. And even if he hadn't, I figured he'd be like the other guys I knew and be too embarrassed to admit his inexperience.

"Yeah, I haven't either. Um... so, yeah. There's that." If we'd been playing poker, I'd say I'd matched his cringe-factor and raised him one.

"Oh, well, that's a relief, I guess. Not that you need to be a virgin, too. I mean, I'd be ok with it if you had... but I guess you not having any experience either means neither of us knows how taking that step goes. So we get to muddle through it together." He ran his fingers through his hair. It was starting to get longer. I was glad; I liked it a little shaggy.

"So… were you thinking you'd want to?" I noticed he looked a little freaked out by this question. I quickly clarified. "I mean, not now! But someday?" I straightened my shirt out because it'd gotten kind of twisted around, and I tried not to blush.

"Before marriage, you mean? That's a little tough for me to answer. I used to just accept that not doing anything, except a chaste kiss, until marriage was the way it needed to be. Not questioning that idea was part of my Amish upbringing. And honestly, it was one of the rules that never bothered me. It was nothing compared to the restrictions on reading the books I wanted to. So, still, in my mind, it seems nice to wait. But the last two months, being with you, my idealism is at odds with my passion."

I worked on straightening my smile. I didn't want to laugh, because I didn't want Zach to think I was mocking him. But it was so charming how sometimes he sounded like a paperback romance novel. "I totally get what you're saying. Maybe we should just take it slowly—maybe try some things that are a little more than what we've been doing—but not actually have sex."

"I like that idea." He carefully chose his words. "But sometimes doing certain things can snowball, yes? And one thing leads to another?"

"Yeah, good point. We should probably be ready for that just in case," I agreed. Good gosh, all of this talking. I knew it was important and everything, but it was hella-awkward.

"Yes. So I will purchase some condoms, just in case. But we agree, we'll keep trying to go slowly?" he asked. A fit of giggles threatened to bubble up from me. He just said, "condom." But seriously, what was better? I adjusted my sweater and cleared my throat while I made a little mental list:

1.   Contraceptive—too vague.
2.   Prophylactic—too technical.
3.   Rubber—too old-school.
4.   Skin—too player-ish.

5.   Burrito poncho—too Ugh! *Seriously, brain? Why can't I get Madison's silly slang terms out of my head?*

"A condom, yes. Sounds good!" I manage to get out with a tone of what I hope sounded like modest enthusiasm. Then I quickly added, "So, how about those whoopee pies, now?" Not the best transition but it'd have to do.

"Oh, yeah!" Zach's face brightened. I imagined he too felt a reprieve. "And I also wanted to show you what my cousin gave me this morning." He led me over to his desk. On it sat a slightly used laptop.

"Oh! You got a computer!" I squealed. I couldn't help but to selfishly think that this meant we could now communicate so much more often when we were apart.

"Yah." His eyes shone with pride. "And I also bought a month-by-month Internet plan, too! Go ahead and try it out. My password is; 'NewLife,' no spaces, capital letters N and L. I'll go get our whoopee pies while you do." He left, and I logged on.

"Milk or water?" he called from the kitchen. It tickled me that he didn't say something modern like "caps" when referring to letters, yet he'd completely gotten over the traditional Amish idea from his past life that women went into the kitchen and always served the men.

"Coke?" I replied. His modem was a bit slow, but it opened to a search.

I heard him laugh. "Wasn't expecting that. Glad I asked!"

I didn't know what to do now that I was websurfing, but I found myself entering "Teagan Markham," Hillary's sister's name, into the search. And what came up when I did made me glad I hadn't taken a bite of my whoopee pie, because I totally would've done a giant spit-take all over Zach's new computer.

We'd all thought Teagan had been waitressing to support herself while she auditioned to break into the industry as an actress, but it turned out she wasn't just a wannabe who'd done a bit part or two looking for her break, as we'd been led to believe. I remembered how I'd gotten so excited seeing she'd played Girl #3 in the horror film *The Corn Mole* when Zach and I had been looking up horror films, thinking that must have been her only break so far. Nope, Teagan already had a lead role in a film. The even more shocking part was it appeared to be a soft-core film produced by a company called Nighttime Distractions. Some of the titles this company produced were: *Cellblock Lovelies*, *Jailbait Dancers*, and *Bikini Wild Ones*!

OMG

Plink! The plate with the whoopee pies rattled on the table next to me, and then I heard a sharp intake of breath behind my left shoulder.

On Zach's computer screen was the image of girl in pink lingerie, Teagan, making out with a man in a business suit whose hands firmly gripped her butt. The photo was from a little gem of a movie titled *The Gentleman and the Ho*.

"Oh!" Zach asked. "Uh, are you doing research on sex for us?"

I whipped around and looked at him. I didn't have any reason to be guilty, but I still almost cleared the screen. I could see by his raised eyebrows and wry smile that he was kidding.

"Oh, geez, Zach, that's funny... but no, this is a movie that Hillary's sister starred in!" I shook my head.

"Hillary? The Hillary from your school who used to be your friend, the one who was so mean to you? The spitter? That Hillary?"

"One and the same," I replied.

"Oh. Wow." He gaped at the screen. "Excuse my Pennsylvania Dutch, but I can't think of another way to say this—that wonders me!"

"Yep, it wonders the heck outta me, too!" I agreed.

CHAPTER FIFTY-EIGHT

Zach and I found the website for Nighttime Distractions, the company that produced Teagan's movie. And it linked to a page, also controlled by the production company, which served as a fan site for Teagan.

We wolfed down two whoopee pies each while reading the comments on her site, many about how hot she was and even a few marriage proposals. But I also saw that a very personal attack had been posted: "You and your sister Hillary are vicious harpies who make other people miserable, and you'll finally get what's coming to you! I can't wait to tell the whole school what you're doing now."

There'd already been a flurry of responses about how "harsh" and "totally uncool" the post was. But then there were also a couple of people who'd upped the ante with comments, calling Teagan a "slut" and Hillary a "bitch."

The city of Lancaster seemed trapped sometimes between its conservative farm roots and the more progressive influences of the last thirty years. Recently, I read about a controversy involving a motivational abstinence speaker invited to an assembly at a nearby school. Unfortunately the practice of "slut-shaming" was rampant in her message.

The controversy of Teagan's film career had generated quite a bit of activity, which I guessed explained why the studio had chosen not to remove the original post. I imagined the decision to leave up things that could be degrading for Teagan was based on the old chestnut, "Any publicity is good publicity!" Isn't that why celebrities in Hollywood released their own sex tapes, allowed themselves to look like fools on "reality" TV shows, and showed up for premieres getting out of limos without underwear, showing all their naughty bits? But wasn't this a form of cyberbullying, too? Especially if Teagan felt pressured by the studio to leave toxic comments up on her page.

It wasn't that shocking to me, a young actress like Teagan taking these roles to get started. But this particular girl... well, I knew her sister. So it felt weird. For better or worse, Hillary and I had spent an awful lot of time together. Heck, to be truthful, up until about a month ago, I would have called Hillary one of my friends. And I was also aware that a lot of our classmates were pretty conservative, and their parents would definitely judge Teagan, even if the kids didn't. I knew of several girls in my school that were very proud of their "purity pledge ceremonies."

"Do you think she was forced to do these films?" Zach asked, his eyes reflecting his worry.

"No, it doesn't seem like that to me," I answered in a tone meant to be calming but hoped it hadn't sounded patronizing. "You know that original post about her and Hillary? It sounds like it was definitely made by someone at my high school. I wonder if Hillary thinks I did it?"

"Oh no, why would she think that?" Zach took a big gulp of his milk.

"Remember how we watched all those horror movies that one Sunday? And remember how we saw Teagan's name in the credits of that one movie? Well, I mentioned it to Hillary and she seemed... odd. Angry even. I didn't think much of it. But a few days later, that whole Facebook thing happened." I was making the connections so fast, it felt like I was realizing them at the split second that they spilled from my mouth. "Then yesterday, she was so pissed at me... and that dis about her sister was also posted yesterday."

"But she couldn't think you'd be so unkind to use something like that against her? To embarrass her? You're not like that." Zach reached over and lightly rubbed my arm.

"Well, I'm not, but I don't know that she totally trusts me." I paused. "I've been told I act kind of aloof sometimes."

"You?" Zach's hand still rested on my arm.

"Yeah, well, I mean, I think I am kinda shut-down about some things, and I'm not always great at letting people know what I'm feeling." I chewed my lip.

Zach removed his hand from my arm, put it in his lap, and literally twiddled his thumbs for a few seconds. "I know that I have no right to ask this, not after I kept my Amish past from you… but I am going to anyway, because I feel like you want me to ask. Do you have any secrets that you want to tell me?"

Oh crap. This was it. And he wasn't wrong. It was like my tone had been begging him to ask me to tell him my secret.

"I'm not perfect, that's for sure. I've done a lot of things I'm not proud of." I knew he'd know I was stalling. I also knew if I didn't tell him now, I'd be officially lying and not just "not sharing." A thin difference, for sure, but one I'd clung to as a justification.

"Oh, I'm sorry, Sam. I don't want you to have to talk about anything you don't feel comfortable talking about. That was wrong of me to ask." Zach looked so remorseful. I couldn't stand it.

"No, it was a valid question. I know I compartmentalize. I think I always have, even before my parents' divorce. It's a coping device, keeping parts of my life separate from others. That's why I didn't want to tell my friends about us dating. I made that choice before I even found out you were Amish." The words came spilling out as if I was an arcade machine on which someone had just hit the jackpot token payoff.

"And then when you found out about the Amish connection, I bet it became more difficult for you to not do this compartmentalizing," Zach said.

"Well, honestly, I make everything a bigger deal than it needs to be." I took a big gulp of my soda and eyed the last whoopee pie, even though I was feeling a little pukey from the two I'd already eaten too quickly. "Dario Argento, you know him?"

"I think I've heard his name," Zach hedged.

"He's the guy who directed *Suspiria*; he's an unmitigated genius, the godfather of modern horror films," I gushed like the fangirl I was but then got serious again. "He said something like, 'Horror is like a serpent which can't be hid away, like we try to do with our guilty secrets.' But see, I think that hiding things we're ashamed of is what makes us sicker. Hiding exacerbates pain and torment."

"That's a good quote." Zach nodded, and I noticed a bit of whoopee pie cream on his cheek. He was so guileless.

Without knowing I was going to, I just came out and said it.

"Zach, I'm a shoplifter. I steal things." It was out, and it hung in the air like the pungent smell of boiling sauerkraut.

Zach smiled a little and nodded, thinking he'd gotten the joke. But then, after a few beats of silence, he could see by my eyes that it was no joke. As it sank in, his face went blank. Then he blinked twice and drained the rest of his milk.

"Sorry, that was pretty out of left field, huh? I mean…" I struggled to find a phrase or word he'd understand. "Well, not what you were probably expecting, huh?" Part of me wished I could grab the confession out of the air and shove it back in my mouth and swallow it back down. But another part of me felt so giddy and silly. I imagined this was what Madison felt like the first time she was very drunk on tequila.

"Oh, at first I thought you were ribbing me. But you're not, right?" Zach asked.

"Nope, not kidding. I started when I was thirteen. Then I stopped because I got caught by the police. We moved here, and I didn't do it for a while. I was good." I bit the lower left corner of my lip. "But then, a few weeks ago, I started grabbing stuff that wasn't mine again." *What the hell? I might as well tell him everything.*

"When I left you to go to the farm? And then all the stuff with the Facebook happened?"

"Yes, but those things aren't to blame, Zach. I need to take responsibility for my own actions and find a different way to cope when things get tough for me." OMG, I was starting to sound like Mr. Evans. Maybe my appointments with him were doing me some good.

Zach was quiet for what seemed like hours but was probably just a minute or two. He walked over to his bookshelf, gave the titles a cursory glance, then paced back. I thought he was figuring out a way to tell me that I would have to leave his apartment, that I wasn't the person that he thought I was, that he'd need time away from me to decide if he could continue to see me. Basically, I figured he'd react to my "skeleton-in-the-closet" reveal in the same way I had behaved when I'd found out about him being Amish.

But then he astonished me. He started laughing. I looked at him like he'd gone nuts. Finally he managed to speak.

"*The Amish Guy, the Thief, the Cyberbully, and Her Porn Star Sister,* that's what they can call the horror movie based on our lives!" he exclaimed cheerfully, nonchalantly referencing the savagely gruesome film *The Cook, the Thief, His Wife and Her Lover.*

We both dissolved into hilarity to the point of tears.

CHAPTER FIFTY-NINE

"She's not going to like this." Madison shifted from one foot to the other. Ever the fashionista, she wore an adorable tweed peplum jacket. Me, I'd dressed down, wearing an oversized green-and-purple sweater.

"Look, we can't do it in school. She'll definitely not be cool with it then, and tomorrow's Monday, so we have to talk to her today," I said. "Are you sure you can handle this?" I worried about stressing out Madison. I knew she'd told Mr. Evans that she was going to try to be sober for two weeks to prove to herself that she could do it. She was only on Day 6, and I didn't want her to fail. But I also knew I needed her to confront my own demon.

It was Sunday afternoon at two, and we were standing in front of Hillary's house. Neither of us had found the strength, the "ovaries," to push the doorbell to start this admittedly not-well-thought-out plan into motion.

Then the door opened anyway.

I think I heard Madison gasp. I know my own heart stopped for a split second as I looked at Hillary's angry face, lips pursed, cheeks flushed, nostrils flaring slightly.

"What the hell do you two want?" she practically hissed at us. Then she turned to me. "You look like Barney the damn dinosaur."

"Nothing," I said, trying to keep my voice steady and calm. "We don't *want* anything from you. Look, we'll probably never be friends again, I mean, 'you and me.' You and Madison, well, that's up to you guys..."

"Hi, Hill!" Madison squeaked. *Ok, not at all helpful but whatever.*

"Even so, I need to clear the air." I cleared my throat for good measure and proceeded. "I'm guessing you think I told people about your sister and the movies she's making. Well, I didn't. I actually just found out myself yesterday. And Madison is the only person I told. And I only did that just this morning to get her to come here with me."

Hillary said nothing. She just rotated her glower from me to Madison and back to me again.

Madison shrugged, smiled, and then rolled her eyes. "Wow! Über-awkward! I can't remember ever wanting to get loaded so bad in my life!" Her cheerful tone was unnerving to me, but I knew acting glib was her go-to. And she wasn't going to admit in front of Hillary that she was trying to stop partying.

"What angle are you working this time, Saint Sam?" Hillary's eyes couldn't narrow any more without them closing completely.

"No angles. I swear," I replied. "I'm not trying to win you over, because I don't think I'll ever be able to forgive you for that whole fake Facebook thing, but I am trying to understand why all this happened so I can move on."

"Yeah, well, I already told that snoopy Mr. Evans that it was all just fooling around and we didn't threaten you or anything, so my uncle the lawyer made the school back the hell down. Besides, WHY do YOU have such a bias against the Amish? What's wrong with being Amish?" She smiled smugly.

"Great, ok, fine. Not here to talk about that." I steeled myself for her inevitable vitriol. "Just tell me, did you think I'd found out about Teagan's movies and then went and told everyone? Is that why you went after me? Because I didn't do that." I wanted to say *Or was all this because you're just a callous, selfish bitch?* but I figured that'd be an assured conversation-ender.

"I know you're lying. Don't try to play me." Hillary had gone beyond hissing to growling. I felt like I was confronting a feral cat.

"O-kayeee." Madison's eyes had a bit of a far-off cast to them. "Like I said, maybe this wasn't such a great idea, Sam." She lowered her voice to a barely discernable murmur, "…and maybe I need to rethink the idea of not getting at least a little buzzed too…" Madison slipping into weakness had the effect of galvanizing me.

"Hillary, I could give a rat's nut what kind of movies your sister does. Truthfully, I've always thought she was super-cool for pursuing her dreams, and I don't see anything wrong with her nude scenes if she doesn't care. I know that some of the people in Lancaster County have parochial views about nudity, but that's not my way of looking at this at all." This was my last ditch effort, and even though I meant every word, I hadn't planned on speaking so bluntly. For just a second, I thought I glimpsed a bit of a glitch in Hillary's death glare before she rebooted it.

"Sure, you might be saying that now to my face, but why shouldn't I think you're the one who told everyone? And now you're posting all sorts of POS comments on her fan site, aren't you? I knew you were sneaky, but this takes it to a new level."

"Um, that doesn't make sense. If I was going to make rude comments online, why wouldn't I have posted something weeks ago when you say I found out? Back when you started bullying me with that stupid Facebook page?" I looked over at Madison, who seemed fixated on the lamp above the door. *Again, not very helpful, Mad!*

"Also, Madison didn't know anything about your sister's movies all this time!" I continued. "Come on, she would have been the obvious first person I'd have told, right? I mean, she's like one of the last people at our school who didn't know!"

"I'm so over all this. Next time I'll use Snapchat to get my digs in so it'll all be gone if a crybaby narcs." Hillary's confidence in her justified hatred of me seemed to be wavering a little more, so I decided to keep going for the brutally honest stuff.

"Look, you've said you think I tried to come between you and Madison as friends, and you know what? I kinda did. Not intentionally, but yeah, I wanted her to be better friends with me than you. So then why wouldn't I have told her your secret, especially when she was mad at me, to bond with her again and get her on my side, not yours?"

The Hillary-logic I was using with Hillary seemed to be working.

"Well, maybe because you were all wrapped up in that stupid Amish guy?" Hillary's voice betrayed her uncertainty.

"No, she did try hard to get me to forgive her after she blew me off and I wouldn't," Madison said quietly.

"Why not? What the hell were you so pissed at her about, anyway? I never understood that." Hillary turned her laser focus to Madison, and I had no idea how to deflect it. I started to panic inside.

"Yeah, but you weren't that concerned about my problems, were you? You were more excited to use it to turn me against her, weren't you?" Madison fired back. Hillary looked stunned. "Truth is, I was lashing out like a vengeful bitch, and you recognized that because most of the time you're a vengeful bitch yourself." Madison's jaw flexed repeatedly. She must've been scared to be standing up to Hillary and having some power in the relationship for the first time. She tapped her heel up and down a bit then faltered a little, offering, "Hey, but you're not a druggie like me… so there's that."

Madison was clenching her jaw so hard, I worried she'd have a muscle cramp, but she did not break eye contact with Hillary. We all stood there, looking from one to another, unsure of what to do. Then it hit me! I'd try something I learned from Zach. A little levity would help ease the stress we were all feeling right now.

"So I'm an Amish-loving loser, Madison's a vengeful druggie, and Hillary's an über-bitch! That'd be a great movie title, huh?" I laughed heartily for a few seconds until I realized I was the only one laughing. Madison looked confused, and Hillary just gave me the "not impressed" face with her mouth squished over to the side like she was trying to kiss her own ear. Massive Face-Plant from the geeky chick. *Ooof.*

Where was Zach when I needed him and his inappropriate but wonderfully dark sense of humour?

CHAPTER SIXTY

Things with Hillary on Sunday ended without any kind of resolution, but I think the visit Madison and I paid her had an effect on her, because Monday she was different. She nodded casually when she saw Mad and me outside before school. And at lunch, when Delia smiled at me from the Sherpa table, Hillary pretended not to notice and didn't ice her out for it. Of course, I couldn't be sure that this was not a part of some greater Hillary scheme, but it seemed that she was going to lighten up. A gesture of détente. I knew we'd never be close again.

Then, after lunch, Simon approached me. "Do you have a second before you go to your locker?" he asked.

"Sure, there's still five minutes before the bell," I said. "What's up?" I felt like this casual thing we were pretending at was whack, since we hadn't been close for a while.

"I just wanted to say I'm sorry. For when you tried to talk to me a while ago. I just didn't know how to... what to say, I guess." Simon's mouth was pinched tight, and he pushed his glasses up higher onto the bridge of his nose, even though they didn't appear to be sliding down.

"No, it's cool. Look, I'm kinda the douche-gargler in this story, not you. You were my first friend when I moved here from Philly, and then I totally blew you off when Madison and I started hanging out. That was rude. And stupid. And immature." I hesitated but decided to be honest. "And besides, I missed our friendship, so I ended up screwing myself over, too. I liked having a friend who understood."

"You did? I mean, I missed you, too. Having a friend who understood my rantings about the theory of entropy and how it related to my bedroom, or my musings about the Fibonacci sequence and how it relates to everything from artichokes to seashells to bee ancestry. Not a lot of people want to put up with that!" He smiled, and his mouth relaxed.

I laughed. "Yeah, well, I read an article online recently about rabbit breeding and its relationship to the Fibonacci sequence, and I thought of you!" *Why did I ever think I couldn't be part of Simon's world if I was friends with Madison?*

"What is it about high school that we feel like we can only be in one group?" Simon shook his head. It was like he'd read my mind! "Seriously, why haven't we moved past the old '80s movies like *The Breakfast Club* and their segregated grouping stereotypes?"

"Well, for me, that's going to end now. I'm not a Sherpa anymore. I'm a free agent. Madison and I are still friends, and I hope some other girls from the Sherpas will maybe still want to hang out, but if they don't, well that's fine, too. And I want to do stuff with you too, if that's ok?" I said. Simon smiled and pushed his glasses up his nose again while nodding. "Besides, I think my dating an ex-Amish guy puts me in an indefinable category that would dissuade any popular clique from wanting me now, anyway!"

"Yeah, about that Amish guy..." Simon looked down at the ground before continuing. "I'm glad you found a nice guy. He is nice, right?"

"Yeah, he's superlative," I said. "And I saw you were dating someone, too."

"Ah, you heard about that? Well, yeah, I was dating Gabby for a while," he said.

"Oh, not anymore?"

"No, but we're friends now, so that's good," he said.

"Oh, that's cool." Then the end of lunch bell rang.

"Hey, one more thing. I just wanted you to know I wasn't trying to make a play for you or anything by writing that post on Teagan's page. I totally respect what you have with your guy. It was just my way of having your back after I found out what Hillary had been doing to you." The words spilled out Simon's mouth so quickly, I almost didn't hear the part about Teagan's page.

"Wait, YOU posted the warning to Teagan that you were going to tell everyone about her movies? That was YOU?!!"

"Yeah. I'm not proud of it. And I totally wasn't planning on actually doing it or anything. It was just because the two of them, Hillary and her sister, have always acted like they were so much better than everyone else, you know? And they're so mean to people behind their backs." Simon pushed his glasses up on his nose for the third time in the conversation. "But my mom owns the shop that Hillary's mom manages, and they're friends, so my mom tells me to just ignore Hillary when she's spiteful."

That was interesting. So that's how Bria knew about Hillary's behaviour before I'd related my experience to her. Yet because Simon was her son, she'd probably thought he was just overreacting when he'd told her.

"After I posted it, I realized a bunch of people already knew anyway. But don't tell anyone I posted that threat, ok?" Simon continued. "My mom and dad would kill me if they found out." Funny, to me Simon's parents were the coolest adults ever. And to him they were just "parents."

Just then Madison walked up. Simon had the look of a mouse without a hole to run into.

"So, I need to vamoose, gotta get to my class… and I'm across the building from it." And with that, Simon took off.

"Hi, Sam." Madison smiled. "Everything ok? You look weird."

"No, I'm good. It's all good," I said. And for the first time in a long time, I really was. "But you know what? I'm about to go to English class to talk about appearance versus reality in *The Great Gatsby* and how nobody is who you think they are. And that's so true. I feel like anyone can surprise you and do things you wouldn't expect them to do."

"Yeah, 'The greatest deceptions men suffer is from their own opinions.'" Madison tilted her head. "I think Leonardo DiCaprio said that."

I wanted to correct her that it was Leonardo da Vinci who said it, but instead I bit my tongue. I just laughed and said, "Good quote!" Maybe I didn't *always* have to blurt things out and hurt people's feelings.

Maybe I was capable of some surprises myself.

CHAPTER SIXTY-ONE

"**M**om, Zach is Amish. Or more specifically, he was raised Amish. Whatever. Anyway, he's my boyfriend, and I don't want to hear any of your criticisms about him or me or…" I was rambling. And I didn't look confident at all. I could see by my reflection in my desktop's screen that my shoulders were hunched and my face was pinched. My hair was piled on top of my head in a scrunchie, and I had spots of pimple medicine on my face. Listening to Ghost of the Robot's "Murphy's Law," I rehearsed confronting my mom, knowing this anxiety was probably causing more pimples. I took a deep breath and took another shot at it.

"Ok, yes, Mom, I am going to Winter Formal with Zach, but no, I don't want your help picking out a dress. Look, there's something else you should know. It's not a big deal or anything, but you were right when you said there was something different about Zach. There is. He grew up Amish."

"Holy crap! Are you serious?" My mom stood in my bedroom doorway.

I froze. Then I did that exaggerated long blink thing you sometimes see the lead actress do in horror movies in a lame attempt to make the dreadful apparition vanish. It never works for them, so I don't know why I thought it would for me.

"Wow, is that true? What a trip!" My mom was wearing a tight green shiny dress and thigh-high white boots. She was home early, even for a weeknight.

"Mom! We talked about you just barging in here, remember?" I fumed, stalling for time. "God, you never respect my privacy!"

"Ok, chill out. My date stood me up, so I came home to have a glass of wine. There's nothing more pathetic than a lady of a certain age sitting in a bar, drinking alone. Anyway, your cell phone was charging in the kitchen when I got in. And the thing started buzzing before I got to pour my second glass. I saw on it that it was your father calling, so I just wanted to let you know. I didn't answer it or anything." She rolled her eyes and held out my phone. "Geesh, give me a friggin' break. I thought you'd appreciate me being cool and relaying the message"

"Ok, all right." I had to resist running to the bathroom to grab a washcloth to swipe the zit cream off my face. I hated that my own mother made me feel so self-conscious.

"So, Zach, he's Amish?" my mom gently prodded. Gentle was unusual for her, so I responded.

"Not anymore. He *was* Amish," I said.

"Oh wow, he left his Amish people for you?" My mom sat on my unmade bed. "That's romantic." I absolutely hated it when she sat on my bed, especially if it was unmade.

"No, he left before we met." I gritted my teeth, waiting for the diatribe about how stupid the Amish were or something similar, but instead my mom just lowered her head and started picking at her cuticle.

"So, your dad, does he already know about your relationship with Zach and the Amish thing? Do you talk to him about this personal stuff?" I almost felt sorry for her. She was trying.

"No, Mom. But the kids at school found out and were riding me about it pretty hard. I'm still getting over this cyberbullying thing that I went through with them, so I don't want to talk about it much." I fully expected her to laugh and to tell me to just brush it off, because when she was growing up kids were much worse and I was too sensitive, yadda, yadda, yadda.

"Those little brats at school harassed you? I hope you gave it back to them as good as you got." She lifted her head, and her eyes burned with a protective fire I couldn't ever remember seeing. It warmed me.

"Well, no, I didn't. I got quiet and didn't tell anyone because all my friends turned on me. Then I started boosting stuff again to feel better." I replied. *Wow, that slipped out before I could set up my usual walls.*

"Oh no, Sam, you didn't. That sucks." I thought she was going to yell at me, but then she shook her head. "I swear, I had this feeling last week that you were stealing again. Did you get caught? Am I going to be getting a call?" *Yeah, that's more like it, worried about yourself, your time, your reputation.*

"No, nobody will be bothering you," I replied and she looked so relieved, I decided to continue. "I mean, a woman did catch me trying to steal back your diamond from that shop you sold it to, but she didn't turn me in to the cops or anything. I had to promise to see my guidance counsellor weekly, though; he's also a licensed psychologist." I looked at my own dry cuticles. "But Dad does know about the pilfering thing."

"Well, that's fantastic, I guess…" My mom's eyes looked far away. "You tried to get my diamond back? That's kinda sad. And then your dad, he wanted to come help you with that, huh? Well, good for him. But you know you can't start shoplifting. Even if your dad goes away again. And he might. I don't trust him."

"Yeah, Mom, I know." I was exhausted. This was a longer conversation than my mom and I had had in years.

"I guess I always worried he'd come back and take you away from me. You're both so alike, so smart."

I felt hot and my throat closed up. "No, Mom. That's not happening." *She loves me.*

She nodded. We were both quiet for a few seconds. "Now, this Zach…" She turned the conversation back to her favourite subject: romance. "You really like him, huh?"

"I love him, Mom." I wanted to trust her, so I put myself out there. She smiled.

"Good for you, Sam. That's good." And then, without a snide remark about me, my dad, or Zach, she quietly got up. "Thanks for letting me into your life, hon." With that she walked to the door and started to close it behind her. Maybe this was a turning point for us, and our relationship was headed in a different, better direction.

Then she abruptly poked her head back in. "He's a hottie, so don't be afraid to go for it with him," she said. Then she got all excited and started spitting out rapid-fire advice. "But tell him it's important for a woman to get her 'cookies' first before the guy. Women warm up slower, so if you get a climax in before you do the deed, it'll be better for both of you. Tell him to study up on the female anatomy. He needs to learn how to rock 'the little man in the boat'!"

"Oh my GOD, Mom! Ewww!!!" I threw myself face-first on my bed and buried my head in my pillows. I heard her chuckling as she shut my door.

Baby steps, I guess.

CHAPTER SIXTY-TWO

Three months later: before the Valentine's Day Formal, with Zach and my mom.

A List of Both the Good and Bad Things That Happened:

Pro: Zach took a cab to my place so my mom could take some pictures before the dance. While waiting for him to arrive, my mom told me I looked beautiful, even though I hadn't chosen the halter-topped black dress she'd liked, instead opting for a Grecian-style lavender-and-green dress. But I could tell she meant it when she complimented me.

Con: Although my mom said, "You should send some of these pictures I'm taking to your dad," she couldn't help adding, "not that the son-of-a-bitch deserves it."

Pro: Zach's face when he first saw me in my dress. Then he half-whispered, "Wow, when it comes to formals, you're the Slayer!" which made me laugh because it was a reference to *Buffy*, one of the first things we realized we both loved. Zach brought me a wrist corsage with lilacs. He put it on me and said, "Lilacs symbolize first love." I wondered if that was an Amish thing. But love transcended Amish vs. English traditions for us.

Con: Zach's family couldn't be here for this. Not that they'd be taking pictures or anything. No phone calls and no pictures. But they were making an effort recently. While they couldn't be supportive of going to a profligate dance and would never be able to approve of any extravagance like that, they were allowing Zach to visit them. Also, his mom said she'd like to meet me someday, which was cool but more unnerving to me than the prospect of a supper with Norman Bates. But if it made Zach happy, it made me happy.

Pro: We got some great pictures. And I did forward some from my phone to my dad. He texted back immediately: You look so happy, beautiful, and grown up. I'm crying and laughing at the same time. I know I don't deserve to have you back in my life but am so happy you are. Thank your mom for me. How weird that my mom and dad still kinda thought the same way, even though they were divorced.

Con: My mom teased Zach, "I know you Amish people probably think at seventeen that Sam is of marrying age, but I don't want her making the same mistakes I made. She's not getting married until she's at least thirty. So don't get any ideas." Mortifying.

Pro: Luckily, Zach got the joke and played along. He told my mom, "No, by seventeen an Amish girl is an 'old maid,' so nobody would be interested in Sam from my old neighbourhood because she's way past her prime." My mom did a double-take; I had to explain to her that he was teasing her right back. (Although I suspected the marriage age of an Amish girl was actually pretty young.)

Con: Then dear old mum told Zach that, in his rented tux, he looked sauve and so mature! The flirty way she said it made me want to dry heave.

Pro: We got out of the house before my mom could bring up the subject of "How to rock the little man in the boat" and whip out detailed diagrams of the female anatomy.

CHAPTER SIXTY-THREE

Zach softly squeezed my hand as walked up to the Lancaster Valley Country Club's main door. Then I stopped as if I'd spotted a Sluggoth monster.

"Are you sure about this?" I asked. "Because I'm fine to ditch the dance and grab a pizza and watch a movie instead."

"I want to go to the formal... but only if you do," Zach replied, pausing.

"Sure, I mean, it was my idea to go, right?" I rubbed the side of my neck but then got my wrist corsage caught on my hair a little. Zach had to help carefully untangle me. "I mean, it's been months since that stupid Facebook thing got taken down."

"You realize that you're allowed to still be hurt about that whole thing." Zach had surprisingly nimble fingers and was more patient than me. I just wanted to rip my tangled hair out by the roots or the flower off my wrist. But I didn't want to destroy the spray.

"Look, I can't promise people aren't going to stare at you. I mean, they might be curious about you growing up Amish and everything," I said. I didn't know why I waited until this moment to bring up my fears. *Better late than never*, I figured.

Zach didn't reply right away, maybe because he was so concentrated on getting my corsage untangled. Luckily, the flowers were fine and I only lost a few strands of hair.

"Yes, well if people are looking at me, I'll know they're staring because they are jealous that I'm taking the most gorgeous girl at the school to the ball." I giggled a little and rolled my eyes. "I mean, I don't even go to school here, and I'm getting to go to this fancy gala with you. I never dreamed I'd be this lucky... and I used to have a lot of wild daydreams when I was harvesting the tobacco!" He could see I was ready to start walking again, so we did.

"Well, if people do get boorish, you have my permission to go all Carrie-telekinetic on them, ok?" I told him.

Zink winked. "Gosh I hope there's no pig's blood dumped on my head. Between you being a vegetarian and how my cousin Isaac, the pig farmer, always smelled, I think that would be particularly unsettling." He put his arm around my waist, and we walked in.

While not all eyes were on us, we definitely caused some drama. A lot of people seemed to be sneaking glances at us, including the teacher chaperones. I knew many of them had thought that when they first saw Zach they'd be seeing a dude in suspenders with a bowl haircut and hay sticking out from behind his ears.

As fate would have it, Hillary was one of the first people I saw when we walked into the room. I averted my eyes to the table piled high with chips, bottled water, and donuts. Before doing so, I'd noticed Hillary was with Adam Stacks, senior, football player, student council president and her co-lead in the fall musical. I couldn't help but to sneak another glance at her. She looked me over briefly with neither disdain nor approval, and then moved on. *Disinterested neutrality... I'll take it!*

"If I was still a Sherpa, Hillary would have probably greeted me with, 'That dress makes you look so much older. But like a grandma-older,' or one of her other famous Comsults," I whispered to Zach.

"Comsult?" Zach was also trying not to stare at Hillary.

"I made it up. It means a hybrid compliment-insult. You're not the only one with fun words now." I preened by sagely nodding my head. Zach chuckled.

Hillary remained the most popular girl at school, but there had been an almost imperceptible shift. Her power had abated a wee bit. The funny thing was, it wasn't because of her sister's films that Hillary's star wasn't shining quite as brightly—it was because of Hillary's reaction to them, trying to ignore them. It made her seem weak. If her slightly diminished control over the student body bothered her, she sure didn't let it show. She acted as if she was just bored with "the Lancaster Township high school games" and had started spending more time with friends from other schools. And she still had enough power to add two new girls to her table: Caitie and Daae. Seems there was always someone willing to be a Sherpa. Though not me, never again.

Then we saw Delia. She was alone. She smiled widely. "Nice to see you, Sam!"

"You too," I said, really glad to see her. "Do you remember my boyfriend, Zach? I think you guys met at that cornfield party." We were slowly forming a new and better friendship. I knew how intimidating Hillary could be and didn't blame Delia for not talking to me when everything went down.

"Sure, I do! Hey, Zach! Glad you could come with Sam." We chatted a bit. It felt surprisingly comfortable. All things considered, Delia was a good egg.

Madison came over and danced with us during a Pitbull song. I couldn't tell if she was a little buzzed or just stoked to be dancing. She'd "fallen off the wagon" so often, it was like the wagon was made of Teflon and her butt was greased with superfluid helium 4 below 4k. She'd promised to look at some rehab camps Mr. Evans told her about, which was hopeful. I wanted her to get better, but I also knew I couldn't make her to do anything; she had to want to change.

At one point, getting punch, we ran into Simon and Gabby. When nobody was looking, I gave Simon a look like, "But I thought it was over," and he shrugged and raised his eyebrows like, "Who knows? Maybe not!"

All in all, it was a great night. A night that never in a million years would I have dreamed I'd have. Zach and I danced to a lot of songs.

Near the end of the night the DJ played "I've Found My Way" by Anime Eyes:

Too many cloudy days

Settling for gray, couldn't see any other way
You showed me sunny days
The pain has finally faded away

I remembered the first time I saw Zach and how he followed me and Madison over to House of Pizza, and another song by Anime Eyes, "Buried," played on the jukebox. I no longer felt that I had to keep secrets or that I'd always be alone. The fact that this song was playing now just felt so right.

Zach held me, and we swayed to the song.

After the song was over, we walked over to a quieter place to sit down. I looked deep into his eyes and asked, "If there was an apocalypse, zombie or otherwise, do you think the Amish would be better prepared? Because they're off the grid already, so they wouldn't be freaked out by power outages and the lack of media guidance. Wouldn't they pitchfork the undead or go about their business ignoring the riots?" He laughed then feigned a grave expression.

"Hmmm... Well, contrary to popular belief, many Plain People do use electricity but often generate it themselves, so that'd be a definite short-term advantage. But because the Amish are pacifists, I think the non-Zombie scoundrels would steal their stuff pretty quickly. As far as killing the potential golems, the Amish might hesitate if they saw them as sick people with souls intact. But if the Amish saw the undead as demons, or even as animals—no better than chickens—that'd be good because the people I come from are pretty good at decapitating poultry by hand with great dispatch without ever getting pecked." Despite my vegetarian leanings, I found that pretty hilarious.

"I think it's critical that I get in good with your family soon, because you never know when we could have that apocalypse... an egghead like me is doomed if I don't have a good plan." I winked.

"I might be an egghead, too." Zach grinned. "I just got accepted to start classes this summer at Millersville University. My cousin gave me a raise and will cut back my hours so I can manage it."

"Oh, that's so wonderful!" I knew the old me would've been fearful about all the "what-ifs?" like *There will be pretty college girls around him. What if they hit on him?* and *What if I go to New York and he's here?* But instead of dwelling in that Land of Fear, I told him, "I'm so grateful that I found you. The world's so different from the way I thought it had to be." His eyes lit with elation.

"There's an old Amish expression, 'We grow too soon old and too late smart.' I'm always feeling like I don't really understand the world. Maybe when we're older, we'll look back and understand everything, and laugh."

"I can't ever imagine feeling like time goes by too quickly! Everything seems to last forever. Do you think it feels like time speeds up when you get older?" I didn't wait for his answer. "Maybe it's a perception thing because when you're sixteen, a year is 1/16 of your life, a good chunk of it, but when you're forty, it's only 1/40, so it feels quicker?"

Zach shook his head. "I think you're pretty wise about many things already. We should probably just enjoy everything while we have it." He pulled me closer and kissed me. Right there in front of everyone! We made ourselves stop after a minute and, in tacit agreement, walked out to my car, where we continued the kiss. And when we did, it felt like time stopped.

Nothing else mattered. Cyberbullying and mean girls didn't matter. Secrets, shoplifting, and shame didn't matter. Sins of the fathers (and mothers) didn't matter. Separations and labels didn't matter. Trying to be "normal" and worrying about Plan P to fit in with everyone didn't matter. Amish and English didn't matter. All that did matter was that I was a girl, kissing a guy, who loved me back.

And life was just *plain* good.

AUTHOR'S NOTE

Dear Readers,
I can't thank you enough for reading my first novel.

I grew up in Lancaster County, PA, but this book is a work of fiction, though many ideas and events are based on things I've experienced or heard about. For example, I never dated someone who was raised Amish, but I did have this strong flirtation with a guy who I used to dance with at this under-21 club. His name was Sam. (Huh. It seriously didn't hit me until just now that I named my protagonist Sam!) Each time, after Sam would ask me to dance all night long, I gave him my phone number, but HE NEVER CALLED. Finally, his cousin took me aside and told me that Sam was Old Order Mennonite and that he had no phone in his house. The first idea for this book came from that anecdote and my thinking, *What if....*

I was bullied, yes. Not cyberbullied, though. I've learned quite a bit about that twist on intimidation and shaming through talking to my students, reading articles, and extrapolating the dynamics of some power plays I've faced by girls who share some qualities with Hillary and the Sherpas. Honestly, I feel sympathy for every character in this book, maybe even empathy. Hillary and Madison are in a great deal of pain themselves. This insight isn't to justify any abusive actions, but it's helpful to remember sometimes that when people aren't happy, they often try to break those around them. But if you're being bullied, it's very important you talk to people. Find support. Know that you'll get through it. Maybe one day you'll even offer advice on Facebook to a former bully of yours about where to find the best pizza in NYC. I know it seems crazy, but that's a true story of mine, too.

Writing Zach's dialogue was challenging. I enjoy writing in Amish dialect (years of immersion language training in Lancaster), but Zach's a guy who's trying to hide his speech patterns. The tricky part for me was that I wanted to let some words, some Amish sentence construction, sneak into Zach's speech somewhat randomly. Members of my critique group and my editor, not familiar with the Amish practice of eschewing most contractions and the odd placement of adjectives and nouns in a sentence, were often confused. But they really helped me to focus on when to use these PA Dutch "slips" and when not to, and how to have Sam react. I decided in times of real stress for Zach, his old vernacular steals into his speech without him even being aware of it.

Obviously you, my readers, probably guessed waaaaay before Sam does that Zach was raised Amish. (Maybe even from their first encounter. I must admit, the title of the book is a pretty big clue.) So it was challenging for me to show how Sam and her friends *don't* figure out earlier than they do that Zach is Amish. If you're a reader who grew up in Amish country, I think you might get why the non-Amish teens are not expecting something like an Amish dating an English. As Bria says in the book, it just doesn't commonly happen that Amish start dating non-Amish. And as far as the verbal communication goes and Zach's gaffes, even non-Amish and non-Mennonites who've had generations in Lancaster often sprinkle PA Dutch vocabulary and syntax into their daily conversations.

I write about some controversial things. Hell Houses actually exist. I went to one in Santa Monica, CA, thinking it was a "regular" haunted house and was blindsided by the true motives of the people running the place, just as Zach and Sam were. Thanks to Rick and Judi Manis, of Rick Manis Ministries, for reading that part and their feedback. My desire is to not only be frank but to also be fair and respectful to all of the cultures, religions, and viewpoints that I present in the book. I also appreciate all my conversations about God throughout the years with Rabbi Dan Wolpe and Rev. Bob Lowdermilk and the insights they've shared.

Furthermore, it was of paramount importance to me that I use care and courtesy portraying the Amish as a culture and as a religion. Members of the Amish culture are often romanticized in fiction, but that's not an accurate reflection. All people and communities have flaws, as well as facets to esteem. Some of the disconcerting things Zach talks about happening in his community come from my own observations, blogs of former Amish, and articles and books I've read over the years. Yet there are beautiful and laudable things about the Amish culture that I wanted to include as well.

For Sam's secret to have verisimilitude, I also talked with shoplifters and read articles and blogs. The idea of trying to fill a void with materialism, while dealing with an attraction to a guy who eschewed materialism all of his life, was interesting to me. The love that Sam and Zach have for education and reading is something I share with them.

Divorce is something I've experienced way too much of. (Maybe any personal knowledge of divorce is "way too much," but it's a reality that exists in our modern culture.) Over my years of tutoring and teaching, many of my students have had the sad familiarity with this occurrence as well. In the course of my work with them, some open up and share their grief and hurt with me. It's heartbreaking when people separate or betray each other or shun each other. Relationships are hard. I wish I had all the best answers about how to deal with the pain of this but situations vary. *Do* find friends or sympathetic adults like the character of Bria in this book and talk with them.

Finally, *secrets*. We've all got them. And sometimes that's ok, and those secrets are nobody's business but our own until we are ready to share them. However, sometimes those secrets control our decisions and torture us. I encourage you to let yourself communicate and to trust others. Sure, some people are douchcanoes, and they'll be disloyal or vindictive. I wish it wasn't this way, but it is. I still believe that you must risk vulnerability and pain to be fully alive in this world. I love this quote by Richard Bach: "Argue for your limitations, and sure enough, they're yours." So don't let fears hold you back. Just like Sam, you're wonderful and special and worthy.

Best always,

Debby Dodds

ABOUT DEBBY DODDS

D ebby Dodds has stories in eight anthologies, including *My Little Red Book* (Hachette Book Group, 2009) and *Things That You Would Have Said* (Penguin, 2012) that led to an interview on the TV show *CBS Sunday Morning*. She was a regular contributor for *The Living Dead* magazine and has been published in *The Sun, xoJane, Portland Family Magazine, Manifest-Station,* and *Hip Mama,* to name a few.

She received a BFA from NYU in Drama/Acting and a MFA in Creative Writing from Antioch University. As an actress, she wrote and performed in shows at both Disneyland and Disney World. She did improv and sketch comedy on stages in Los Angeles and New York and also appeared in a special with Jerry Seinfeld. She also had roles in several independent films. In Portland, she still performs occasionally, often with the comedy show *Spilt Milk*.

When she's not writing, she might be SAT or ACT tutoring, but her favourite days are spent cosplaying at Comicons or watching *Buffy the Vampire Slayer* with her daughter, Dory.

Connect with Debby online:

Blog: www.debbydodds.com
Facebook: www.facebook.com/debby.dodds.tutor
Twitter: @DoddsDebby
Goodreads: www.goodreads.com/user/show/32547595-debby-dodds-author
Instagram: www.instagram.com/debbydodds/

BOOK CLUB DISCUSSION QUESTIONS

1. How does Sam and Zach's relationship mirror those of other "forbidden relationships" between different cultures or groups? How is it different?

2. Cyberbullying is a real problem. Adults are becoming more aware of this and how it's not the best strategy to "just let the kids work it out." How has the use of intimidation and bullying affected teen culture? What are good steps to take when you learn about bullying?

3. What do you think of the idea of the "Hell House?" Do you think Sam and Zach overreacted? In a case like this, do you think the creators of the "Hell House" believe that their passion for their mission justifies some trickery?

4. Every character seems to have a secret—what are they? Is it ever a good idea to keep a secret? Is it wrong to tell others' secrets?

5. Some characters have unlikable qualities (Sam's mom, Hillary, Zach's dad, etc.) Do you have any empathy for these characters? Why?

6. Do you make lists? Are Sam's lists different from the ones you make? Are the lists helpful for Sam, or do they prevent her from communicating?

7. Desertion is a theme. How many ways do the characters desert each other?

8. What assumptions does Sam make that aren't true? What are assumptions made by other characters? How does our past shape our assumptions?

9. Zach and Sam share a love of horror movies and the TV show *Buffy the Vampire Slayer.* Does this interest say something about them as people?

10. Did you learn anything new about the Amish reading this book? Did anything surprise you?

ABOUT BLUE MOON PUBLISHERS

We love discovering new voices and welcome submissions. Please read the following carefully before preparing your work for submission to us. Our publishing house does accept unsolicited manuscripts but we want to receive a proposal first, and if interested we will solicit the manuscript.

We are looking for solid writing—present an idea with originality and we will be very interested in reading your work.

As you can appreciate, we give each proposal careful consideration so it can take up to six weeks for us to respond, depending on the amount of proposals we have received. If it takes longer to hear back, your proposal could still be under consideration and may simply have been given to a second editor for their opinion. We can't publish all books sent to us but each book is given consideration based on its individual merits along with a set of criteria we use when considering proposals for publication.

For more information, please visit us at www.bluemoonpublishers.com

THANK YOU FOR READING
AMISH GUYS DON'T CALL